CW01641973

# CRADLE OF DEATH

MATT JAMES

SEVERED PRESS
HOBART TASMANIA

# CRADLE OF DEATH



WWW.SEVEREDPRESS.COM


This novel is a work of fiction. Names, characters, places and incidents are the product of the author's imagination, or are used fictitiously. Any resemblance to actual events, locales or persons, living or dead, is purely coincidental.

*ISBN: 978-1-922323-57-6*

ALSO BY MATT JAMES

THE JACK REILLY ADVENTURES
*The Forgotten Fortune (2020)*

STAND-ALONE NOVELS
*The Dragon*
*Dark Island*
*Sub-Zero*
*Cradle of Death*

THE DEAD MOON APOCALYPTIC THRILLERS
*Nightmares are Born*
*Home Sweet Hell*
*Song of Sorrow*
*In Memoriam*

THE DEAD MOON SHORT STORIES
*Nightmare at the Museum*
*Scared to Death*

THE DANE MADDOCK ADVENTURES w/David Wood
*Berserk*
*Skin and Bones*
*Venom*

THE HANK BOYD ADVENTURES
*Blood and Sand*
*Mayan Darkness*
*Babel Found*
*Elixir of Life*

THE LOGAN REED THRILLERS
*Plague*
*Evolve*

OTHER STORIES
*The Cursed Pharaoh*
*Broken Glass*

PRAISE FOR MATT JAMES

"Matt James is my go-to guy for heart-stopping adventure and bone-chilling suspense!"

—Greig Beck, international bestselling author of BENEATH THE DARK ICE

“Matt’s novels need a pause button. They do not stop!”

—Lee Murray, award-winning author of INTO THE MIST

“A talent voice in the action-thriller genre!”

—Richard Bard, *Wall Street Journal* bestselling author of BRAINRUSH

“Matt James is electrifying!”

—Rick Chesler, bestselling author of HOTEL MEGALODON

“Matt James has cemented his place among the finest talents!”

—SUSPENSE MAGAZINE

“Matt James has proven that true adventure is found in the fine line between myth and reality. James walks that tightrope with a master's touch.”

—J.M. LeDuc, bestselling author of SIN

“Matt James is definitely an author to watch!”

—David McAfee, bestselling author of 33 A.D

“If you like thrills, chills, and nonstop action, then Matt James may just be your next favorite author!"

—John Sneeden, bestselling author of THE SIGNAL

For the amazing Richard Bard

*Wall Street Journal* bestselling author of the *Brainrush* series, former USAF pilot, and an all-around great guy

R.I.P.

You are missed

# PROLOGUE

Giza, Egypt
2559 B.C.

Building Khufu's pyramid was no small task. Luckily for Zadmarr, the king's Grand Architect, he was given the power of the gods. He didn't quite understand what the object was, but he did know how to wield its might. Still, even with the added strength, it had taken him fourteen long years to get to this point. Now, all he had to do was raise the precious capstone, and his work would finally be complete.

It was going to be Zadmarr's greatest challenge, but also his greatest accomplishment. He felt the strain on his soul. His very essence was being drained, stripped away into the cosmos. Being the empire's architect was an honorable position to hold. Unfortunately, for Zadmarr, and those that came before him—and after him—it was also a death sentence.

The sun scorched his exposed skin, yet Zadmarr felt cold. His skin was paler than usual too. He knew his lifeforce was nearly gone, but he still had a job to do, a calling to fulfill.

*With the 'Will of the Gods,' I will complete what I started.*

Zadmarr knew more about the gods than most. The pharaoh had given him insight into who they were. Though, he knew he hadn't been told everything. Unknown to most, a collection of archaic texts was handed down from king to king. They explained, to an extent, who had provided Egypt's great dynasty with the Will of the Gods. Holding the object up, Zadmarr was lost in its electric green glow.

Within the cube-shaped artifact was a strobing, swirling viscous liquid. It crackled with the energy of a thousand lightning strikes and softly vibrated in Zadmarr's hands. Only he, his apprentice, and the pharaoh could feel it. It proved that they, like their king, were of an ancient, royal bloodline. There were more like them too, but they wanted the Will of the Gods for more nefarious purposes.

Gratefully, Khufu ordered that sect to be put to death for fear of losing his prize, a prize that was to be buried with him in his pyramidal tomb. Zadmarr didn't agree with his king's decision to break tradition and steal away the object back to heaven. He believed that it should be passed on to the next pharaoh to be used to construct a better, vaster empire…as well as a deterrent against the kingdom's enemies.

And they had many.

But Khufu felt differently. Time had worn him down. He was

perpetually sad, speaking of atrocities in his sleep, horrors that he said that he was responsible for. Zadmarr didn't know of anything in his king's past that was that atrocious. As far as he knew, Khufu had been an honorable leader.

*What's he hiding?* Zadmarr asked himself. *Stop it!* he scolded. *You still have a duty to your king.*

Cradling the Will of the Gods in the crook of his left arm, Zadmarr closed his eyes, pulled it into his chest, and held out his right hand, palm down. He tapped into the artifact's power and felt an invisible force tug on his stomach. Slowly, he turned his hand over and raised his open hand to the sky. From beside the base of Khufu's pyramid, the enormous, beautiful capstone, and the strange mechanism hidden within it, rose.

The mechanism had been found with the Will of the Gods. The artifact had been locked into place and could only be moved when the current pharaoh grasped it.

There was more to the Will of the Gods than power. Within the object was a living source of energy. At least, that's what they believed. No one quite understood the artifact, not entirely, anyway. Legend says that it was discovered by accident by Khufu's predecessor's army, Sneferu. He slowly realized what he found in the caves beneath the future pyramid grounds. He had accomplished it through intense prayer and experimentation.

He begged the gods to give him the ability to remove the object. Eventually, Sneferu's prayers were answered, but in the form of Khufu.

The Will of the Gods and mechanism weren't the only thing they had found down there. The cavern was the single largest, enclosed space anyone had ever seen. Within it was something no one could adequately describe. No one within the kingdom had ever laid eyes on such a…vessel. They were so engrossed with it that they had attempted to recreate it. They called them "solar barges," and they were used for ceremonial purposes, to ferry the deceased to the sun god, Ra, in the afterlife. Zadmarr wondered what else the gods used the impossibly large vessel for.

*And what else could the Will of the Gods be?* Zadmarr asked himself, gripping the relic tight.

He was in control of it, but he was also in agony. His steadfast beliefs and determination let him push through it, however. Refocusing, he lifted his outstretched hand higher and higher. With each passing heartbeat, Zadmarr felt his life slip away. He knew he was going to die, and it didn't bother him in the least. He would perish for a noble cause. Not only was he about to complete his king's tomb, but he was also finishing construction on the Will of the Gods' final resting place.

Khufu's army had dug up the artifact's dock based on a location proven by the king himself and transferred it to Giza. Khufu refused to say how he knew where to find it. There was no evidence of it anywhere in their collection of texts. Then, Zadmarr and a team of the best and brightest went about designing and constructing the exquisite capstone covering.

*Just...a little...higher.*

Zadmarr's vision blurred and his head swam. He collapsed, but not before lowering the capstone into place. Folding in on himself, he handed over the Will of the Gods to his protégé and breathed his final breath. Hopefully, Mankesh would do as he'd been trained to do. If he didn't, the world would feel his failure.

Within that final exhalation, Zadmarr prayed to Ra above to protect his apprentice and guide him in his journey. He was now the empire's Grand Architect.

Mankesh stood, cradling the Will of the Gods like a newborn child. His eyes were wide, filled with wonder and anticipation. He knew he could do more with the artifact than his master ever could. Mankesh was bigger, faster, and stronger. He had a warrior's heart. Not only would he fulfill his destiny as the next Grand Architect, but he would also help usher in the next great army of the world...even if the pharaoh were unaware.

The thought of a group of devout followers, his prophets, infiltrating the kingdom made him smile. On its face, he'd do everything that was asked of him. But behind closed doors, in the cover of night, Mankesh had plans to change the world as they knew it. He'd dug deep and found a beautiful truth about the gods.

He didn't know how, but as the new Grand Architect, he would bring the gods home even if it meant sacrificing the population of half the known world to do so. Genocide was a small price to pay to bask in his master's light.

Mankesh looked up to the heavens and closed his eyes and visualized the lands of Egypt being turned into a raging inferno.

*Let it be done.*

Qumran National Park, West Bank
Modern Day

Shoving his assistant deeper into the cave, Elliot Oxley retook his position just inside its entrance, gripping the only weapon he had in one of his gloved hands. Under normal circumstances, a tactical knife wouldn't do much good against the four extremists wielding AK-47 assault rifles.

Unless you were a man of Elliot's *talents*, that is.

Some forty feet in the air, Elliot had a perfect view of the landscape below. The low-roofed cave, like a handful of the other Dead Sea Caves, was situated halfway up a steep rock face. The only way inside was with climbing gear. In his mind's eye, Elliot imagined the last people to step foot inside the natural opening, some 2,500 years ago. They would've been forced to rappel down the peak of the rock formation with nothing more than a crudely fashioned rope and a handful of men holding the daring adventurer aloft.

*No thanks,* he thought, spying on the commotion below.

Beneath his perch was a long, bowl-like valley of stone and sand that stretched and wound on for miles. Elliot was kneeling atop one of the valley's highest, northernmost points. If he left his post, there'd be no way of escaping the twisting bathtub of a labyrinth without first running into the men with the guns. Unless he retreated to the cave, he'd be stuck in an oversized, overheating desert ditch with a small army of radical assholes.

*Decisions, decisions...*

But there was no decision to make now, because Elliot had already made up his mind. And even after having removed himself from the combat world over a decade earlier, he was trained to engage the enemy, regardless of any circumstances. The present situation was no different.

"Get back and keep quiet," he whispered, speaking to the only other person with him.

Still surveying the newly christened battlefield, Elliot quickly took stock of everything it offered in the way of cover. Unfortunately, there wasn't much besides the naturally formed offshoots, random boulders, and rises. Five people were already dead, including one of the five gunmen.

He knew about the unfolding chaos via radio when one of the park's security team had informed Elliot before he had been silenced. The dreadfully understaffed outfit, stationed at the edge of the excavation, had been completely overwhelmed in seconds.

Elliot's assistant, a Brit named Harry, was twenty-five years his junior. Typically, the younger man was full of piss and vinegar, eager to show Elliot and the others how awesome he was at life—a real pompous "college bro." Just thinking about it made Elliot's eyes roll. But even at twenty years of age, the forty-five-year-old archaeologist still ran circles around the entitled brat.

"You hear me?" Elliot asked, annoyed by his assistant's lack of response. Borderline angry, he forcefully shoved his two-way radio into the *boy's* shaking arms, stirring him awake.

Harry snapped out of his stupor, and emphatically nodded his head. Tears streamed down his dust-covered face. The twin streaks reminded Elliot of Eric Draven, the *Crow*. The intern had none of Elliot's background, just the me-first attitude of someone who'd been coddled his entire young-adult life. The kid looked like he was going to pee down his leg, and honestly, Elliot wouldn't have blamed him if he did.

Taking a deep breath in the stale cave air, Elliot reeled back in disgust. It stunk of ammonia. Harry had already pissed himself.

*Why me?* he asked himself.

"What…are you…going to do?" Harry asked in between blubbers.

Elliot grumbled a series of incoherent curses to himself.

"What?" Harry asked, not hearing them.

The archaeologist quickly snapped up an open hand, hopefully silencing any other incoming queries. "It was nothing… Just stay here until I'm done, and," he shoved his walkie into Harry's chest, "radio in what you see."

The Brit's eyebrow raised. "Done with what?"

*So much for not being questioned.*

Elliot sighed. "What I was trained to do."

Sucking in another deep gulp of air, Elliot made his move.

Bolting out of the low, trapezoidal entrance, he clipped onto the braided rappelling line. He needed to get to ground level before he was spotted. Without wasting another second, he leapt out over the three-story drop, already planning out his next move. Unlike with Harry's frantic, emotional outburst, Elliot stayed calm. In times like this, the world around him slowed to a crawl.

Falling like a bomb, he reached his gloved left hand around his back and squeezed the line with just enough pressure to arrest his descent. His landing was hard—harder than he would've preferred. He was out of practice, after all. But he successfully turned the jarring impact into a graceful roll, finishing off the maneuver up onto one knee. Weapon up in a backhanded grip, he scanned the grounds before him and waited.

"Just like riding a bike." Elliot groaned as he stood. "A rusty bike…"

His *Volbeat* shirt was caked in dirt, and the seam across his left shoulder was torn. His worn blue jeans had survived the fall, looking as tattered as usual.

Instead of attempting to skirt around the shooters and head for the nearest encampment, as any sane person would do, Elliot went straight for the closest gunman. He was just under a hundred yards away from him, a distance he wasn't excited about. It'd be a miracle if he made it without being seen. Gliding heel-to-toe on the dry terrain, the only noise he made was the slightest of grinds and crunches.

The sun was on Elliot's back. Even if the gunman turned and spotted him, the sun's low, blinding rays would make Elliot all but invisible.

Happily, the killer never took that look behind him.

*Lucky me.*

A strong gust of wind buffeted Elliot's back, hiding his approach. He slowed and calmly strolled right up behind the assassin. The unidentifiable goon wore a beige hood and face covering. From the front, all you'd be able to see would be his forehead and eyes.

*And they'd be as wide as saucers right about now,* he thought.

Elliot had seen that "Oh, shit!" look many times back when he killed the retched refuse—like this guy—while on Uncle Sam's payroll.

Moving like a ghost, Elliot wrapped his free hand around the man's veiled mouth, instantly hearing a muffled yelp of surprise as he did. But it was too late. Before the gunman knew what hit him, Elliot swiftly yanked the knife across the killer's throat, effortlessly slicing through the thin fabric between his jugular and the stainless-steel blade.

Knowing his target no longer had the ability with which to warn his comrades, Elliot shoved the wheezing man to the ground without a second glance. He picked up the felled Kalashnikov and immediately decided against using it. He depressed the magazine release and manually unloaded every bullet from within the banana-shaped cartridge.

Elliot could've simply used the rifle to mow down the remaining enemies, but stealth was vital in situations like this. He didn't want to draw the attention of this one's friends. Hostages were sure to be in custody. If the other assailants discovered what happened behind them, and decided to cut their losses and run, his co-workers' deaths would partially be his fault.

*No, I can't let that happen*, he thought, determined.

He was, at the moment, doing damage control. Blood had already been spilled. Plus, he always preferred his SOG knife over bullets in the past.

"Where are you?"

In reality, finding the other three gunmen wouldn't be hard. All he'd have to do was follow the gunshots and screams. These men weren't a squad of Delta operators. The men that opened fire on the excavation wanted pandemonium. Pandemonium led to newsworthy, global headlines. That's all assholes like this wanted. They wanted the world to know who they were and what they represented.

Pausing his counterassault, Elliot ducked behind a low rise of rocks in the center of the main path. Up on his tippy toes, he peeked over the formation. He confirmed that this was where the valley split up. He was at the base of the upside-down Y. The left arm, he knew, deadened after a series of sharp, switchbacking turns. The tributary on his right was the way to go. Like the other side, it cut back and forth. It also broke off into secondary branches, making it very easy to get lost.

But not for Elliot. He and his team had marked the trail, so Elliot knew where to go.

The frightful shouts of his coworkers, melding with the metallic report of two separate, yet similar, weapons echoed through the valley.

He'd been up against worse odds in his life. Though, he usually had something that packed a lot more punch than his SOG knife.

*Hmm.*

Elliot looked back and second-guessed not bringing along the dead man's rifle. He shook his head. No, he'd done the right thing.

More than most, Elliot understood the value of the element of surprise. It was generally the better option in any scenario.

Besides the racket an AK-47 made, it also had less-than-ideal accuracy, unless you were standing within spitting distance of the other guy. The reason that particular rifle was so prevalent in the world's militaries and private militias wasn't because of its reliance. It was because they were cheap and massively overproduced. If you knew where to look, and Elliot did, you could easily find one, as well as an excessive amount of spare ammunition.

"A suppressed M4 would be pretty nice right about now," Elliot muttered to himself. It was his old unit's weapon of choice and one he'd grown accustomed to using during their missions.

Moving fast, he slid to a stop and ducked down on one knee. He took a moment to catch his breath, then popped up like a meerkat, and observed the scene. He quickly found the cause of the commotion. Coming from around the bend ahead, Elliot watched as another of the *terrorists* backpedaled toward him, laying down cover fire for an injured ally.

And they were *definitely* terrorists.

If you shouted into the air and praised your god while slaughtering unarmed noncombatants, it made you one. It defined you as one in Elliot's book. He'd seen it a dozen-plus times before. Gladly, most of those animals lost their lives before they finished their worship. His prior crew was superb at what they did.

"Wish I had those guys right about now…"

He didn't need his entire team, though. All he'd need was one of them. Between Lincoln and him, they'd be able to wage a small war on whoever they deemed worthy of their combined wrath. They were the best, and no one ever argued the fact. They did, however, disagree with Elliot when he announced he was walking away from the military and retiring.

Of the two radicals, the wounded one was doubled over, holding his stomach, bleeding heavily. Elliot could tell that it was taking everything the other man had to leave his comrade to die. The commitment impressed Elliot. He could tell there was more to the relationship than just being brothers in arms. These two were friends.

*Cute,* he thought.

So, Elliot would take the decision out of the guy's hands.

Springing to his feet, Elliot flipped the knife into the air. After half of a rotation, he snagged its blade. Then, with a flick of his wrist, he launched it forward. As it silently whirled through the dry air towards the unwounded terrorist, Elliot moved for the injured, but still very dangerous gunman. Meanwhile, the knife struck its target first, burying itself into the back of the upright man. He dropped just as Elliot dove atop the shooter with the stomach wound.

Upon contact with the prone man, the barrel of his gun swung around, and he opened fire. Elliot spun to avoid taking a bullet to the chest, and instead, the projectile grazed the edge of his left trapezoid. It hardly did any real damage. At most, it'd need a butterfly bandage—maybe a couple of stitches.

His momentum carried him forward, and he promptly disarmed and overpowered the wounded, hollering man, slamming him onto his chest with an audible "Oof!" Using his six-foot-four, 220-pound frame to his advantage, Elliot grabbed a handful of the man's greasy black hair and drove his face deep into the hot, stifling sand. Locking his elbow out, Elliot leaned into him, riding the feeble man as he bucked and flailed.

Suffocation was a horrible way to die.

*And these assholes deserve it,* he thought, snarling.

Keeping his left hand engaged, Elliot reached back toward the other gunman, the one that now had his SOG knife in his back. The extremist with the stomach wound, the person currently beneath him, was laying atop the only other nearby weapon, another AK-47. But the man's positioning made it all but impossible for Elliot to obtain it.

So, Elliot concentrated on reacquiring his knife instead.

His fingers grazed the bloodied hilt several times before eventually wrapping around it and swiftly plucking it free. The killer was roused by the sudden movement of the blade exiting his body and reacted by going straight for his rifle.

Gritting his teeth, Elliot drove his knife back into the same man, this time, aiming for his kidneys. After the second such strike, Elliot jammed the blade in as deep as it would go and twisted it back and forth until, with one final whimper, the assailant's breath caught, and his wild eyes went still.

*Now,* Elliot thought, looking around, *where's your gun?*

He looked around and saw that it was way out of reach. And, as it was, he was out in the open. Elliot knew he'd be a sitting duck if he didn't get moving soon. The guy he thought had suffocated was still alive beneath him too. He had to get to cover before—

*Crunch.*

Three things happened at once. Firstly, the gunman beneath him finally stopped struggling. Secondly, Elliot yanked his knife free of the other corpse's lower back with a sickening *slurp*. And thirdly, a pair of booted feet impacted the scorched earth behind him.

The last extremist arrived.

Elliot sighed, his shoulders dipping.

"Don't move!" the newcomer yelled in Arabic.

"What?" Elliot asked, pretending not to understand.

Unbeknownst to many, Elliot spoke the language fluently. He was as familiar with the Middle East as any American alive. He had spent a lot of time there in the past. He had hated every minute of the constant billowing sand and heat. It was a terrible combination, but he had been there for noble reasons, so he put up with it without complaint.

"Drop your weapon!"

"What?" he shouted back, cracking his voice like a teenage boy.

"Knife down!" the assassin ordered, switching to broken English. "Hands in air."

Still straddling the suffocated man, Elliot abided the killer's demands and let go of both the dead killer's grungy hair and his knife. Slowly, Elliot raised his hands and pretended to be frightened. "Please, I'm unarmed." He faked a sob. "I'm an archaeologist, not a soldier!"

Both were *technically* true. Elliot was, in fact, an unarmed archaeologist, but for seventeen years of his life, he was an active-duty soldier, enlisting directly out of high school. He rarely ever revealed what his job had been in the military. Even now, if someone asked, he'd just broadly say, "I was in the Navy." Again, he wasn't lying. He just wasn't telling the whole truth.

Once known as Chief Special Warfare Operator Elliot Mason Oxley, "Ox," as his teammates called him, was the leader of Red Squadron's Titans. They were an elite arm of the United States Naval Special Warfare Development Group (NSWDG), also known as DEVGRU, as well as Task Force Blue. Around the world, they were more commonly referred to as SEAL Team Six.

"On feet!" the radical shouted.

*Well, here we go.*

Elliot nodded and put his hands down against the torched, grainy earth. As he pushed off, he dug his fingers deep into the compressed sand. Keeping up the charade of being scared, he spun and stumbled forward, closing the gap between himself and the lone gunman. Opening his eyes wide, he stared at the rifle and put his shaking hands—his closed fists—around the back of his head, hiding his twin fistfuls of sand.

The bearded gunman was close, only a few feet away.

While facing his would-be executioner, Elliot mentally walked through every situation possible, trying desperately to avoid getting shot point-blank. The sand would be a useful distraction, and with any luck, it would momentarily blind the bearded assassin after Elliot threw it. But if his plan didn't work, what then?

The fact that Elliot could see his face, plain as day, told him that this guy was the leader of the team, and more than likely, a wanted man. He was more than likely known throughout the region. His exposed face was intended to be used as a weapon. It would instill fear into those who recognized him.

Elliot didn't know the man. It didn't matter anyway. He wasn't intimidated by anyone based on who they were. The only time he felt unsettled about another human being was because of how big of a stick the other person carried.

Their proximity was another reason Elliot held out hope of surviving. All he had to do was toss the sand into the air, stay low, and bullrush the smaller man. But could he avoid getting shot worse than the close shave he had sustained only minutes earlier?

*Let's hope so*, he thought, deciding he'd lead with his shoulder.

He'd been shot there once before. He even recalled the hell-fire in which it burned.

Elliot laughed every time a *hero* in some overproduced Hollywood movie got shot. The film industry didn't know dick about gunshot wounds and the debilitating result they had to the area surrounding the injury. But Elliot wasn't dumb. He recognized that moviemakers were meant to entertain, not resemble real life. If they made movies out of his past experiences with the SEALs, they wouldn't be marketed as action-adventure romps.

They'd be R-rated military-horror films.

The only reason you ever heard stories of men toughing it out and finishing the mission was because the alternative was always Death's noose. Pain was a blessing compared to that. So was the accompanying adrenaline rush. Epinephrine was a soldier's best friend.

It was pumping itself through Elliot's system at the moment.

A strong gust of hot, disgusting air snapped through the high rocks surrounding the site. As a result, Elliot's overgrown, rust-colored hair billowed, sticking to his sweat-soaked, lightly freckled face. He'd been meaning to get his locks cut but had been in the field for months, bouncing from country to country, job to job.

His employers, the higher-ups at the British Museum, loved his enthusiasm and his eagerness to do anything the profession required. Yes, from leading his own digs, as he did now, to assisting others with their efforts, Elliot had quickly built a reputation as the hardest working field man around.

He owed his work ethic to the lessons learned while serving his country—a country he didn't represent anymore. Elliot was in the process of becoming an English citizen. It only seemed fitting, and it would make the paperwork a hell of a lot easier on him. He lived in London, after all.

*God save the Queen and what-have-you.*

Sidestepping to his left, away from the body beneath him, Elliot feigned a fall and rolled, throwing the sand at the shooter's face. The buffeting wind took the payload and delivered it as Elliot hoped, right into the man's eyes. Rolling one more time to his left, Elliot was now "safely" out of the wailing man's sights. He jumped to his feet and charged him. With only feet until he impacted the terrorist's gut, his gun barrel swung Elliot's way.

For a split-second, Elliot's eyes went wide, and he waited to die.

Death never came, though. The trigger was never pulled.

He was too close, and his momentum was too great. Instead of being shot, he barreled into the blinded gunman with the force of a wrecking ball. Elliot had no knife, but that didn't mean he was entirely unarmed.

Both combatants went to the ground hard. In a brawl, Elliot was far from honorable. He didn't mind fighting dirty. The first thing he did was jam his right thumb into the bearded man's left eye, driving the gritty sand in deeper. Bullets shot wildly into the sunlit sky. The noise caused Elliot to flinch. The reports were deafening. His head was only inches from the gun barrel.

Twice did the muzzle sway back toward his face.

Elliot grabbed the radical's right hand, the one holding the rifle. Like the world's deadliest game of Thumb War, Elliot wrapped his thumb around the gunman's finger, and trigger, and squeezed as hard as he could. Together, they rapidly emptied the weapon's magazine harmlessly into the sky above. With that part of the threat neutralized, Elliot solely focused on his foe.

Elliot drove his right palm into the terrorist's left eye socket, purposely abusing the same eye again. The blow was meant to concuss, possibly even incapacitate. It did the former. The local's hold loosened on the empty AK-47's handgrip, and Elliot quickly ripped it away, tossing it somewhere behind him.

Balling his fist, Elliot clubbed his adversary in the throat with a quick, cobra-like strike, landing the blow before it could be blocked. Gasping for air, the bearded man hid his face from Elliot's fury. One after the other, he beat the killer with his bare hands. He was so lost in his rage that he didn't hear the authorities shouting for him to stop. Only when he was thrown to the ground and cuffed did he understand what was happening.

He was being arrested for saving lives.

Elliot was detained for nearly eight hours due to his part in the explosive conflict, even after a number of his colleagues came rushing to his side, pleading his case. Still, the police refused to set him free. It didn't surprise him, either. Things operated differently in this part of the world.

In the West Bank, he was the outsider. If something like this happened back in the U.S., he would've been seen as a hero, not a troublemaker. Tensions were elevated all over the world, especially in a place like the West Bank. The Middle East was always centimeters away from boiling over and turning into an all-out war.

After being cuffed by two cops, Elliot was hauled to his feet, easily towering over the pair. Staying calm, he glanced over his shoulder and was happy to see that the last gunman was flat on his back, eyes closed.

*At least the asshat is down for the count,* Elliot thought.

"Stop!" Janet shouted, climbing out from beneath a nearby truck. "Don't! He saved us!"

Peter said the same thing—everyone that witnessed Elliot's daring counterstrike did. Last to arrive was Harry, and he still had Elliot's two-way radio in his hand. He'd done as Elliot asked and called out what he'd seen from high above.

A third local, not a cop, stepped up. Elliot recognized him. Elijah worked as a ranger in the Qumran National Park, and he took his job very seriously. Elliot respected that. Elijah was the one park officials sent out to investigate any, and all, disturbances occurring within the park.

Elliot had witnessed two other disruptions since stepping foot in West Bank, though, neither were like this. The first time was a theft, and the other incident involved a person having some fun with some spray paint.

*He's probably the one who called it in,* Elliot thought, nodding to the man.

"More trouble, Mr. Oxley?" Elijah asked in perfect English.

Elliot shrugged. "You know me. One thing leads to another, and—"

The injured terrorist leapt to his feet and cried out to the heavens. Brandishing a wickedly curved blade, he raised it and targeted the person nearest to him, Elijah, the park ranger. The attacker had only been playing possum, feigning his unconsciousness.

With his hands bound behind his back, Elliot was still able to yank free of the startled policemen. In one fluid motion, he spun and landed a strong back kick to the killer's wrist. Lunging forward, he then smashed his forehead into the terrorist's swollen face, dazing him and causing him to drop the blade. Elliot's assault was halted by the echoing reverberation of a gunshot.

The last of the radicals was down again. This time, it was for good. One of the cops had finally reacted and drew his pistol.

Elijah's stunned expression flicked back and forth between the body and Elliot half a dozen times before finally settling on the American. Like Elliot had done before, the park ranger gave him his own nod.

"Thank you, my friend," he said, still flabbergasted.

Elliot shrugged. "All in a day's work."

# 1

Qumran National Park, West Bank
Four Months Later

"What a day…" Elliot muttered, brushing away a layer of earth. He was back inside the thirteenth Dead Sea Cave, doing what he loved. It was peaceful and—

"What was that?"

*Oh, right,* Elliot thought. He wasn't alone.

Long gone was Harry. He'd transferred out of Elliot's team the day after they were attacked. The blonde that took his place was around the same age, another college student—but an American, like Elliot. She was tall, lean, and unbelievably beautiful.

"Nothing, Ava. It was…it was nothing."

Ava Towns was intelligent in her own right, but her father, not her qualifications, was the reason she had been thrust onto Elliot's team, with little to no field experience. Her dad was a powerful man back in the States, the Chairman of the House Armed Services Committee. The fact that Elliot was a former SEAL wasn't a coincidence either. The Congressman knew what he was doing—knew who Elliot was. He had played politics and thrown his weight around at the same time. Who better to watch over his little girl than someone like Elliot?

Elliot sighed. "Stupid bureaucrats…"

"What?" Ava asked.

He waved her off and got back to work. If there was one thing most soldiers despised, as much as the terrorists they fought, it was a politician who routinely dragged his feet. House Representative Michael Towns dragged his feet so much that Elliot swore the man was standing still. The Congressman was notorious for "thoroughly thinking things through," even in moments of crisis.

*And now I get to look after his baby girl. Yay me.*

Since the assault on the excavation, security had gratefully tripled. Chairman Towns was responsible for that, but only after his daughter had been assigned here. There were a couple of nervous days in between when Elliot's people had little safekeeping at all. Once Ava moved on from Dead Sea Cave 13Q, Elliot figured the extra protection would leave right along with her. The entire incident made international news. It made Michael Towns look like a man that got things done.

Elliot shook his head at the ridiculousness of it all, smiling to himself. There was nothing he could do, nor was there anything he wanted to do. The increased protection would at least give him some peace of mind, for the time being. Until the added security detail left, Elliot would get as much work done as he could.

So far, they had found five clay jars. Three were in mint condition. Another was in good shape, having only suffered a hairline fracture at its base. Unfortunately, one of them was smashed to pieces. It took everything in him to stop himself from imagining that another lost book of the Bible had been in at least one of his sealed jars. It's what the Qumran Caves were famous for, after all, the Dead Sea Scrolls.

Elliot was a digger and a project leader, not an expert on the scrolls themselves. He didn't understand ninety percent of the jargon inscribed on them. Each new jar they found was carefully packed into custom-made, foam-insulated crates and whisked away for a detailed examination.

The thirteenth cave was about thirty-five feet deep, and it slowly descended, merging with the back, curved wall. Elliot was kneeling in front of that wall now. Brush in hand, he gently swept away centuries of grime from a sixth jar. Gratefully, this one was still intact, from the looks of it.

"Easy does it," he said to himself.

The jar stuck up at an awkward angle. It was wedged in tight. Elliot wasn't sure if he could remove it without chipping at the stone beneath it. He hoped he wouldn't have to. The vibrations could shake the artifact to pieces if he wasn't careful.

"Easy does it."

By nature, he was a patient man, though. So, he continued to remove whatever sediment he could, until the majority of the relic could be seen. A figure knelt beside him and huffed an annoyed breath.

"Anything interesting?" Ava asked.

*Seriously?* Elliot thought. He motioned to the jar.

Ava rolled her stunning blue eyes. "Like I said…"

Elliot softly chuckled and gently nudged the jar with his free hand. It didn't give an inch. Blowing out a long, annoyed breath, he procured a small hammer and chisel set and laid down on his stomach. His knees were killing him, anyway, so the change in posture felt wonderful. The rock beneath his body was cool too.

"I'm gonna go check on the others," Ava said, getting up. When she turned, her heel nearly struck the top of the jar.

Elliot's growl was answered by a "Huh?"

Instead of scolding her for her near-catastrophic mistake, he stayed silent and got back to work. He wanted her gone to begin with, so he didn't fight the fact that she was supposed to stay by his side at all times. Whatever he could do to get her to go away, he'd do it. Her professors didn't need to know that she was the laziest of the bunch. They probably already knew.

Placing the miniature, flat-head blade near the base of the jar, Elliot softly tapped the stone with barely enough force to scar it. Surprisingly, that's all the rock needed to split and fold in on itself.

"Shit!" Elliot yelled as the world around him came apart.

"Elliot!" Ava cried out. Her voice was distant, echoing from above.

He fell what he figured was about ten feet, into darkness and dust. He landed on a downslope and instantly barrel-rolled down it, hitting another drop and then landing and rolling back the other way. It was a switchbacking network of vertically cut, angled tunnels. He could tell they had been cut that way on purpose because there was no way that this set up was natural.

Rolling another twenty or so feet, Elliot dropped into a hollow of some kind. It was pitch black, so he was unable to gauge its breadth. Moments later, he struck the ground hard and felt his shoulder separate. A typical person would yell out in excruciating pain if something like this happened to them, but not Elliot. His left shoulder was a disaster from a series of injuries and surgeries. It could easily slip free if jostled properly.

That didn't mean it still didn't hurt.

"Ow," he groaned, rolling onto his back.

Slowly, he brought his knees to his chest and slid his wrist between them. With one quick jerking motion, he popped his shoulder back into place with nothing more than a soft whimper. He'd be sore for a few days—a week, tops—but it wasn't anything that would debilitate him for too long.

Before getting to his feet, he pulled his small Maglite free from his pocket and flicked it on. Shining it straight up, Elliot found his entry point. It was fifteen feet off the ground and cut into a perfect square. The rock itself was dark grey, which made no sense.

The rock back in the cave was colored in shades of brown and red. Then again, he was pretty deep beneath 13Q, after all. Who knew what was below it?

Carefully, he held his left arm against his chest and sat up, splaying his light around the room. He focused it on the wall directly in front of him. Elliot instantly knew he'd found something incredible. Beautiful pictographs covered it, and like the stone above him, the cave wall was also grey.

"What are you?" he asked, getting to his feet.

The image before him was perfectly etched into the stone, possibly laser cut. It also depicted a dreadful scene of death. It didn't shock him that an ancient culture would proudly display such heinous artwork. The people of the past didn't know anything about nature and biologics. Their focus was to ensure bad things were not repeated so they'd routinely put focus on the bad.

The pictograph featured a group of people kneeling in reverence to something in the middle of a broad, flat valley. The object sat on a pedestal and seemed to be radiating an energy of some kind. Elliot had seen images of the Ark of the Covenant, and this looked eerily similar. Twelve rows of people prayed, hundreds in all, before what must've been a weapon of untold power.

"Just wonderful," Elliot said, his voice sounding muted from being deep beneath the ground. It was as if he was inside a soundproof recording studio—not that he'd been in many in his life.

He stepped closer to the wall-sized image and noticed something he hadn't seen at first. The first couple of rows of worshipers weren't inscribed in as much detail as the others. Indeed, as you followed the energy flow from the core to the outer edges, the people seemed to be in better focus.

It struck him.

"They aren't worshiping it," he said.

Yes, the people depicted were praying, but they were also begging for it to stop. The thing at the core of the crowd was killing them. The object, the weapon, looked like a small box.

"Hmm."

To Elliot's left and right were more pictographs. Each one, like the one before him, showed, in vivid detail, the death of a group of people. The evidence that some ancient weapon of mass destruction existed shook something inside of him. He spun, averting his eyes, closing them, and breathing hard.

His knowledge of the ancient world wasn't as in-depth as some, but his sponge-like mind retained just about everything he learned. Something from antiquity was described in such a way. It made what Elliot had found terrifying and all too real.

Greek mythology tells of a container occupied with all of the world's evils.

"Pandora's Box…" he muttered, stunned at the possibility.

The air was dank, and it rushed in from the hole above his head, creating a makeshift air conditioning system. The switchbacking tunnel he fell through was currently acting as the ductwork.

Opening his eyes, Elliot found a pedestal similar to the one in the picture behind him. On it, was a small square object constructed of a milky, foggy material. Now, he could see that it wasn't stone at all. He had no idea what it was.

He stepped forward, shining his light upon the artifact.

With each step he took, something odd happened.

The floor beneath Elliot's feet vibrated with a subtle tremor. It wasn't much, but it was nevertheless there. Whatever Elliot had just stumbled upon wasn't as ancient as he thought. Contemporary technology was present here—technology that the people of the Qumran Caves didn't possess. Either this fissure was recently constructed, or it was as old as the Dead Sea Caves, but built by someone with far more ingenuity.

*Impossible,* he thought.

Elliot didn't believe in that nonsense. He didn't think that a race of advanced beings influenced the world thousands of years ago. He looked around him and frowned. There's no way this was built in secret.

This cave had been here for a long, *long* time.

He felt a dynamic power flow through him as he continued forward. His curiosity drew him nearer, and as he closed in, the tremors intensified.

"What are you?" he asked again, this time focusing on the object and not the pictographs.

He recalled his earlier thoughts about the Ark of the Covenant and realized that he was as close to being Indiana Jones as he'd ever been. The box in front of him was his "fortune and glory." He was living *Raiders of the Lost Ark* in real-time.

Kneeling as Indy did, Elliot set his flashlight down and raised his hands out beside the artifact, one to the left, and the other to its right. The object's corners were impossibly smooth, and no, it wasn't made of stone. It was made of a type of foggy alloy. It was hard to describe. He'd never seen anything like it.

His fingers closed in on it—but stopped as the room around him came to life. Previously extinguished lights ignited above him. Even the relic began to glow from within. The alloy was more of a plastic polymer, like one of the light-up, fake ice cubes they served in some cocktails.

"Are you a type of battery?" It did kind of look like one, now that he thought about it.

Once more, his curiosity outweighed his risk assessment, and Elliot laid his hands atop the artifact's icy surface. Quickly, the lights within it strobed, heating up. Elliot screamed in agony, though it wasn't his body that was assaulted.

It was his mind.

The images that flashed across his mind were like the ones he saw etched into the chamber's walls. Hundreds of millions were dead. All because of the six-inch-by-six-inch box. Additional visions of destruction attacked his consciousness until he couldn't take it anymore. With one final, anguish-filled wail, Elliot released the unknown object and collapsed in on himself.

# 2

"The Cradle has been discovered," the agent confirmed.

The person's identity was concealed on video through a series of voice filters and dark lighting. Osiris knew the informant could be trusted because the language being spoken was one only a handful of people on the planet knew.

It was the "Language of the Gods."

The dialect was a combination of the ancient languages predominantly spoken in places like Egypt, Greece, China, and Mesoamerica. Unless you were fluent in them all and had the mental capacity to transition between them with ease, you wouldn't have stood a chance trying to decipher it.

In ancient Egypt, Osiris was the lord of the underworld, and in his organization here, "Osiris" was also king. Like the other men of his given moniker that preceded his station, he led the Prophets. They had one unified goal: Finish the work of their creators.

"You're sure it's our Cradle?" Osiris asked, understandably skeptical.

Until now, the Cradle had been missing for over a thousand years, hidden away by the last of the god-like race of humanoids responsible for mankind's advancement. It's what the Prophets believed, anyway.

Legend says that the last of the gods whisked the Cradle away after he fell in love with a mortal woman, having a change of heart about deleting the evidence of their race's existence on Earth. As the last of his kind to inhabit the planet, it was his responsibility to do so. Osiris himself had doubts about ever seeing it with his own eyes.

The descendants of the gods, Osiris included, were charged with caring for the Cradle, and since they had no artifact to watch over, their calling shifted to recovering it at all costs—violently, if need be. In the not too distant past, some of their tactics were described as extreme or terroristic.

Osiris and his followers believed that they contained a strain of the ancient god's DNA inside of them. If a geneticist knew where to look, he or she would've noticed a small anomaly fused to the code within a very select populace. Only a hundred or so existed that Osiris knew about.

Each one of them was either brought into the fold, sometimes forcefully, or they were terminated because they had been seen as future threats. Soviet-style brainwashing was used on occasions. Most of the time, they only had to surgically implant an explosive into the recruit's brain and occasionally refer to it to get the person to comply.

It was brutal and farfetched, exactly how Osiris wanted it.

"Yes, Osiris, I am sure it is the one true Cradle."

He nodded. "Excellent, Hel. Continue with your operation."

Before they disconnected from their untraceable call, Hel spoke up. "What about the man who discovered it? There are rumors that he may have activated it."

Osiris' greying brow raised, and his eyes widened. "Impossible! Only a child of a god can do that!"

Hel's blacked-out form shrank away at his outburst. Rarely did he ever get this worked up.

The agent bowed in apology. "I'm sorry, but that's what is being said. He's been rambling on about seeing images of annihilation and despair. All of it coming after touching the Cradle."

Sitting back in his plush office chair, Osiris wiped the sweat from his bald head. He took a minute to properly think things through before giving his agent his next orders.

Only a few knew of the existence of the room that Osiris found himself in. His prized agent, Hel, was one of them. His location was always labeled as "UNKNOWN" in all his communications. The room was located beneath his office and was lined with lead, doubling as an emergency fallout bunker.

"Where is he now?" Osiris asked.

"At a hospital in Jericho."

He nodded. "Good. Visit our new friend and see if what he says is true."

"It won't be easy," Hel replied. "He's under twenty-four hours a day armed watch."

Osiris grinned. "Then, use your training and get close." He leaned forward. "I want to know…" He leaned in even closer, "Now."

**Hel's name came** from the Norse goddess of death, not to be confused with the fictional variation, Hella. Her real identity, like Osiris and the others inside the Prophets, was a closely guarded secret. Outside of the order, she appeared to be an everyday woman. That's precisely what the Prophets wanted too. The participants in the organization had a pact to never give up their identities and would protect that secret until their dying breath. One way or the other, no one would ever know who they are.

Given her age and physical stature, it was surprising how lethal of an assassin Hel was. She'd become something of a legend within the Prophets because of the abilities she displayed. Osiris took her in after her parents were murdered when she was young, and after her godly DNA was confirmed, she immediately began her schooling.

"What are they?" she once asked Osiris.

"Gods," he replied, steadfastly, "and we are their children."

Even now, Hel was somewhat skeptical that the ancient beings he spoke of were truly gods. She did, however, believe that they were incredible creatures, the likes of which people on the planet hadn't seen in centuries. She mostly stayed with the organization because of the wealth and status it had created for her. But she also remained with the Prophets out of fear.

She was terrified of her father.

Every significant culture throughout the globe had similar beginnings. Teachers of incredible, life-changing knowledge seemed to have randomly popped up all over the world. Hel knew it wasn't random, though. The Cradle was responsible and had what was described as otherworldly power contained within it.

"What is it?" she asked.

"What is what, my child?" Osiris replied.

"The Cradle. What is it?"

He contemplated how to reply. Hel was still very young, only eight-years-old at the time. She held an off-the-charts IQ and was easy to hold a conversation with despite what seemed appropriate for a child of her life experiences. She was what some described as an "old soul."

Osiris sat Hel on his knee and explained.

"We Prophets believe that the Cradle is a source of unimaginable power."

"Like a nuclear power plant?" she asked, showing off a bit of her intelligence.

He shrugged. "In a way, yes. But no, that's not what I would call it. You see, the Cradle is supernatural in a way, yet entirely technological as well."

"I don't understand," Hel said, looking annoyed.

Osiris laughed. "You mean I stumped the great Hel, Goddess of Death?"

She giggled. Hel loved her new name, though, she knew she'd have to use her birth name, when required, like when she was out in public. Some would say Hel had been brainwashed, or indoctrinated, into a cult. She didn't care what others whispered about her. She was being taken care of and had anything she'd ever need.

Her master, while also her father, had never let her down. If she asked for something, he'd given it to her without question. Hel knew not to push him, something she'd learned a year before when she had mouthed off to him. As punishment, Hel was put in an insulated isolation chamber for a week.

No sound—no human contact for 168 hours. The only exception was for her meals, which were delivered through a rectangular slot at the base of the door.

It was the last time Hel had defied her master.

Her face said it all. Hel still didn't understand.

Osiris turned her around so she could easily see him. Looking him square in the eyes, she was floored by what he said.

"I think our Cradle is what some believe to be Pandora's Box."

From that moment forward, Hel immersed herself in everything revolving around the myth of Pandora's legendary box. She quickly became the organization's foremost mind on the subject, working side by side with Osiris himself.

*It's still so hard to believe,* she thought, strutting onward.

Hel was a beautiful specimen to behold. It helped her in her work. She could get close to anyone she desired, man or woman. In this case, she was headed upstairs inside the Jericho Governmental Hospital to visit Elliot Oxley. He was a hero to some, having taken down a small group of terrorists before becoming the first man to discover alien technology on Earth.

Even Hel wasn't sure whether or not the gods of old were extraterrestrials or not. The Prophets' historians didn't have information that dated back far enough. Hel was fascinated by what she did know and that was that one day the ancient beings just appeared out of nowhere.

*Where did you come from?*

It was one of a million questions she had for the Cradle. Hel hoped that her questions would be answered once she had it in her possession. She had no idea how that would happen, but she hoped it would. She was excited about the fact that this Oxley character had a reaction to it when he touched it. It gave her hope. She prayed that she might have a similar experience once she laid her hands on it. She expected amazing things. After all, the mutation in her DNA, the "god levels," were among the highest ever recorded.

"Why you?" she asked herself, wondering why, out of all people in the world, it was Oxley that was chosen. As far as she knew, he was nothing special.

Her spoken question got the attention of a nurse.

"Excuse me?" the woman asked in fractured English.

Hel put on her practiced smile. "Where can I find Elliot Oxley?"

The woman's face soured. "I'm sorry, but Mr. Elliot is not seeing anyone today." She motioned to the men with guns stationed down the hall of the hospital.

Hel's smile turned into a predatory sneer. "Tell him I'm a special friend, okay?"

Hel closed her hand into a fist and squeezed so hard that the joints audibly popped. The local woman flinched and nodded.

"Please," Hel pleaded, "you have no idea how much it'll mean to me if I can speak with him."

# 3

Elliot climbed to the peak of a smoking husk of land. He was still too low to see much of anything, but the intense heat that rolled down the grade told him that something terrible awaited him. His brain made him instantly think of a nuclear bomb denotating. Elliot looked skyward and had his premonitions confirmed.

A mushroom cloud was easily visible. A bomb had gone off, and Elliot knew he was too close to it to survive. So, Elliot climbed higher and faster. If he were going to die, he'd at least see it for what it was. He'd meet his maker head-on and give him the finger before he turned to dust.

Stumbling forward, Elliot finally made it to the top of the enormous, city-sized crater. With him were three people, none of whom he recognized. Mostly because he couldn't see their faces. Every time he tried to identify one of their faces they would conveniently be veiled in shadows.

He knew he should feel frustrated, but he didn't. Elliot, instead, turned his attention back to the mushroom cloud. The blast was rolling down a hill. It resembled a pyroclastic cloud belonging to that of an erupting volcano.

*Is that what this is?*

No, Elliot knew better. This wasn't some natural disaster. He could feel it in his bones—in his soul. The destruction was being caused by his hands. Looking down at them, he saw blood. The metaphor was too perfect. The blood was, quite literally, on his hands.

His mind slipped back into the chamber beneath Dead Sea Cave 13Q. He watched over the shoulder of the past Elliot, as he grabbed the artifact. When he touched it, the fogged material lit up and pulsed. Each *whump* of energy hit the other Elliot like a gunshot. His body jerked backward, but he didn't let go. His hands seemed to be glued to the relic's surface somehow.

*Radiation?* Elliot thought, peacefully observing.

He had no idea how or why he was being shown what had happened to him, or whether the out-of-body experience was real or just a figment of his imagination.

After the first pulse hit, Elliot was shown an image of the Great Pyramid of Giza. Next, the Colossus of Rhodes. Then, the Lighthouse of Alexandria. One by one, he was jolted by an unknown energy source. Following each impact, he was shown a glimpse into the past. Each time, it was like a short movie, and every time, it revolved around one of the Seven Wonders of the Ancient World. He saw all of them perfectly intact, and they were glorious.

After the seventh such pulse of energy, he was thrown back into the scene depicting the cataclysmic event. He rolled down the incline and stopped, feeling a series of small pebbles dig into his palms. It felt so real.

*Can't be…*

Elliot tried to catch his breath, but he couldn't. He wheezed for what felt like an hour before finally inhaling a long singular gulp of oxygen. Stumbling to his knees, Elliot looked back up to the hill. With no end to the *vision* sight, he got up and rejoined the trio of shadowy figures. He dusted himself off and crossed his arms.

"This is a dream, isn't it?"

The three shaded faces returned his gaze and spoke in unison. Their voices were identical, deep and booming.

"That may be, but…" Their bodies were swiftly turned to dust by an incoming wave of heat, "you're our only hope."

While the famous *Star Wars* line should've been comical, it wasn't. Not at a time like this. The world, or at least the piece he was standing on, was ending—and ending violently. Why was he their only hope? How could someone like him save them from something as devastating as a nuclear explosion?

He woke up before he could get an answer.

**Covered in sweat**, it took Elliot a second to realize where he was. The last thing he remembered was clutching the artifact in his hands. Then, he screamed and blacked out. Strangely, nothing hurt physically. He was tired, though. He felt mentally worn out. Nothing since the SEALs had made Elliot feel like this. Nothing. He'd never felt this exhausted since retiring.

"What the hell…" he said, squeezing shut his shaking hands.

Gone were the irritating stones from his hands. The abusive heat had vanished too.

He was spooked, terrified by the dreams—the images—rattling around in his brain. He felt as if he'd personally lived the life of the people that had perished so horribly. It wasn't just the crowd bowing before the pedestal that he saw. It was dozens of other events as well. And at the center of every one of them was the artifact.

Sitting in his bed, Elliot frantically searched his room for the object. Not seeing it, he forced himself to calm down, knowing it wouldn't be here. A find of that magnitude would've been spirited away immediately after it was discovered. He knew he'd probably never see it again.

"Good riddance," he moaned, laying back.

A lover of history, he tried to focus on the Seven Wonders of the Ancient World. His arms were still broken out in goosebumps. The beauty of them all at their zenith gave him a feeling that he'd only felt one other time in his life. That was fifteen years ago, however, when he realized that he truly loved a woman by the name of Magdalen Bitar, a young Egyptologist who worked for the Museum of Egyptian Antiquities in Cairo. Currently, there were murmurs that she was about to accept a promotion that would make her the museum's next director.

Their jobs made it almost impossible to have a long-term, worthwhile relationship. They had tried to make it work over the years, staying in contact for some time before finally calling it off. Elliot had been the one to end it actually, and he wasn't proud of the way he'd gone about it. Like a coward, he wrote a letter to the love of his life, instead of talking to her like a real man would've. He had wanted to do it right, but he just couldn't get himself to speak the works out loud, so he'd turned to the pen instead.

*Dammit, Maggy…*

He grabbed his head. "What's happening to me?"

Elliot hadn't thought about Maggy in years. It's not that he didn't still care for her. He did. He thought that time had healed those wounds long ago. Elliot was smart enough to see that his feelings for Maggy had only been buried, not extinguished. His work kept him busy, which kept his mind off the Egyptologist.

The artifact had jarred something loose inside of him. He found it hard to focus on one single thing. It was like he had instantly developed ADHD overnight. Elliot blinked hard and shook his head, hoping it would help clear his thoughts.

It didn't.

He was an exceptional soldier when under duress. He was able to stay calm and focus no matter the situation. His squad mates had joked that he owned an iron will the likes of which no one had ever seen. Lincoln, his number two, said it was also his large set of brass balls.

He shook, uncomfortable with his surroundings. Elliot wasn't sure why he was so on edge. Hospitals had never bothered him in the past.

"The thing."

He knew it had to be it. Whatever it contained, it broke something loose inside of his mind. So, being the seasoned veteran that he was, Elliot decided to meet the newfound discomfort instead of running from it. He closed his eyes and pictured the Great Pyramid of Giza.

*Okay, you can do this. Focus. Remember what you saw.*

Elliot gripped his bedsheets as he was jetted away to Egypt…ancient Egypt. He was soaring over the pyramids like a bird, experiencing the sights like never before. He'd been to Giza twice before, but that was in their current state and at ground level. Now, he was seeing them as they were in their prime.

"Woah."

The trio of megaliths was encased in polished, white limestone. They gleamed against the setting sun and showed off Khufu's greatest feature. Its long-lost capstone.

The Great Pyramid of Giza was the first of the Seven Wonders. Remarkably, being the oldest, it's also the only one that still stands today. Named after the pharaoh of the Fourth Dynasty, Khufu was a sight to behold.

*Especially now,* Elliot thought. *Let's see if I can get a closer look.*

Excited, he willed himself lower and was practically thrown atop Khufu's pyramidion, its capstone. A capstone was typically constructed of granite or additional limestone, like its casing stones, but unlike the casing stones, the pyramidion was finished in layers of gold leaf. The ancient rulers wished for their tomb to be seen from great distances. Khufu's peak kind of reminded Elliot of a rudimentary lighthouse.

Carefully he landed just below the base of the pyramidion, not understanding why he didn't slip off and tumble down the 450-foot pyramid. The gleaming capstone added another thirty feet of height, and it towered over Elliot's head. Stepping forward, he placed his hand on its radiant surface and was stunned when it vibrated—just like the artifact beneath 13Q.

Reacting to his touch, the pyramidion broke away from the rest of Khufu with a burst of compressed air. It rose into the afternoon sky, revealing a hollow space beneath. The capstone really was just a cap. Hidden beneath it was a space similar to the one Elliot found the artifact in.

The cap paused twenty feet above his head, hovering in midair like it was nothing. Elliot tried to wrap his head around what he was witnessing, but he couldn't make heads or tails of it. Like the core, this…outer body experience…was something new for him. He wasn't a lucid dreamer. Elliot never lived inside his own mind while he was sleeping, as some people did.

He stepped beneath the hovering cap as walls of light shot down and met Khufu's presently flat peak. The only thing within the space was a pedestal. It was an exact duplicate to the one he'd seen with his own eyes.

"Where's the core?" he asked.

He lifted his hand and the artifact suddenly appeared in his right hand.

"Uh…"

Maybe he was lucid dreaming? The object wasn't in his hand until he started thinking about the location where he'd found it. The pedestal had a one-inch indentation in it. You'd have to be an idiot not to understand that it's where the core belonged.

Elliot shrugged. "Eh, what's the harm?"

It was a memory, after all. He knew, memories, no matter how vivid they were, couldn't physically harm you. Mental pain, however… Memories could definitely do a number on you.

His back and legs were still sore from his tumble down the apocalyptic hill and his real-life unsteady entry into the core's underground chamber. Still, something drew him forward. Elliot *had* to know what would happen if the object was docked.

Once the artifact passed over the edge of the metallic pedestal, it was ripped free from his hands and floated itself into position. Elliot glanced up and down, figuring it had to be some sort of magnetic field or something. The air turned cold, too, causing him to shiver in the desert sun.

The core lowered and slipped into the square cutout on top of the dock. An audible click followed, and the world went dark once more.

Elliot waited for the lights to bloom back to life. When they did, the other Seven Wonders appeared to him again in sharper detail. Was this his path? Was he supposed to go to their sites, a few of which had never been discovered?

He heard the door to his room open, and he was forcefully expelled from the vision, dropping two feet to the bed. His body had been airborne, a sight he wished he could've seen for himself.

"Mr. Elliot?"

Breathing hard, he wiped his sweaty forehead with his bedsheet and replied. "Yes?"

A local woman wearing all white, a nurse, poked her head in. She was about his age and had a full, cheerful face. "You have a visitor."

"I do?" He looked around the empty room. "Who is it?"

# 4

Trouble was in the air, and Agent Ryan was up to the challenge of defusing it. He'd spent a lifetime of "taking care of the situation," first when he'd been in the Armed Forces, then while a member of the CIA. Now, he worked for a division of the "Company" that few knew existed. Even Ryan knew nothing about it until he was "asked" to join.

When he was first approached about the group, Ryan thought it was a joke. His recruiter, someone he knew well, threw it at him one day at lunch.

"We're a little like the *Men in Black*, but this is real."

"Aliens?" Ryan asked.

Mark Conners waved his hand. "Um, sure, we can go with that. What we are is the first and last line of defense against an ancient organization that predates the Giza pyramids."

Ryan's eyes opened wide. "Really? So, the stories within the agency are true?"

Mark silently nodded his head. "Think of it as an arms race of the extraterrestrial kind."

"Alien weapons?"

"And sciences."

"What if I say, 'no?'" Ryan asked, smiling.

But there was no way in hell he wasn't going to join. Even in his early forties, Agent Ryan was still a little juvenile. He loved worldly adventure, never wanting to stay put for too long, and he had an awful, raunchy sense of humor. But he was also one hundred percent loyal to his work.

He was a little rough around the edges. Other than that, he was a damn-fine agent.

Mark leaned in close. "Don't say no."

Ryan wasn't a dummy. He knew what Mark's warning was meant to do. A) Scare him. B) Terrify him. If he openly rejected his friend's offer, Ryan would be on his own. Just like that. Gone.

Also, if he did reject the offer, there wouldn't be anyone who believed that he'd been let go because he refused to transfer to the government's special alien division. Even now, as he threw open the front door to the Jericho Governmental Hospital in the West Bank, he had a hard time believing what he did for a living.

But he'd seen the enemy up close. Never the same person twice, either. Women and men. Young and old. The Prophets recruited them all. One singular goal was shared between the Prophets and his organization: Find the Cradle before the other group did.

Unfortunately, there were other devices hidden around the world that

Ryan and others were after as well. However, none of them were of a higher priority than the Cradle. It was everything to them, which meant it was also everything to Ryan.

After his twenty-three-minute lunch-time interview, Agent Ryan was officially a member of an outfit called Prometheus, a deep, black-ops arm buried within the CIA. Over the years, agents heard that the group may be out there, but no one could ever confirm that it existed. It was always labeled as an old wives' tale or a wild goose chase.

Or just plain fucking stupid.

*Prometheus,* he thought.

The name was fitting. Even with all the evils Pandora released upon the world, there was still hope left inside her box. Prometheus, the Titan, was the one who had stolen fire from the heavens. He was credited for creating mankind out of clay, but in reality, he was *only* to thank for humanity's eventual advancement. The "fire," as it was described by the poet Hesiod, was really the energy source found within the Cradle.

Agent Ryan grinned. The things he learned in the coming years were all astonishing. Hesiod was a rogue agent of what predated the inception of the Prometheus organization. He was trying to let the world know what had happened without being identified. The poet failed, though, and he was silenced forever.

The most fascinating tidbit Ryan had learned was that the archaic god, Prometheus, was real. He was the last of an ancient race of beings and was responsible for what they and the Prophets sought, the Cradle—his fire. At the time of their presence, humankind did not understand technology or put much faith in the sciences. Instead, the Cradle's creators were deemed as heavenly deities and all the high-tech stuff was considered supernatural, or magical.

Agent Ryan stopped at the front desk to get directions to a patient's room.

"Good morning, sir," the receptionist said. Her English was pretty damn good. "How may I help you?"

Agent Ryan grinned and took off his sunglasses.

He slipped into the local dialect, getting a smile out of the attractive young woman. "I'm here to see a man by the name of Elliot Oxley."

**"Ava, hi," Elliot** said, a little embarrassed that she was seeing him like this.

Elliot was, after all, only wearing his boxers. He wasn't expecting his assistant to come and check on him. Normally, he wouldn't care what he was or wasn't wearing. It was different now. He felt more anxious than usual. Something had undeniably come loose inside his brain following the incident. He just didn't feel right.

The door shut. "How are you, Elliot?"

He would prefer it more if his assistant wasn't acting so casual with their relationship. Given the informal setting, though, he couldn't expect the formality he wanted. After all, she was speaking to him as a concerned friend, not a colleague.

"I'm okay," Elliot lied, "a little tired, I guess." He speedily moved the conversation away from his condition. "Any news from the excavation?"

Ava's eyes lit up, excited. She also looked a little wired.

"There's so much to discuss, but first…"

She reached around the small of her back, beneath her jacket. Elliot had no idea why she was even wearing one. They were in the desert, after all. It was too damn hot for such a thing. The leather garb did accentuate her cleavage, though. Maybe that's why she decided to adorn it.

Elliot's instincts told him to jump out of bed and subdue the woman. She was about to pull a gun on him and shoot him. He had no idea if the hospital had metal detectors. He honestly doubted it.

"Ava, what—"

"Look at these!"

She snapped up her phone and hurried forward. Elliot's grip on his bedsheets eased, and his mind relaxed. Laughably, he'd just mistaken his research assistant for an assassin.

*What the hell, Elliot?* he thought, blinking his eyes hard.

Looking down, he watched in awe as Ava scrolled through a series of pictures.

"They're all blurry," he remarked, looking up at the tall woman.

She shrugged. "I know. I tried several times to get my phone to focus, but it just wouldn't. I even tried every Instagram filter I could think of. It's like the pictographs didn't want me taking pictures of them."

"And the cube, where is it?"

Ava frowned. "It's still there."

"Really?" Elliot asked.

She nodded. "No one can get close to it."

"Why…not?" Elliot asked, wincing as he sat up.

She smiled like a shark. "It won't let us."

He had no idea what that meant, but he needed to see it with his own eyes. Not caring about the fact that he was practically nude, Elliot leapt out of bed. Ava didn't seem to mind either. Glancing back at her, Elliot saw her staring at his abs, then the slight bulge in the front of his boxers. She was biting her lip and blushing too.

*Down girl,* he thought, turning away before they made eye contact.

He chuckled and looked for something to wear. If he still had his boxers, then maybe his clothes were somewhere close. He found them moments later in a drawer across the room. His jeans, socks, and black Volbeat shirt were neatly folded and washed. The treatment he'd been given here was impressive. Of course, he had no other clothes with him unless someone was willing to go back to his apartment and gather them.

Swiftly throwing everything on, Elliot snagged his wallet from the nightstand, slipped into his work boots, and headed for the door. He was about to break a major rule and leave without being properly discharged. He was a man on a mission, and no orderly was going to keep him from his destination.

*What has gotten into me?*

Prior to touching that core, Elliot would have never acted like this. Usually, he'd be in complete control, no matter what, like he had been up in 13Q with Harry. But not now. At this moment, he felt uncomfortable in his own skin.

Throwing open the door, Elliot and Ava dashed out. Directly across the hall was the central nurses' station built of two large semi-circle desks with a path through the middle. Past it was another hall identical to the one Elliot now stood in. The workstation was circular and filled with different sized monitors, each displaying an array of information regarding the admitted patients.

Unexpectedly, to his right, fifty feet away, a man with a woman that looked remarkably similar to Ava rounded a corner and drew pistols. Each quickly snapped off two shots, directing their aim at Elliot's guards. He turned and shoved Ava back into his room, just as the four projectiles sizzled right between them and hit his armed protectors in the chest. Before the shooters could get off another volley, the elevator situated further down the hall dinged. Elliot and Ava were now pinned between a pair of assassins and whoever was about to join them.

A lone man, dressed swankier than Elliot, stepped out and raised his already drawn gun. He fired two quick rounds. Both hit the male gunman in the chest. The woman disappeared back around the corner before the newcomer could get another shot off.

More surprising than the shootout itself, was the man who had come to his rescue. Elliot hadn't seen his old friend in some time.

"Lincoln?"

"Hey, Ox," Lincoln said, grinning like an idiot, "how's it hangin'?" Ava stepped out from inside Elliot's room and immediately got the man's attention. "Oh, well, hello there…" Then, his eyes darted back and forth between Elliot and the much younger woman. "Ahhh, I see." He gazed at Ava and winked. "You have good taste in men."

Lincoln Ryan was Elliot's second-in-command back with the SEALs. They were close, best friends even. Unfortunately, once Elliot retired, Lincoln fell off the face of the earth. At the time of his own resignation, Elliot knew Lincoln was close to calling it quits himself. Back then, there were rumors that one of the agencies had interests in him.

"How?" Elliot asked, pointing at Lincoln. Next, he motioned to the end of the hallway. "Who?"

Lincoln laughed and slapped him on the shoulder. "Come on, Ox. I'll explain on the way."

"Where are we go—?"

Ava's question was interrupted when two more assassins stepped into view and opened fire on their position. The woman, the one Lincoln had missed, was joined by another armed man.

"Now what?" Elliot asked, pulling Ava down to the floor behind the nurses' station. He was unarmed and didn't even have his knife this time.

Joining them, Lincoln got to one knee, keeping his weapon, a Sig Sauer P226, leveled at the corridor. From there, they could barely see past Elliot's room. The rest of the hallway was obscured by drywall and plaster.

Concern was plastered on Lincoln's face. He didn't intend to be met with conflict. "Now," he glanced behind them, "we run."

# 5

The positioning of Elliot's room made it easily defendable for the local security force that had swiftly been taken out. Elliot was surprised that the two men had stuck around long enough to be killed. They held no real interest in what was clearly somebody else's fight.

Re-entering it was out of the question, as was using the elevator. The latter was too slow and could be shut down with the flick of a switch. They were all sitting ducks if they got stuck in between floors. So instead, Lincoln led them straight through the spherical nurses' station, shouting for everyone to get down. Everyone that didn't run, hid, and most of them were women. Elliot wanted to stop and help them, but it was because of him that these people were in danger to begin with.

The first gunshots had been directed at the men protecting him, after all.

Ava was falling behind after only a few steps. She wasn't moving as quickly as Elliot and Lincoln. He wasn't surprised at Ava's reaction to the violence. The guards too had been stunned into inaction. Ava was a civilian, and a young one at that. She wasn't an Elliot or a Lincoln.

Behind them, their previous hiding spot was torn to shreds by automatic gunfire. Elliot covered his head and looked back, eyes wide. Ava was nowhere to be seen.

"Ava!" he shouted.

There was no answer.

"I see her!" Lincoln yelled. "She took off down another hallway." The monitors above the desks were obliterated next. "Smart girl," he added, jaw clenched

"You wouldn't happen to have another gun, would you?" Elliot asked. "I'd rather not be empty-handed at a time like this."

Lincoln rolled his eyes and reached around to his back. He handed Elliot a second P226 and smiled. "You're welcome."

Elliot took the offered firearm and checked it over before readying it. He had used a similar Sig Sauer variant many times before and loved the make and model.

A third barrage shredded the workstation further. Lincoln pulled Elliot to his feet, and the two men scampered into a nearby office before it was turned to swiss cheese.

*How many of them are there now?* he thought.

Back on their hands and knees, the pair of former SEALs crawled through the rear door and zig-zagged their way further away from the ever-growing group of gunmen.

"Who are these assholes?" Elliot asked.

"The enemy," Lincoln replied.

"No shit, but who?"

"They're a group we've been at war with for years."

"We?" Elliot asked, wanting more information.

"Yeah, *we*," Lincoln replied, apparently not ready to give up the ghost just yet.

They slid behind a secondary counter and kept watch, listening carefully to anyone who came close. On two occasions, Elliot almost shot a member of the hospital staff. It had been a while since he'd been in a firefight like this, plus he wasn't entirely focused and was dealing with whatever happened inside his head.

Elliot was armed and twitchy. It was a recipe for disaster.

"Here," he said, offering his P226 back to Lincoln. "I don't trust myself with this—not right now."

Lincoln stopped and turned. "You're kidding me, right?" He shoved it back toward Elliot. "You may not fully trust yourself after a decade away from it, but I do."

"No, Linc, you don't under—"

"No, you don't understand," Lincoln interrupted. "We die if you don't help me!"

Elliot bit his lip but nodded in agreement. Even if he wasn't at full strength, he was still better than most.

*Just stay calm and follow Linc's lead.*

After a minute of silence, one of the killers stepped into view directly behind Lincoln. Pushing his friend to the ground, Elliot snapped up his gun and pulled the trigger. The result was devastating.

Blood, brains, and bone fragments splattered everything behind the assassin, including the killer's buddy, who had been following closely after him. Elliot put two bullets in the sneering man's chest, killing both of their assailants in seconds.

Breathing heavily, Elliot looked at Lincoln.

"You good?" Lincoln asked, plainly seeing Elliot's inner struggle.

Elliot nodded.

Together, the duo stood and sent a volley of gunfire back the way they'd come. A scream told them that they'd successfully disabled at least one additional gunman.

The immediate area went silent once more. Elliot and Lincoln both scanned the smaller, secondary nurses' station and found no other adversaries. Looking back at Elliot, Lincoln gave him another shit-eating grin.

"Not too bad for a has-been."

**Hel couldn't believe** that her men had missed their chance, especially with an agent of Prometheus here. While dangerous in his own right, the outnumbered operative should've still been easy to take down. He'd proven to be a difficult target thus far, though. She recognized Lincoln Ryan from surveillance photos captured by Prophets spies. Thankfully, he didn't seem to recognize her.

Hel had done well to keep her head down over the years. Few people outside her organization ever discovered who she really was. The people who did find out who she was had died either by her hand or under "accidental" circumstances.

Alone, she cautiously stalked forward. Four of her men were down. Three of them were dead. The man that hadn't been dispatched appeared from behind the remains of the ruined nurses' station. His shoulder was bloodied as was his side. He was in bad shape, possibly suffering from life-threatening injuries.

"Report," she ordered.

He took a deep breath before speaking. "They're gone."

"Gone?"

The agent nodded. "Yes." He grimaced in pain. "Osiris will not be pleased."

Hel drew her pistol and shot the man in the head.

"Nor am I," she said, grinding her teeth.

Raising her hand to her left ear, Hel tapped the small device buried inside it. The comms link held a direct line to her master.

"Report," he said, ordering her as she had just done to the man lying at her feet.

"Failure," she said flatly. There was no reason to sugarcoat things.

"This is…disappointing," Osiris replied.

"Yes, it is," she agreed, quickly relaying what had occurred.

"Hmm," Osiris mumbled, "this may present a problem."

Hel stayed silent and waited. She'd be given another set of orders.

"Do not pursue. Wait for reinforcements."

The line went dead.

Now, she had a decision to make. Hel could either follow Osiris' hold order or pursue her target on her own—and she'd be on her own. She could expect no backup if she openly defied her master.

Never one to back down from a challenge, Hel shrugged and procured the earbud/tracking device. She dropped it on the ground and stomped on it with the heel of her boot. Then, she casually kicked the remains aside. There'd be no tracing the gadget's origins. It would be swept up with the rest of the debris and discarded without being discovered.

She'd surely be reprimanded for going rogue, but if she succeeded… If she didn't, she could always disappear under the guise of a false identity. She owned seven of them and could recite their backstories without hesitation. Even Osiris was only aware of three of them. An agent had to watch their backs and cover their tracks—even from those they worked for. She had money hidden around the world and could live comfortably for the rest of her life. If this was the end of her time with the Prophets, then so be it.

"It was fun while it lasted," she said, recalling all the horrible things she'd done in the name of a belief she didn't fully accept.

*And that's IF I can stay alive.*

Hel pounded around the nurses' station, calming as she peeked out into the next hallway. All was calm. She needed to move before she was discovered by the police. They'd arrive shortly. If Hel was imprisoned, then her mission would, indeed, be over—and so would her life.

Walking softly, heel-to-toe, she listened for any clue to her quarry's whereabouts. If she could end it, here and now, she would. If not, she'd discontinue her pursuit as Osiris had ordered.

After passing a dozen or so rooms, Hel was beginning to doubt that her targets were still in the immediate vicinity.

But then, she saw *her*.

**"Elliot!"**

Ava sounded scared. It was evident that someone was attacking her, and Elliot and Lincoln were already en route to her. They needed to get to her fast. Apparently, the Prophets held no qualms about killing innocents.

*Unless they take her hostage.* She was a Congressman's daughter, after all.

They were close enough to hear a dense *thud* as Ava was struck. Then, a crash as she fell into something. Edging down the main hall, guns up, Elliot and Lincoln froze when they saw Ava appear from around the corner. She went down hard, bleeding from a cut to her temple. Then, she was dragged away, kicking and screaming.

"Where are they?" someone shouted. The voice was also female, and she snarled her words, seething with rage.

"I don't know!" Ava cried back. "I swear, I don't know where they are!"

Elliot heard Ava get struck again. He needed to stop this before his assistant was killed, all because of him.

Without waiting for Lincoln, he darted out into the center nurses' station and leveled his Sig Sauer at Ava's assailant. It was the woman from before, the one who had opened fire on them as they were exiting his room. She had a maniacal look on her face, crazed and deranged.

Then, she was gone, diving behind one of the desks before he could get a clean shot off. Elliot went straight for Ava. Her face was severely beaten, and her hairline was slathered in blood. Her left forearm was bleeding too.

Lincoln stepped out and covered Elliot long enough for him to pick up the whimpering girl and head for cover back into the corridor behind them. Shots rang out as Elliot and Ava disappeared. Lincoln had opened fire on someone, most likely the woman with the fiery eyes.

"What happened?" Elliot asked, setting Ava down and checking her injuries. Everything looked superficial at best, but still, Ava was in pretty bad shape.

She shook her head, terrified to answer.

"Ava."

Elliot placed a gentle hand under her chin and forced her to look at him. "You're okay now."

With watering eyes, the young woman burst into tears and threw herself into his chest. For a moment, he did nothing but let her cry. He noticed it was the only sound he heard. Lincoln had stopped shooting and stepped up next to them.

"Time to go," he said, checking his magazine. He replaced it with a sharp click, startling Ava in the process.

Elliot looked up at him and nodded. Standing, he helped Ava to her feet. Luckily for them, her wounds didn't extend to her legs. She could walk just fine, but they'd need to hurry. Gripping one of her shaky hands, he pulled her along behind him.

They entered the stairwell at the end of the hall and quickly descended two floors. With one remaining, Lincoln stopped them.

"Gun."

Elliot lifted a questioning eyebrow.

"We're bound to run into police," Lincoln explained. "Best not be armed when we do."

Agreeing with his friend's assessment, Elliot handed over his weapon and watched as Lincoln wiped down the handgrips with a handkerchief. He opened the door to the second floor and quickly peeked out. With the coast clear, he hurried to the nearest wastebasket and tossed them in.

"Ready?" Lincoln asked.

Seconds later, he rejoined Elliot and Ava, and the trio continued their descent. In a hurry, Elliot scooped up Ava in his arms before exiting the stairwell. Lincoln threw up his hands and shouted like a madman when a foursome of local cops aimed rifles at them.

"Don't shoot!" he cried. "Up there!" he pointed back to the stairs. "People with guns!"

Elliot faked a stumble, clutching the injured Ava hard. The policemen's eyes went to her, and their barrels lowered.

"Mr. Elliot!"

It was his nurse.

"You know this man?" one of the cops asked.

The local woman nodded. "He's one of my patients."

"He's a patient?" the police officer asked, looking him up and down.

Elliot smiled, not at all looking injured. With Ava still in his arms, he shrugged. "What can I say, I'm a quick healer."

# 6

Amid the late-afternoon chaos, and the lack of a real police presence, Elliot, Lincoln, and Ava slipped away from the scene unnoticed. After he was positively identified as one of the hospital's patients, the local cop and nurse turned their attention back to the other people exiting the hospital. The policeman was shouting for everyone to keep moving while the nurse conversed with her coworkers.

They darted in and out of alleyways until finally arriving at a beat-up Toyota 4Runner. Lincoln keyed open the vehicle with a wireless FOB, something the ancient-looking car shouldn't have had. It was at least twenty years old and looked like it barely ran.

Throwing open the rear, passenger-side door, Elliot laid Ava down on the pristine, leather seats. The 4Runner wasn't what it seemed. Everything inside of it was brand-new. The heavily tinted windows hid that fact from the outside world. The body had been doctored to make it look worthless. Elliot wasn't sure if that was true, or maybe it was the other way around, and the interior had been gutted and replaced instead.

"Nice ride," Elliot said, sliding into the front passenger seat.

Lincoln joined them, plopping in behind the steering wheel. With a wink of his eye, he started the engine and grinned when it roared to life.

"Who was that back there?" Elliot asked.

"Which one?"

"The woman," Elliot replied. "Who was she?"

Even Ava was curious. She sat up and leaned forward, sliding her head in between the two men. She wanted to know who her attacker was too.

Lincoln shrugged. "No idea. They aren't the most open of people, you know?"

Ava's hand found Elliot's shoulder. He glanced at her and shook his head. He had no idea what was going on. All he knew was what little information he'd gotten out of Lincoln back in the hospital.

"Let me start from the beginning," Lincoln said. "I'm a part of a black-ops organization buried deep within the CIA called Prometheus. We do things on our own, more or less. Very few people inside the government know we exist. Most of them think we're ghosts wrapped in myth and drizzled with even more conspiratorial hot sauce."

"What's your goal?" Elliot asked. Every agency had a reason to exist. They never existed for no reason at all.

"To protect the world from annihilation."

Both Elliot and Ava stared at him.

"You're kidding, right?" Ava asked, blinking against a swelling eye.

Lincoln's face softened. "I wish I was."

He explained further while guiding them through the city.

"We oppose the Prophets."

"The Prophets?" Ava snickered. "Really, that's their name?"

He nodded. "Yep. We think it's an old translation, back when a name like that would be intimidating. Now," a smirk formed on his face, "it sounds cheesy."

"Definitely," Ava agreed.

"They didn't act cheesy back there," Elliot said, quieting the two. "They were well organized and ruthless."

Lincoln nodded. "That they are. They have their fingers in most of the world's governments."

"As I'm sure you do," Elliot added.

Lincoln quietly shrugged his reply, confirming Elliot's supposition without verbally saying anything.

No one spoke for a few minutes, not until Elliot realized that they were headed back to the excavation.

"What are you doing?" he asked, looking at Lincoln.

"Taking you back to the Cradle." He glanced at his friend. "I need to see it with my own eyes."

"The Cradle?" Ava asked, sitting back.

"Yep…the Cradle," Lincoln answered, sounding far off. "This is all about the Cradle. No one has seen it in centuries."

Elliot asked the obvious question.

"Why is it called the Cradle?"

"Well," Lincoln replied, "cradles hold things, right?" Elliot and Ava nodded. "In this case, our Cradle holds an otherworldly power."

"So," Elliot said, thinking back to his visions, "it *does* contain an energy source."

Lincoln glanced at him and raised his right eyebrow. "You seem to know a little about this already, huh?"

Elliot quickly recounted his time with the core—the Cradle. He decided to keep his out-of-body experience in ancient Egypt to himself. It's not that he wanted to hide anything from Lincoln or Ava, it's that he wasn't sure whether it was relevant or not.

Lincoln bit his lip, thinking hard. "Hmm."

"What?" Ava asked.

"Ox's description of what happened matches our reports from antiquity, and the ones from local law enforcement here." He continued. "When someone of their bloodline touches the Cradle, it activates."

Elliot's eyes narrowed. "Wait, *their* bloodline? Whose bloodline am I supposedly a part of?"

Lincoln looked uncomfortable.

"Linc?"

He grumbled but answered Elliot's question as they pulled into the parking lot outside of the Qumran National Park. From there, it would be a short walk to the excavation site.

"Better wait until dark, just in case," Lincoln said. Then, he threw the 4Runner into park and turned sideways in his seat so he could fully face Elliot. Clearing his throat, he said, "You, my friend, are part alien."

Both Elliot and Ava broke out into laughter. Lincoln, for his part, crossed his arms and patiently waited for them to quiet down. Once they did, he explained.

"Only those of 'royal blood' can activate the Cradle. We have evidence back at HQ that confirms it."

"I mean," Ava added, "that could mean anything. Maybe Elliot's parentage is royal in a normal, hierarchal sense?"

Lincoln sternly shook his head. "Nope. That's not what it means."

Elliot's grin faltered. Lincoln was dead serious. So, he decided to bite and go along with the ridiculousness of it all until it was factually proven to him that he was of alien ancestry—part of him, anyway.

"The ancient teachers of the world—of the ancient cultures—were simply known as 'the gods.' They had no other name that we know of. They are who they are because that's who they were. Their existence, as you'd expect, is clouded in mystery and mythology."

"Like Prometheus himself," Elliot said.

"Exactly," Lincoln said. "He was the one who brought an ancient fire—a weapon from above."

"I know the story," Elliot said.

"No, you don't," Lincoln quickly added. "Not all of it." He continued. "Zeus was pissed, like super pissed, when Prometheus stole the fire, binding the Titan to a rock—"

"Where an eagle, the symbol of Zeus, tore at his liver until Hercules finally released him," Elliot finished. "I told you, I know the story."

"No," Lincoln said, "you know the version that was allowed to be written. What you don't know is what really happened next." He took a breath and explained. "Zeus wanted vengeance against the trickster, Prometheus, especially after he gave us the knowledge we needed to advance. Prometheus broke the chains of our lack of ingenuity and gave our race the final push that was needed to move forward. The 'creation' that Prometheus is credited for was mistranslated over time. He isn't our father. He's the father of everything we've become."

"An advanced race of cosmic beings..." Elliot said, staring past Lincoln and out the window.

Ava said nothing, sitting back with a blank look on her face. Lincoln had just hit them with a mind-boggling bomb, and she was having trouble processing it.

"Zeus hated our development. As it was, he despised us from the beginning. We weren't worthy of being on the same planet as him. So, he ordered Prometheus to destroy his children—his followers—us, with the very fire he stole. He defied Zeus, of course. Then, he disappeared, and was never heard from, or seen, again."

"As did the fire," Elliot said, putting it together.

"What happened to Zeus and the other gods?" Ava asked, looking pale.

"Without the fire, the energy source, Zeus had no real way of obliterating the world the way he had planned. The alternative was to set forth a series of curses on the earth. Illness, war, planetary upheaval..."

"They cursed us?" Elliot asked.

"Not in the sense of the word that we know, no. They infiltrated the planet with their science, something that I don't even understand. It's said that the only thing that can cure it is either Prometheus himself, or his fire. But..."

"There's more?" Ava asked, sounding exhausted.

"There's always more," Lincoln said, looking sad. "If someone of Zeus' bloodline finds the Cradle first, they can fulfill their ancestor's will and annihilate us all."

"Can we destroy the Cradle and stop the war?"

Lincoln shrugged. "I don't know. As much as we know, we're still in the dark about a lot. Records have been destroyed over the years. Only so much has survived to present day." He blinked hard, looking tired. "What we do know is that any person in the bloodline can wipe out the other—and before you say anything—no, we don't want to kill anyone, even if they're a part of Zeus' family tree. The Prophets, on the other hand, they, like the ancient people they inspired, want to kill us all and rejoin their creator in heaven." He sighed. "Some of the worst people ever have followed their model: Kill everyone and be rewarded by their god."

Everyone went silent. It was a lot to take in, but Elliot had no reason not to trust his friend. Lincoln had never lied to him in his life, and he could tell that he believed every word he had just said. The tale didn't sound too dissimilar to the extremists in the surrounding lands. They also believed that their deaths would be supernaturally rewarded.

"Why are you telling us this?" Elliot motioned to himself and Ava. "Don't you have a code to live by, like not to tell us your deepest, darkest secrets?"

"Normally, yes, but you're what we've been waiting for. The waiting is finally over." He leaned forward, eyes wide. "A direct descendent of

Prometheus, the last of the ancient gods here on Earth."

"It all sounds pretty fanatical to me," Elliot replied, leaning away.

Lincoln blinked away the slightly maniacal look. "No, Ox, I'm just a believer. After everything I've seen…" He smiled when the sun finally set beneath the horizon. "Trust me, before tomorrow morning, you'll be as 'fanatical' as me."

"Are you one of them—a descendant of Prometheus?"

Lincoln shook his head. "No, I just work for them."

Elliot wasn't so sure about anything, but he did agree that something weird was going on. His dreams, the visions into the past, were too real just to dismiss.

*Alien blood?*

He'd heard the hypothesis before. Some people within the scientific community believed that humanity was, in fact, alien in a way. Not in the E.T. sense, though. They hypothesized that life began after organisms from space crash-landed on Earth. If that were true, then yes, everyone would technically be of alien blood. Elliot didn't care much about life's origins. He was in the here and now, and that was all that mattered to him.

Before exiting the 4Runner, Lincoln swiped his thumb across the face of the glove compartment. The result was a soft tick and the lid opened. Inside were two more Sig Sauer P226 pistols. There were also two extra magazines to be had. Both Elliot and Lincoln took one of the loaded weapons and a spare "clip." Ava didn't seem upset about being unarmed. Elliot doubted that the young woman had ever fired a gun before anyway.

Lincoln headed for the rear of his SUV and popped the hatch. He grabbed two backpacks, handing one of them to Elliot. Then, Lincoln procured a long rope and a trio of climbing harnesses. Apparently, Lincoln was already prepared to come here whether Elliot was with him or not.

"More rope in the packs, BTW."

"BTW?" Elliot asked, not understanding the acronym.

"*By the way*." Lincoln grinned. "Geez, you really are getting old."

Between the walk ahead of them and then the climb, Elliot inwardly groaned. He was hurting, and the last thing he wanted to do was scale a rock face. Then, they'd have to rappel down into the chamber that held Prometheus' Cradle.

He sighed. "Sounds fun…"

**After his operative** failed to apprehend Elliot Oxley, Osiris decided to calm himself down with meditation. His anger sometimes got the better of him, but for the most part, he kept it in check and kept his cool.

Osiris was lean and well-built for a man of his age. Outwardly, he appeared to be in his early fifties, when in fact, he was actually in his mid-sixties. His shaved head displayed a wicked scar ranging from just behind his left ear all the way up to his temple. It had happened after an attempt on his life had failed. The injury required to stem internal bleeding.

The man that had tried to kill him was one of Prometheus' top agents, a man who had successfully infiltrated the Prophets a decade ago. It was an embarrassing moment in Osiris' tenure as head of the organization. From then on, he decided to personally vet the recruits and they either lived or died on the spot.

If you failed your initial interview, you perished.

Since becoming directly involved, extreme measures were set in place to protect his identity. He had friends in every government. Most of them were involved in both of his lives too, though none knew both his identities.

The nude Osiris sat with his legs crossed in the lotus position. He breathed with long, steady inhalations and exhalations. His eyes were closed, and his mind focused on a singular goal: The Cradle. In the past, the Prophets hunted for all sorts of ancient relics. The Nazis had done this under Hitler's reign, a man that had also been a Prophet. The *Fuhrer* desired the Cradle as badly as Osiris did now but had foolishly spread his people too thin while looking for other trinkets. Decades later, once Osiris was sworn in as society head, he narrowed their sights onto the Cradle and the Cradle alone.

He also lessened his people's footprint around the world. Enlistment was at an all-time low. Now, they only brought in the best, brightest, and most ruthless. Secrecy meant everything to them. The fewer mouths there were to speak, the less of a chance they'd be found out.

Osiris' private office was his sanctuary. The only two people that had access to it besides him were Hel and Izanami. Izanami was Osiris' aide, named after the death goddess from her home country of Japan. She, like Hel, was a deadly assassin but had retired after an injury left her without her left eye and deep scarring on her lower jaw. After her veiled recovery, the woman was moved to Osiris' secret compound. And as time went on, Izanami became more than just his professional confidant.

The door behind Osiris opened, and someone entered without a whisper. Her physical presence could not be heard either. Izanami said little and moved silently, as she had learned from her years of repetition while killing people for a living. Wearing only a traditional kimono, she slipped out of it and slid up behind Osiris. Pressing up against his back, she massaged his shoulders and neck, occasionally reaching her hands around to his chest. Speaking softly, she updated him on the happenings in the West Bank.

The news of Elliot Oxley's disappearance enraged Osiris, but his practiced breathing, again, kept him under control. But the news of Hel defying him and going underground caused him to blow up. He wheeled around on his lover and pinned her likewise naked body to the ground.

Snarling like a beast, he dove into her and kissed her hard, reeling back when she bit his lip. The passionate act caused him to bleed. It also caused him to smile like a predator. He liked it when Izanami presented him with a challenge.

# 7

The desert night gave Elliot, Lincoln, and Ava the cover they sought. The air was crisp, refreshing to a degree, and as the minutes passed, the temperature would continue to drop. The trio was just about to clip onto the peak above their entrance, a feat made possible by drilling directly into the stone. There, heavy-duty, steel rings were attached. Their ropes hooked onto it via carabiner clips.

"I'll go first," Elliot said, tossing his line over the edge.

Lincoln shrugged. Ava, for her part, stayed silent.

*Click.*

"No, you won't."

A light source came to life, and with it, a shadow approached from the north, startling everyone. From his current distance, no one could make out who was speaking, but Elliot knew. He recognized the man's voice. It belonged to the park ranger, the one he had saved.

"Elijah, what are you doing here?" Elliot asked.

The local stepped into view, lit by the aura of an electric lantern. He was casually dressed, and he looked angry. Elliot had no idea if the man had ever smiled. His current attire gave Elliot the notion that he'd come while off duty.

"The same could be said about you," Elijah said, hand resting on his hip-holstered pistol. He'd yet to draw the weapon, however. That was a terrific sign to Elliot. Maybe, if he played his hand right, he'd be able to talk Elijah into helping them.

Stepping away from the cliff face, Elliot greeted the park ranger.

"Everything finish up okay down there?" Elliot asked, sticking a thumb out.

Elijah nodded. "Yes. The police came and went, as did a few government officials. They suggested that we close the park until more is discovered. After the last attack and now this…"

Elliot frowned. "Sorry about the mess."

He didn't want to be the reason that Qumran shut down. Lots of people would lose their jobs.

"Yes, well, I think we can all be sorry about that." He took his hand off his pistol and crossed his arms, still standing incredibly rigid. "I'll ask you again… What are you doing here?"

Elliot decided to be honest with him. If they didn't get his blessing, Elijah could just simply phone it in and ruin everything. Elijah was dedicated to his job. Elliot desperately needed him to be on his side.

"I need to examine the artifact."

Elijah's eyes opened wide.

Lincoln jumped in. "We need to determine if it's dangerous or not."

Elijah's head tilted slightly to the right. His eyes squinted. "You don't know, do you?"

"Know what?" Elliot asked.

"Three people attempted to reenter the chamber after you were recovered, but none were successful."

"Did the passage collapse?" Lincoln asked.

Elijah shook his head again. "No, but there's absolutely something strange going on down there. No one can get close enough to the artifact without becoming ill. There's an energy of some kind down there that no one can explain. Not only does the…radiation, for the lack of a better word, cause the person to feel sick, but the pulsations cause the room to shake. I'm afraid that if someone enters, it'll shake the cave to pieces." He looked off into the darkness. "Maybe the entire park."

*Energy?* Elliot asked himself, focusing on the single word. *Hmm…*

"I think I can turn it off," Elliot said, unsure of what he was going to do. He had to try something, though. He recalled the vision of him successfully holding the Cradle. "I've touched it before."

"And you ended up in the hospital because of it," Elijah said, not buying it.

"Honestly, Elijah, I have no idea what'll happen, okay? It's hard to explain." He stepped up to the ranger and held out his hand. "I need you to trust me on this. I think it'll work, but we won't get a chance if you call the police. This is our one shot to see exactly what we discovered before it's whisked away and studied in some lab."

"Elliot," Elijah replied, looking uncomfortable, "I'm not so—"

"This could be the greatest discovery in history," Elliot interrupted. "Don't you want to see what it is before it's gone forever?"

The ranger looked away, back at his park.

"Look, buddy," Lincoln said softly, "at the end of the day, all we want to do is keep people safe, and we can do that by seeing what we have."

Elijah faced the Prometheus agent. "And you are?"

"An old friend with knowledge about what's going on," Elliot replied before Lincoln could.

"Government?" Elijah asked.

Lincoln nodded.

Sighing, Elijah ran a hand through his hair. He had worked longer at this park than anyone else and loved his job. If there was something historic waiting below, Elliot knew the man would want a piece of the action—and some of the credit.

"Come with us," Elliot said, hand still out. "See it for yourself."

Finally, he took the American's offered hand and shook it.

"Okay, but only because you saved my life." Following one quick pump of his hand, he let go. "After this, we're even."

Elliot grinned. "I'm good with that."

"Give me five minutes to get my things."

They watched the ranger turn and head off.

"Can we trust him?" Lincoln asked in a hushed tone.

"I think so," Elliot replied. "He just wants what's best for the park."

Lincoln smiled and held up his right hand and rubbed his fingers together. It was the international symbol for money. If something more important than the Dead Sea Scrolls were found on Elijah's watch, then the ranger would surely see some of its benefits, maybe even a substantial raise.

Elliot didn't think Elijah's primary motivation for helping them was all about fame and fortune. He'd seen the man talking to tourists about Qumran in person. His knowledge of this place was second-to-none. That made him an invaluable ally.

The ranger returned with his own climbing gear and quickly slipped into his harness. He also adorned a helmet with a light attached to it.

"Ready?" Elliot asked the group.

Everyone nodded except for Ava. She stayed silent and held herself, gripping her arms tightly, shivering. The younger woman still looked a little shellshocked, though she seemed to be coming around. Elliot figured it was both her nerves and the sting of the sharp breeze that caused her to shiver.

"Stay here, Ava," Elliot said.

She shook her head and blinked out of her stupor. "No…no…I'll be okay. I want to see it with my own eyes."

"You sure?"

She nodded. "I'll be fine," she blushed, "as long as you're there."

"Don't forget about me," Lincoln said, giving Ava a playful wink.

Ava rolled her eyes as she, Elliot, and Lincoln quietly slipped into their gear. The only sound heard was their boots scraping across the stone, and the wind swirling around them. Light was provided by Elijah's lantern and the stars above. Everyone carried small flashlights, but they had initially planned on keeping them off until underground and away from prying eyes.

*So much for that,* Elliot thought, glancing at Elijah. His team was getting bigger than he would've liked. But it was also becoming more specialized.

Like he did before, Elliot volunteered to go first. Starting backward, he leaned away from the ledge until his backside was nearly horizontal with his feet. Then, he shoved away from the rock face and began his journey. It was a short trip, maybe twenty feet or so. When he arrived, he pointed his flashlight up and quickly clicked it on and off, signaling for the next person to start their descent.

It was Ava. Impressively, she'd done precisely as Elliot had. It seemed that the college student was an experienced climber. Her body type was perfect for it too. Tall and lean. As long as she had a good grip, she'd be able to move along a rock face with little difficultly, covering more distance in one stride than most.

Her foot came into view, and Elliot snagged it and steadied her as she lowered herself down to him. Back on solid ground, Ava unhooked her line and fell into her boss' arms. A split-second later, Lincoln appeared and spotted them.

Midair, he hung there with a sad look on his face.

"Not a word, Linc," Elliot warned. His friend opened his mouth but was quickly shot down. "Not. A. Word."

So, Lincoln did as he was told and stayed quiet. It didn't mean he wasn't going to react at all, though. He flicked his eyebrows and grinned. Then, he swung inside and likewise unhooked himself. The line went tight once more as Elijah began his descent.

"So," Lincoln said, "where's our booty?"

"Back there," Ava said, turning on her flashlight. Everyone added their lights to hers, and they all swiftly spotted the void in the back corner of the cave.

After the ranger joined them, they moved in slowly and stepped carefully up to the edge of the hole. Splaying their lights into it, Elliot saw something he hadn't noticed the last time he was here.

"Are those steps?" Ava asked.

"Sure looks like it," Lincoln agreed.

Elliot's body had taken a beating when he fell here. If only he'd had the time to examine the entry, he would've most likely avoided any injury at all. Elliot knelt and took off his backpack. He procured a second rope and tossed most of it down the hole.

"Linc, add your rope to mine and tie the end to the one outside."

Lincoln did just that and pulled out a rope of his own. Adding his to the chain, Elliot threw the rest of it down into the shaft.

"Alright. Here we go. Wait until I give the all-clear, okay?"

Everyone nodded their agreement.

Like he had done outside, he turned and gripped the rope with his hands, using the newfound, albeit shallow footholds to walk himself backward down into the entry. It was slow going, but he quickly got into a rhythm and found himself at the first of two switchbacking passages.

Eventually, his foot found nothing but air.

"Woah!" he shouted, getting the attention of someone up above him.

"You okay, Ox?" Lincoln yelled. His voice was muted by the tons of rock.

"Yeah," he replied, blowing out a long, nervous breath. "I'm good."

He wasn't okay, though. He'd been lost in his thoughts, and he'd almost fallen out of the vertically cut passage...again. He told himself to focus, gripping the rope tighter. Then, he lowered himself down into the chamber. The room was ignited with a strobing green light. The artifact and its perch were behind him, out of sight.

He dropped the last few feet and staggered back, feeling nauseous, his body concussed by the waves of energy. It was just as Elijah had described. It felt like his organs were being torn apart molecule by molecule. Still, he needed to try something. He needed to shut it down before something terrible happened.

Elliot stepped closer to it, stunned when its intensity increased. Growling against the discomfort, he reached his hand out in front of him and continued onward. His growls quickly turned into cries of agony. He was only a few feet away now, but he was unsure whether or not he'd make it before he passed out.

Only inches separated him and the relic now. His eyes closed, and he fell into the Cradle. As soon as his fingers made contact with it, the light winked out, and the energy wave reversed course and was sucked back into the sleek cube with a bellowing shriek. It was like a thousand voices screaming as one. The blood-curdling sound must've been just as intense topside because he also heard his partners shout.

Breathing hard, Elliot looked around the room. The beautiful pictographs were gone, scorched by the powerful pulsations. Strangely, he hadn't felt any heat of any kind. Elliot had no idea how he survived.

One after the other, his team arrived and was in awe at what they saw. Elliot held the active Cradle. Lincoln's reaction was an emotional one, he lifted his attention away from the artifact. His eyes met Elliot's, and his breath caught. The Prometheus agent had come to a realization.

"You..." he said, pointing at Elliot. "You really are one of them, aren't you?"

# 8

Everything within the Cradle's chamber was burnt to a crisp except it and the human holding it. Being the true believer of the group, Lincoln backed away from the object rather than rushing forward and squealing with joy. Elijah muttered something incoherently to himself. Ava held her hands over her mouth, eyes wide.

Steam rolled off Elliot's body like it would a hot cup of coffee on a cold winter night. The clouded material that encompassed Prometheus' fire mostly hid the device's contents. The circular windows on each of its six sides didn't, however. Inside the cube, pulsed a green plasma of sorts, intermittently swirling and flashing.

Elliot was the first to speak. "Kinda reminds you of Greek fire, huh?"

Lincoln nodded, snapping out of it. "Yeah, that, uh, was one of its interpretations. One of the last groups of people to possess the Cradle were the ancient Greeks."

Greek fire was an incendiary weapon first used by the people of the same name. It was later perfected by the Byzantines to set enemy ships ablaze. Even upon contact with water, the flammable material continued to burn at incredibly hot temperatures. Impressively, the Byzantines launched the fire from what was described as a rudimentary flamethrower, a pressurized nozzle called a *siphon*.

Elliot loved archaic warfare practices. For years he had wished he had the time to go back and study them in college. He dabbled in it a little since retiring from active duty, but he was nowhere near an expert on the subject.

Lincoln spoke up again. "The first person to come up with Greek fire was supposedly a member of the Prometheus bloodline that defected and joined the Prophets." He inhaled deeply. "This discovery will shed light on so much."

Then, awkwardly, Lincoln just stood and stared at the Cradle. His jaw was clenched shut, and his arms hung loosely by his side.

"Earth to Lincoln." Ava waved her hand in front of his face. "Hellooo… Anyone home?"

She snapped her fingers in front of his face, finally getting a reaction out of the half-comatose man. Lincoln blinked his eyes and peered around the room, looking confused at the attention he was getting. Slightly embarrassed, he chuckled to himself and adjusted the straps of his backpack.

"The visions," Ava said. "Did you see any this time?"

Elliot shook his head. "No."

After taking a few seconds to calm down, Lincoln stepped up in front of Elliot and gave the Cradle a quick once-over. He leaned forward and put his hands on his knees, trying to look through one of the holes in its side. He must've seen what Elliot had.

"So, it's a gelatinous compound of some kind. Interesting…"

"Why is that interesting?" Elijah asked, staying put directly under the entry shaft.

"Nothing important to us," Lincoln replied, "just another one of my people's theories being proven right. One of the scientists thought it was a plasma, while a second one said it was most likely an alien crystal brought from space via a meteor."

"So," Ava said, "now what?"

That's what Elliot was thinking too. They, more or less, knew what the Cradle was, but what were they supposed to do with it besides keeping it out of the Prophets' hands? They couldn't risk destroying it. It might go off and do precisely what their foe was planning.

"Here you go," Elliot said, holding the Cradle out in front of him.

Lincoln knelt and opened his pack. He produced a thick, flat piece of padded metal. Then, Elliot watched as he unfolded the object, turning it into a three-dimensional square. It appeared to be the same size as the Cradle.

"In she goes, Ox."

Elliot raised an eyebrow. "You can't do it?"

Lincoln grinned. "I could, but seeing as you're Frodo, and I'm Samwise…"

Elliot rolled his eyes. Being saddled as the "ring bearer," he concentrated and gently placed the planet-killing weapon into its portable containment housing.

"Lead lined, just in case."

"It's radioactive?" Elijah asked, looking mortified.

Lincoln shrugged. "Not sure, but that's why I have the case." He held it up, just barely being able to see the glow within.

"Where to now?" Elliot asked.

"Washington," Lincoln said. "I have to get this back to HQ on the double."

Elliot felt used, and he expressed it. "So, that's it? All you needed was for me to help you. Then, you get to go back home and play the hero?"

Lincoln raised a hand. "No, Ox, that's not it at all."

"Well, that's what it feels like."

"I was about to ask you to join Prometheus."

Elliot laughed out loud. "You've gotta be joking!" He laughed again, making Lincoln's blood pressure soar. "Look around you, Linc! Did it ever occur to you that I'm happy right where I am?" Elliot stepped around the agent but stopped when he was beside him. "I got out of this line of work for a reason, and I'm never going back."

As Elliot started off again, Lincoln grabbed his arm. "Sorry, Ox, but you finding this place sealed your fate. You either help me or—"

"Or what?" Elliot asked, leaning in close. Now, he was only inches away from the other man's nose.

Lincoln let go, his hardened face faltering. "Or you condemn us all to death."

Elliot pushed past Lincoln but stopped when the agent spoke up again.

"I'm sorry for dragging you into this, Ox, I really am. But there are people out there far worse than anything you've ever faced—people who want to wipe us all off the map." He turned and faced Elliot. "This isn't about borders or religion, Ox. It's about us—our planetary race. Humanity is at risk in all this, not just a chosen few. It's all or nothing, and I know I'd much rather it be the *all* side of things."

Elliot lifted his eyes to the hole in the ceiling, then closed them. There, he took a moment to collect his thoughts. He knew what he had to do, even if he didn't want to.

"Fine."

"Fine?" Linc asked, perking up.

"Yes, fine." Elliot turned around and faced him. "I'll help you, but when we're through, I never want to see you again."

Lincoln held up his hands. "Good enough for me. When we're done saving the world and all, I'm gone, out of your life forever...again."

He winked as he passed Elliot, grabbing the rope and hauling himself back up into the cave above. Elliot was the last to leave, helping Ava and Elijah get started. Neither were expert climbers. Not even Ava had the strength to get herself up the line without a boost.

Alone in the Cradle's chamber, Elliot looked over the pictographs again. The once beautiful artwork was utterly ruined. Even if they had never found the alien device, this place would've still been the find of a lifetime. It proved that there was something else out there—that we weren't alone in the universe.

With care, he made his way back up the vertical entrance. The discovery of the stairs made it quick and easy work. Even with them being cut shallowly into the rock, they served their purpose.

By the time he crawled out of the hole in the back corner of the Dead Sea Cave, Elijah was already gone. Ava was right behind him too. From here, Elliot could see her booted foot disappear back up the cliff face. He and Lincoln were alone. He felt bad about blowing up on his friend. Lincoln was in a rotten place. Prometheus was the rock, and his friendship with Elliot was the hard place. Elliot didn't want something as monumental as this to be the reason they'd never speak again.

Dusting himself off, Elliot stood and made his way over to the edge. There, he stopped and admired the cool breeze slapping him and Lincoln in the face. No one said a word. They just stood still and waited for Ava to finish her ascent. The rope wouldn't hold them all. Like their descent down into the chamber, they'd have to go one at a time.

Seconds later, Ava called down to them. "All done!"

The former SEALs faced one another and waited for one of them to tell the other to go. But neither said a word. They just stood there in the still desert night.

A boom and a scream got them moving, however. Both men flinched when something came streaking toward their perch forty feet up the canyon wall. An object seemed to be towing a trail of fire behind it.

"RPG!" Elliot shouted, diving back into the cave alongside Lincoln. Someone had fired a Rocket Propelled Grenade at their position. It had come from down below in the valley of stone.

As soon as they hit the stone floor, the projectile detonated on the top lip of the cave opening. Shards of ancient rock flew everywhere, assaulting the two men with shrapnel of all sizes.

Shortly after the explosion, they were already moving, darting back toward the trashed cave mouth. Thankfully, there was still an opening large enough for Elliot and Lincoln to climb through. Unfortunately, the rope up to their vehicle was gone, severed in half by the attack.

# 9

Bullets pinged off stone, causing Elliot and Lincoln to duck behind the low outcrop of their newly formed cover. After the cave's mouth was destroyed by the RPG, the pieces that weren't initially thrown into the air fell into the entrance, threatening to bury them alive.

Intertwined with the barrage of automatic gunfire was Ava's screams. She must've still been on the rockface when the attack commenced. Peeking over the small mound of rubble, Elliot spotted the muzzle flashes of four separate shooters. Armed with only his Sig Sauer P226, he tracked the muzzle flashes to their origins and quickly brought up the weapon. With a steady hand, he depressed the trigger six times, aiming for two of the gunmen. Lincoln, likewise, squeezed a burst toward the other pair of attackers.

Their return fire seemed to do the trick. Even over the slight ringing in his ears, Elliot could hear Elijah shouting for Ava to run. He hoped neither were seriously injured, and the fact that they were on the move gave him the faith that they weren't.

"So," Lincoln said, ducking his head and gritting his teeth as another volley of bullets impacted their hiding place, "any ideas?"

Elliot's mind was in overdrive. His options were limited, so he promptly made up his mind. He knew what they had to do. The only thing that could make his plan go terribly wrong was if their attackers were sporting night-vision goggles or a second RPG.

*Or both.*

Elliot searched the littered floor and found what he was looking for. The severed end of the rope leading down into the chamber was still present, pinned beneath a smoking boulder. He quickly went about retrieving the remains of their line, pulling it up as fast as he could, leaving the trapped end where it was.

"What are you—?"

Elliot interrupted him and answered him all the same time when he flung the rope back the other way. It wouldn't reach the full length of the cliff, but it would be close.

"Going down?" Lincoln asked, raising an eyebrow.

Elliot hurried past Lincoln and slapped him on the shoulder. "Goin' down, buddy."

Slipping out of his backpack, Elliot quickly found his flashlight. Lincoln followed suit and held it aloft as he did.

"On three, toss it as far as you can and get moving."

The agent's mouth hung open like a fish. "*This* is your plan?"

Elliot gave him a nervous grin. "Do you have a better idea?"

Lincoln pounded the stone barricade with the base of his closed fist and shook his head. He softly chuckled and met Elliot's eyes.

"Just like the old days, huh?" He shrugged. "Eh, screw it. What could go wrong?"

Both men holstered their sidearms, moved into position, and got to one knee. Elliot counted them down.

"Three…two…one. Now!"

They clicked on the distractions and hurled them outside, Elliot leapt over the waist-high cover, gripping the line as tightly as he could. Lincoln was right on top of him as they both fell like bombs to the ground below. At first, Elliot failed to get his feet beneath him. When he did, he pressed his boots together and used them as a makeshift brake. Elliot slowed his descent as much as he could before his boots slid off the end of the rope. He fell the rest of the way.

Elliot's estimation of the eight-foot freefall was off by about four feet. Luckily, for him and Lincoln, the desert valley met the rock face in a gentle, weather-worn slope. It *eased* the transition from drop to tumble. Still, it hurt like hell, especially when Lincoln ended up on top of Elliot's back.

"James Bond…eat your heart out," Lincoln muttered, grimacing.

Elliot's reaction wasn't as lax. "Get. Off."

Breathing easier, Elliot wished he had the time to stay put and collect himself—but he didn't. Though the plan seemed to have succeeded, it didn't mean they were out of the woods yet. They still had a squad of enemies to deal with.

*At least we're on their level now,* Elliot thought, pushing himself up.

Elliot and Lincoln climbed to their feet and redrew their pistols. Staying together, they moved swiftly and silently. He moved in the same manner that he had four months ago when he terminated the radical terrorists. And, instead of this assault occurring in broad daylight, the sixty-foot wide, rectangular terrain was shrouded in darkness. Neither man attempted to recover their flashlights either. Both of the devices had shattered upon impact with the canyon floor, extinguishing as soon as they struck.

Up ahead, twin beams of light came to life. Two of the shooters had just given themselves away to what Elliot believed was a more-dangerous force—Lincoln and him. It didn't matter that the duo was only armed with a pair of 9mm pistols. They still had the upper hand. As former SEALs, they preferred to work in the dark.

Elliot was still shocked at how quickly his soldier mentality had returned. He didn't feel out of practice at all. He felt as if he'd been fighting the war on terrorism this entire time, not digging in the dirt for the last decade.

*Once a soldier, always a soldier,* Elliot thought. It's what Lincoln had said to him when he said he was retiring.

They made it to a somewhat narrow passage. It's what separated the grounds below the newest Dead Sea Cave from the rest of the canyon's system. Elliot had an idea of where to go next, but first, they had to get rid of a few nuisances. Backs up against either side of the nine-foot-wide, hourglass-shaped entry point, Elliot and Lincoln waited for their prey to come to them. No longer were they the hunted. Elliot and Lincoln had instantly become predators after they successfully escaped the cave.

Elliot was just able to see Lincoln in the starlight. He put a finger to his lips and quietly slid his P226 back into his pants at the small of his back. They'd use their hands on these two. Both men got low and readied themselves.

Elliot was about to grab his masked target but stopped. The killers were dressed the same as the terrorists that had previously attacked the excavation. Their presence here, at this very moment, wasn't a mistake. The Prophets must've hired these men to hit them, right here, right now. It also meant that there was a traitor in Prometheus' ranks. No one else could've known they were here.

*Or it meant someone was following us.*

Elliot's indecision allowed the man to swing his flashlight-mounted rifle toward his face. He doubted he was fast enough to dodge a point-blank burst to the head. So, instead of tempting fate, and his luck, Elliot ducked even lower and struck the barrel with an open palm. The upward motion startled the assassin, and he reflexively squeezed the weapon's trigger.

The bullets sprayed overhead, only missing Elliot by inches. With the gunman's midsection exposed, Elliot dove into the killer and drove him back into the side of the high, stone entrance. Lincoln seemed to be having better luck with his guy. Elliot spotted him wrapping his arms around the second gunman's neck. All he'd have to do now was to apply sufficient pressure and wait.

"Oof!" Elliot's assailant grunted when he struck the stone.

The jolt caused him to squeeze the rifle's trigger again. This time, instead of harmlessly sending a volley of projectiles into the air, the rounds drove themselves directly into assassin number two…and Lincoln. Happily, Lincoln had seen it coming and let go of his man. Grabbing the back of the guy's shirt, Lincoln dragged the dazed killer in front of him and held him in place. The gunman took the barrage head-on.

With one man down, both Elliot and Lincoln turned their attention to the other cloaked man. Facing away from Elliot, the assassin lifted his rifle to shoot Lincoln but was stopped when Elliot kicked out the guy's right knee. He stumbled and turned but dropped when Lincoln leapt into the air and drove his elbow into the base of the shooter's skull, right where it met the spine.

Down, but not dead, Elliot was stunned when Lincoln casually pulled his pistol and executed their injured foe. In the end, he fully understood why his friend killed the man. If he wasn't dead, he was still dangerous, and if the Cradle was what they thought it was, then they needed to proceed ruthlessly.

Solemnly, they retrieved the deceaseds' rifles and extra ammunition, looking them over while they caught their breath. Elliot expected the men had used AK47 assault rifles, like before. These hadn't sounded the same, however.

Lincoln let out a low whistle, surprised as well.

"This isn't good," Elliot said. "What are these guys doing with these?"

The weapons were German-made *Heckler & Koch* HK417 battle rifles. They'd only been in service for a couple of years before Elliot had called it quits. He never had the privilege of using one, though he did witness them being fired during their test phases. Now, they were employed by several countries between both the military and their local law enforcements.

Lincoln shook his head. "Doesn't matter. These guys are well-funded either way." He picked up one of the weapons. "These things cost a fortune!"

Elliot looked up at Lincoln. "The Prophets?"

"Possibly."

Shouldering the hard-hitting rifle, Elliot tipped his chin to the passage. "Come on, Linc." He took another deep breath. "We need to find the others."

**Ava and Elijah** ran for their lives. Ava was just happy to be able to run at all. The explosive had detonated just under her feet. Her back and legs were peppered with golf ball-sized remnants, but gratefully, she hadn't sustained anything worse than a handful of superficial cuts and bruises. For his part, Elijah had campaigned for her to hold on and not let go. That made him feel like a genuinely decent person, one that Elliot trusted.

Ever since Elijah had hauled her to her feet, the two of them had been running for his truck. Elijah had parked far enough away so that he wouldn't be noticed by the trio of Ava, Elliot, and Lincoln.

*Or he knew we'd return, and he'd been waiting for us.*

If he knew where they were going, then maybe he was secretly a member of Prometheus or the Prophets? It was something she'd have to keep an eye on. People like that wouldn't be easy to spot. And unfortunately for Ava, she had no weapon of her own.

*Just keep playing the part,* she told herself. *Pretend you're oblivious.*

"Where…are we…going?" she asked, feigning exhaustion. Even though she was tired, Ava wasn't anywhere close to dropping. She ran track and hiked rough terrain regularly. If she had to make a run for it, she knew she could outrun most people.

But could she outrun a bullet?

The footpath dipped and rose as it banked right then left. Ava could tell it was used regularly by its smooth, worn surface. It was slightly slick, mostly from a layer of dirt that she figured was brought in by the gusts at her back. The weather was brisk and dry—everything you'd expect from the desert at night.

"We're almost there," Elijah called out, glancing over his shoulder. "Just over this next hill and we should be—"

Cresting the next rise, both Ava and Elijah yelped in surprise when a handful of flashlights bloomed to life around them. They were of the barrel-mounted variety, attached to identical tactical rifles. The six men in front of her were either the local police or the bad guys.

*Possibly both,* she thought, immediately snapping her hands up in surrender.

"Don't shoot!" she cried, cowering away from the closest man.

Elijah, in a rare act of modern-day chivalry, stepped in between the gunman and her. Ava would've smiled at the gesture but was too zoned-in on the rifle pointed at them.

**Elijah had no** idea what to do next. He wasn't armed, and while he was an above-average boxer in his own right, he doubted that his hours spent sparring other padded fighters would do much good here. The worst thing was that he recognized one of the men pointing a gun at him.

"Yezid?"

Yezid Ganim was an old friend of Elijah's. In the past, the two men had been members of the Jericho police force. A decade later, Elijah was shot in the line of duty and decided to call it a day, and moved to a career in history, his second love. A few years later, the two men reconnected after Elijah was hired as a park ranger, though Yezid had disappeared since. Elijah had no answer for the reason Yezid was in the park now with these men. Rumors swirled around his departure from the police force—none of them good.

The former police officer grinned like a shark. The malicious look grew more profound when he turned his sights on Ava.

"So, Elijah, who do we have here?"

"No one!" Elijah shouted. "She is…just a friend."

"Is she now?" Yezid smiled, leaning around Elijah. "How come you haven't told us about her?"

"Us?" Ava asked.

Yezid laughed. "You have not told her, have you?"

"Elijah?" Ava asked, tears streaking down her face. "What's he talking about?"

Three of the five riflemen turned their attention on Ava. Two of them shouldered their weapons and forced her to her knees.

She shook her head. "The Prophets… That's how they got here so fast."

One man bound her wrists with zip ties. The other stuffed a rag in her mouth. While she was being detained, Elijah pleaded with them to stop. He also swore on his mother's grave that he had nothing to do with the Prophets.

Elijah wasnt being treated the same as Ava was. He was being left alone, entirely. Yezid was purposely making it seem like Elijah was in cahoots with them.

"Why are you doing this?" Elijah asked.

The other man grinned. "You, of all people, should know. This is merely protocol."

"I—" Elijah started to say.

"Now," Yezid interrupted, jabbing a finger back toward the valley, "we sit and wait for your friends to come to us."

"I—" Elijah tried again.

"Shhh," Yezid warned, pulling a pistol and training in on Ava. "I would hate to ruin this pretty face."

# 10

Bullets tore through the air above Elliot and Lincoln. They'd just stepped out into the next section of the canyon when they were forced to hit the dirt and scramble for cover. The cratered terrain gave them ample hiding places, but they had no way of knowing exactly how many adversaries there were. They'd have to take it slow and be as precise as possible.

*Ava and Elijah don't have that kind of time,* Elliot thought.

Backs against a cylindrical column of rock, the two men laid out the next phase of their plan.

"Split up," Elliot said. "Stay dark and take these guys out quietly."

Lincoln bit his lip, but eventually nodded in agreement. They each slung their battle rifles over their shoulders and got moving once the next barrage struck their cover.

Elliot rolled right and sprinted away from the formation. Lincoln went left and instantly disappeared into the night. Seconds later, the rocks were hit again with automatic fire. The muzzle blasts gave away the positions of four more gunmen. It also confirmed that the enemy weren't outfitted with night vision equipment. They were oblivious to Elliot and Lincoln's escape.

These assassins were not Special Forces soldiers. They were local militiamen that did what they could with their shoddy training. Only, this time, they were using far superior weaponry.

Elliot kept his footfalls light and came up behind the closest shooter. His eyes had adjusted to the near pitch-black lighting. Instead of going airborne as Lincoln had, Elliot dipped forward and bull-rushed the gunman from behind. His rifle went sailing into the air and landed with a clacker.

Voices rose up, calling out someone's name.

The gunman tried to respond and got to one knee, about to warn his comrades. Elliot slid up behind him and wrapped the crook of his right elbow beneath the man's chin. He squeezed. Being much larger than the shooter, he quickly forced the local to one knee, releasing him after ten seconds of not breathing.

Staying low, he shouldered his rifle and waited. If his takedown was noticed, he'd be met with a forceful retaliation. Nothing came. No one had detected his ghostly attack. It caused the left side of his mouth to curl up.

He still had it.

"Gah!"

To Elliot's right, someone choked out a gurgled surprise. With as quiet as the landscape was, he was sure the remaining assassins had heard it too. Bullets tore into the area where the gag originated. But he couldn't see the rounds hit anyone. At least he knew the locations of the other two shooters now. Taking aim, he visualized where the pair's midsections might be and squeezed off twin three-round bursts. Then, he swiftly darted to his right.

One muzzle flash returned fire, and Elliot slowed but didn't stop. Sidestepping, he shouldered his rifle again. Gently, Elliot depressed the trigger twice and was happy to hear his target shriek in pain. He immediately took another dozen or so steps to his right, trusting that his trajectory wasn't being tracked. Satisfied that the enemy was either incapacitated or dead, he knelt and took a moment to collect himself.

"Linc," he called out, quietly.

Nothing.

"Linc," he said again, only louder.

"Over…here."

Happy to hear his friend's voice, Elliot got to his feet and hurried towards it.

"One more time, Linc."

"Keep…going."

His voice was muffled, and it sounded like he was having trouble breathing. That was a common problem with chest injuries. Had Lincoln been shot? After another moment of silence, Elliot found him and it took everything he had to not laugh.

Lincoln was pinned to the ground beneath a man a hundred pounds heavier than either of them. Usually, Lincoln would've been able to push the unmoving lump off him, but when they had fallen to the ground, Lincoln got stuck on his side. His left arm was caught at an awkward angle under his own body. Even now, Elliot watched his friend flounder like a fish, struggling to gain enough leverage to escape his man-bondage.

"Uh…a little help?"

Elliot snickered, but helped Lincoln up, nonetheless.

"He was a big one, huh?" Elliot asked.

Lincoln winced as he rotated his shoulder. "Eat me, Ox."

"No thanks, I'm good."

"Ava and Elijah?" Lincoln offered, stretching his back.

Elliot nodded and patted the pack on his hip. "Then, we figure out what to do with this thing."

"What do you mean?" Linc asked, picking up his felled gear.

"The Cradle…?" Elliot replied. "We need to figure out what to do with it."

Lincoln snorted out a laugh. "Uh, you're gonna give it to me."

Now it was Elliot's turn to laugh. "Not a chance."

"What?" Lincoln didn't like that answer.

"Come on, Linc," Elliot said, rubbing the sleep from his face. "Look what you're asking me to do."

"I'm asking you to serve your country and save the world."

Elliot chuckled, bending down and rubbing his right knee. "Put yourself in my shoes for a second… You want me to give an ultra-secret organization the power to destroy the planet?"

Lincoln raised his hands and opened his mouth, but nothing came out. After a second of no reply, he relaxed. "Well, when you put it that way…"

Elliot stepped forward and put his hand on his friend's shoulder. "Look, Linc, I trust you, but I don't know a thing about the people you work for. There's always more than 'king and country.' There's *always* somebody with a nastier ulterior motive." He stepped away. "Can you honestly tell me that no one in Prometheus fits that bill?"

Lincoln shrugged. "I'm sorry, Ox, but I can't give you that assurance."

He nodded. "Then, it's settled. The Cradle stays with me until we find the best solution for it."

Lincoln didn't look happy, but he didn't argue with Elliot. The two had grown to trust one another over the years, and just because they each led different lives now, didn't change that. Elliot was hopeful that Lincoln hadn't been brainwashed by a cult within the government.

They turned and slunk away deeper into the darkness.

*Could a man of Lincoln Ryan's ilk be programmed like that?*

Elliot shook his head in disbelief but had an inkling that it could be somewhat true.

Everyone on the planet, to a degree, was conditioned by something. The two biggest influencers are politics and religion. Some people took what they believed to another, scarier level. The same could be said for military personnel. Elliot would be lying if he didn't admit he hadn't been propagandized. His rigorous, elite training wasn't just physical, it was also mental.

He owed his strictest habits to his time in the Navy. Even outside of a war-based setting, it had affected him. It made him the man he was now: Determined and loyal. He became a respected archaeologist because he wanted to be one, plain and simple. He knew he could do it, and he followed through with his goal. Now, he was confident that he would survive the night. Regrettably, he knew he could only control his personal survival, not anyone else's.

They needed to find Ava and Elijah before it was too late.

**A set of** bright lanterns showed off Ava's nearly ruined face. Her lip was split, and both sides of her face were developing deep, purple bruises. Between getting slugged by the woman at the hospital, and being backhanded by Yezid just now, she was beginning to look like a victim of domestic violence. She'd protested against her bonds and let out a garbled cry for help. That's when the leader of the armed men swiftly responded. He did so with a smile.

"I am going to ask you one last time," Yezid said, staring at Elijah. He jammed the muzzle of his pistol into Ava's temple. "Where are the other two Americans?"

Elijah, who was still free to move about, threw his hands up in frustration. "I do not know! Like I have said, we were separated from them when you tried to blow us up. Maybe, if you had not acted so brashly—"

"Watch your tongue, dog!"

Elijah took a step away from the psychotic man.

"What happened to you, Yezid?" he asked. "I never pictured you running with such a wicked bunch."

The other man smiled wide. "What happened to me?" He took a second to collect his thoughts. "I was allowed to better myself. I was given an offer I could not refuse."

"So, you sold your soul."

Yezid swung the gun around on Elijah. He heard the deranged gunman grip the pistol harder, but he didn't pull the trigger. Instead, Yezid's hardened face faltered, and for a split-second, the man looked frightened.

"You do not say no to these people. You—"

The back of Yezid's head exploded. A single report of gunfire followed closely behind. His body dropped to the dirt, followed by Elijah, who dove for the dead man's weapon. Confused about who the new enemy was and where the kill shot had originated, Yezid's men shouted at one another to get down. Elijah, gun in hand, pulled Ava to the rear of his truck and quickly went about cutting her wrists free with his pocketknife.

Another shot rang out, and yet again, one of Yezid's men was sent sprawling to the earth. The report came from the east. One of the assassins saw it too, and he stayed low and ran toward it. Elijah and Ava watched as he passed them. He didn't make it ten feet before being taken down like the others.

Except, this time, it was by Elijah's hand.

With steady aim, Elijah put two rounds in the killer's upper back. He'd never ended another human's life before, after all, he'd been a policeman assigned to do mostly office work. The only thing he saw regarding a shooting was what was in the aftermath of the reports. He'd never been part of one until he himself was shot. He had been trying to prevent mugging while off-duty.

Ava's eyes flashed up to his, and she smiled in thanks. He'd just saved both of their lives. Being a good bit older than the beautiful American, maybe fifteen years or so, Elijah felt uneasy with the way she was looking at him. Unlike men of Elliot and Lincoln's backgrounds, Elijah hadn't done anything very heroic in his life.

More gunfire erupted somewhere on the other side of his truck. Instead of engaging the people that had just tried to kill them, Elijah decided to stay put and protect Ava. He wanted to keep her safe and had no qualms about doing so while keeping himself out of harm's way too.

Two more of Yezid's men went down in a harmony of anguish, each shouting as their bodies were impacted with bullets. The last man standing turned and tried to run but was killed before he could even take a single step in the other direction. All he could do was turn his shoulders, and then, *poof*, his head snapped to the side.

The grounds returned to the silence that Elijah had grown accustomed to over the years. Then, like a pair of ghosts, Elliot and Lincoln stalked toward them, rifles up, arms, and heads unmoving. It was impressive to watch the two in action. Elliot quietly lifted his hand, instructing them to stay put as he passed.

They did, and in doing so, Elijah felt something incredible. Ava laid her head on his shoulder while gripping his shirt hard. She wasn't about to let go.

# 11

They left the Qumran Caves in a hurry. Lincoln drove with Elliot sitting beside him, up front. Ava had refused to leave Elijah's side, even after he and Elliot had successfully cleared the area. Instead, she clung to the ranger's arm, looking very shellshocked. Lincoln thought it was weird that she was clinging to him so badly. It wasn't like they were on the same level at all, though honestly, Lincoln didn't care.

To put it simply, Ava was way out of Elijah's league—not that Elijah wasn't a good looking guy. Lincoln was mature enough to admit when another man was handsome. Elijah seemed to be a solid-enough guy and he wasn't terrible to look at either.

Lincoln rolled his eyes. *Seriously, dude, THIS is what you're thinking about?*

He had a place back in town, near the northern border of Jericho. It was a safe house that had been used by several Prometheus agents over the years. With the discovery of the thirteenth Dead Sea Cave, his organization had received reports of movement within the Prophets. Evidently, they thought that their missing thunderbolt was somehow involved.

*And, boy, were they right!*

He still couldn't believe that he'd found the Cradle. Well, he couldn't believe that the Cradle had been found. Technically, it was Elliot who discovered it, not him. Still, this region was his domain. He was the lead agent in the area, and he would get the credit for the find. As much as Lincoln enjoyed his job, he wanted more.

There were things within Prometheus that he'd yet to be trusted with. The higher you climbed the company ladder, the more you were privy. While battling the Prophets was *numero uno* on his people's list, there were other, lesser things they were watching too. Hardly anyone knew that Prometheus was working hand-in-hand with the government at their Area 51 site.

But what they did there was way above Lincoln's pay grade. He had a couple of ideas, though. There was definitely a spacecraft there—that much he knew.

Arriving at his apartment, Lincoln swiftly ushered everyone inside and locked the door with twin deadbolts. It was one of the nicer places on the outskirts of Jericho, but not too nice. His presence here was already under scrutiny by the local authorities. The last thing he needed was to be seen entering one of the area's few "mansions." The larger, stand-alone homes were few in numbers and belonged to a variety of people, mostly government higher-ups.

Lincoln's place was modest in size and featured one bedroom and a small, motel room-sized kitchenette. It was all an agent of Prometheus needed. He was hardly ever there, anyway.

His group was exhausted and could use some much-needed rest. Sadly, they'd need to get moving soon—at sunrise at the latest. For now, they'd discuss what they learned and where they'd go from here.

"Alright, Ox, let's see it," Lincoln said, procuring an icepack from his freezer. He handed it to Ava and sat in one of four chairs around the kitchen table. Everyone joined him and groaned as one when they sat, reflexively sighing once they got off their feet.

Ava's right eye and cheek were still swollen but had since lessened a bit. She'd said that the cool desert air felt wonderful on the injuries. Gently, she applied the icepack, wincing in discomfort. She took a deep breath and nodded her thanks.

To her right, Elijah grabbed her free hand and squeezed it, leaving it there for a moment. Then, he released it when he found Lincoln staring at him. Unhappy at not being the one to *get the girl*, the confident American cleared his throat and turned his attention to Elliot and the alien relic.

"So, tell us again what you saw when you touched it. I'm talking vivid detail."

Elliot nodded and started.

"Down in the…docking chamber…I acted impulsively and tried to grab the, uh, device." Elliot held his air. Just talking about it gave him the chills. "As soon as I laid a finger on it, I saw the aftermath of mass killings—exterminations. Entire populations were wiped off the face of the earth." His eyes watered. "Women… Children… Anyone and everyone."

They all stayed silent and waited for him to continue.

"Then, later in my hospital room, I saw the Giza pyramids, not like they are today, but as they were in their prime." His voice softened, more distant too. He was still awestruck by their beauty. "I was there *in* ancient Egypt. The detail was so...extraordinary!" His heart was racing now. "There's no way I could've made it up on my own."

Lincoln's eyes darted to Ava and Elijah. They looked concerned.

"I know it sounds insane, but…I know what I saw. I was there. Then…"

"There is more?" Elijah asked, sitting back in his chair.

Elliot nodded. "Yeah, but this is where it gets kinda weird."

Everyone laughed in unison. Everything about this was strange, and Elliot was happy that no one called him out for sounding crazy. He looked at the concealed cube and got an idea.

"What if I show you?" Lincoln, Ava, and Elijah sat bolt upright at the mention of activating the object. "I think I can control it."

"You *think* you can?" Lincoln asked, rightfully looking unsure.

Elliot shrugged.

He was surprised when it was Ava that stood by his side.

"Do it," she said, eyes glued to the relic.

Elliot eased the artifact from the protective casing. It was pulsing like crazy, filling the apartment with different shades of green.

"Now, hang on a sec," Lincoln said, sliding his chair away from it. "We don't know what will happen."

Ava's wide eyes danced in the light of the Cradle. They snapped up to Lincoln and then traveled around the table to Elliot and Elijah. "Elliot says he can control it. I believe him."

"Actually," Elijah corrected, clearing his throat, "he said he *thinks* he can control it. What if he cannot, and something bad happens?"

Elliot shook his head. "I don't think so. I don't know how, but I think it wants me to do something for it."

The room went silent again.

This time, it was Lincoln who spoke up.

"Ah, what the hell, do it. You only live once, right?"

Elliot waited to get confirmation from the three people sitting around him. Lincoln and Elijah appeared to be on the fence, but neither one verbally argued against it. Ava, on the other hand, was strangely ready to go. It was as if she needed to see what Elliot was about to show them.

So, with a shaky arm, Elliot raised his right hand and gently placed it on top of the Cradle. The room instantly flashed, and time stood still. His friends were paused by the energy pulse. It was as if they were on the screen of a buffering smart TV. And he was the only one that could move. Besides that, nothing else happened.

Doing the only thing he could think of doing, Elliot focused on the artifact and told it where he wanted to go.

"Take us back."

He and the others were whisked away to ancient Egypt and deposited at the foot of the Great Pyramid of Giza. Khufu's megalith was as beautiful as he had recalled it. Lincoln, Ava, and Elijah all "un-paused," looking down at their hands and bodies. Then, as a group, they realized where they were.

Locals nonchalantly skirted around them, but no one paid any attention to them. It was as if they only existed in spirit. The sun was high in the sky, and the smell of camel dung slapped Elliot in the face.

Lincoln noticed the stench too. "Woof." He pulled his shirt up to his nose. "That's awful."

Ava and Elijah didn't say a word. Both were standing in stunned silence at the thought of actually having been transported back in time. Though they weren't living in real-time, so to speak, Elliot knew what they were experiencing was more of a replay of the past, like stepping foot into a VR chamber centered around Giza.

"Pretty cool, huh?" Elliot asked, smiling.

Elijah finally spoke up. "You could say that, yes."

Lincoln spun in a circle, taking it all in. He stopped and faced Elliot. "Not to sound ungrateful or anything, but I thought there'd be more. The Cradle has to be more than just some space-age DVR."

Elliot grinned and looked up at the gleaming pyramidion atop Khufu's peak. On cue, the quartet of time travelers rose away from the ground and took up individual positions on each of the pyramid's sides. On its northern face, Elliot held out his hand and willed the Cradle to appear. It did, and the capstone activated similarly to the first time he had tried it.

"Oh," Lincoln said from the eastern face, shocked as the capstone lifted and separated, "okay, now that's cool!"

"Incredible," Elijah said with his mouth hanging open.

Ava still hadn't said anything. She was just standing there, eyes darting around, taking in everything they could. Soon, Elliot would be forced to bring them back to reality. He could feel himself weakening from the effort of transporting four living beings into the past.

*Well, that's a new one,* he thought. *Elliot Oxley, Chauffer of the Ancients.*

They witnessed the Cradle hover into position above the futuristic device that was hidden within the capstone. It activated and began strobing in a similar fashion to the Cradle. Both pulsed with the green energy until they were perfectly synced. Then the artifact lowered and locked into place in another dock of some kind.

"Same as the chamber beneath 13Q," Lincoln said.

Elliot hadn't seen this before.

Once it was docked, a beam of light shot into the sky and disappeared into the upper atmosphere. That same energy then came pulsing back down, stronger and hotter. The Cradle flashed in time with the returning light.

*It's an antenna—a charging station!*

After three quick pulses, the world around them stood still, pausing as it did before. Only, this time, all four of them could move and converse with one another. They looked around, confused.

"What the heck?" Lincoln asked, looking at Elliot. "Someone paused the movie?"

He shrugged. "I guess so."

"End of side," Lincoln added.

"What is he talking about?" Elijah asked, apparently not understanding the reference.

"Books on tape used to end with a voice that said, "end of side."

Elijah put it together. "The Cradle does not have a recording of what happened next."

Elliot nodded. "It seems that it contains only snippets of their history."

"Anything else you can show us?" Ava asked, finally speaking up. "This is all just too incredible."

Elliot looked around at the scene beneath him and wondered what the Cradle could remember and why it did so. From what Lincoln had told him and from what he gathered on his own, the Cradle was supposed to be a weapon of mass destruction, not a visual history book.

*Maybe it had more than one purpose?*

Elliot held out his hand and retrieved the Cradle. It vanished from the docking mechanism and rematerialized in his hand with the blink of an eye. He was tired but needed to try something else before they called it quits and returned to Lincoln's safe house.

Closing his eyes, Elliot told it where to take them. "To the beginning."

Now, telling an alien artifact to take you to the beginning seemed pretty vague when Elliot said it, but he had a picture of where he truly wanted to go in his head. He wanted to see when Khufu's pyramid was built.

The world around them shimmered and blurred. Then, *snap*, they found themselves back at the foot of the Great Pyramid. It was standing mostly complete, except for the capstone. Amazingly, they watched one of the builders raise his hand out in front of him, as Elliot had done. An invisible force lifted the entire pyramidion high into the sky. Once in place, the builder's hand dropped, and so did he.

"They used the Cradle to build the pyramids…"

Elliot was flabbergasted. He didn't know what else to say.

The others were quiet, too, and watched as a group of locals gathered around the master builder. One of them laid a hand on top of the unmoving man's chest. After a few seconds of inactivity, the "doctor" shook his head and dipped it in prayer.

Khufu's architect was dead.

"Um, Ox," Lincoln said, "don't be that guy, okay?"

Elliot didn't reply. He could only stand there and stare at the dead man. He didn't know how, but Elliot knew the builder had burned himself up using the Cradle. It wore him out so much that it had killed him.

He'd seen enough. The revelation that he could die if he overexerted himself was too much. Elliot held up the Cradle and said, "Take us home."

# 12

The four travelers were thrown back into the apartment. Lincoln and Elijah were tossed to the floor, crashing hard. They picked themselves up and found the pair of Elliot and Ava still seated at the table. They were both breathing hard and staring through the other. Elliot's face was slathered in perspiration, though the room wasn't warm.

"Well, that was neat," Lincoln said, holding his stomach, and plopping down in his chair.

His hands shook. Even as a former soldier who'd seen a lot, Lincoln was having problems processing what he'd just experienced.

Elijah was breathing heavily. "Seems like the Cradle has a lot to do with the Giza pyramids."

"Yuh think?" Lincoln said, sitting back. "I'd say it has *everything* to do with it."

"But what exactly?" Ava asked, eyes still unblinking. She shook her head and locked in on Elliot. "The device within the capstone, what is it?"

Elliot shrugged. "I'd say it's probably similar to the one we found beneath 13Q, but who knows? There are still too many unanswered questions." He sighed. "We need to go there."

Lincoln looked at him. "Where, Giza?"

Elliot nodded. "I think I can figure it out if I'm there in front of the pyramids."

"But, my friend," Elijah said, "the capstone is gone."

That fact deflated everyone. If the capstone was stolen away, or maybe even dismantled and sold off piece by piece like the casing stones were, what then? Why was the Cradle pushing them to Khufu's tomb if there was nothing left? They needed answers, and Elliot knew who could provide a few of them, but he refused to bring *her* up.

Lincoln, on the other hand, had no qualms about it.

"I know someone."

"No." Elliot's eyes were full of anger, but they were also terrified.

"Who?" Elijah asked.

Knowing Lincoln was right, Elliot took a deep breath and then blew it out, calming his nerves. The next word to come out of his mouth was a hard one to say—painful even.

"Maggy."

Ava and Elijah looked at one another in confusion.

"Who is Maggy?" Elijah asked.

"Magdalen Bitar," Lincoln explained. "She's a bigwig at the Museum of Egyptian Antiquities—renowned Egyptologist." His mouth curled into a smirk. “She also happens to be Ox’s ex.”

**The rear of** the second-floor safe house, Lincoln’s room, was barely big enough to fit his bed, let alone a second human being. So, Elliot, Ava, and Elijah spent the night scattered around the living room. Ava was given the sofa. Elliot let Elijah choose his spot. He was surprised when the man decided to lay out a sleeping bag on the floor. His reasoning was sound enough, though.

“I’ve spent the majority of my adult life sleeping out under the stars. The floor of a furnished home is a luxury condominium compared to that.”

Elliot could relate. Back in his military days, he routinely slept outside. Whether it was in the freezing Siberian wastelands or the humid, disgusting jungles of Central America, Elliot was used to making do with what he was given.

He was currently near the only window. He propped himself up between two chairs and watched nothing. There wasn’t a soul to be seen wandering the streets of Jericho—not that he was paying attention. His mind was on the next day. It was going to be the first time he’d seen Maggy in years.

He’d found pictures of her in magazines and had watched her interviews online. A few years ago, she had done a vlog mini-series about powerful women in archaeology. The show was impressive. The comments weren’t because they were steered in a juvenile direction, focused more on her looks rather than her work.

*I guess I can’t blame them,* Elliot thought, picturing the beautiful Egyptian woman in his mind’s eye.

“Can’t sleep?”

Ava’s question startled Elliot, who pushed the chair away from him with a screech of wood on wood. Elijah’s soft snores rose to a crescendo of grunts and snorts. Both Americans smiled, holding back their laughs. With the second chair now vacated, Ava sat and turned to face the window.

“You either, huh?” he asked.

She shook her head. “Not a wink. *Thomas the Train* over there isn’t giving me a chance.” Elliot smiled. “Plus,” she continued, “I’m a light sleeper, anyways—have been ever since I was a kid. I could never fall asleep right away. Not without—”

“Night terrors?” Elliot asked, genuinely curious.

She nodded. “Debilitating. So much so, that my father used to drug me to get me to sleep.”

“Geez,” Elliot said, feeling sorry for her. “I’m sorry to hear that.”

She shrugged. “Better than going to the nuthouse because of sleep deprivation." She sighed. "Eventually I grew out of it. Though..."

Elliot sat up a little. "Though, what?"

"I, uh," she blushed in the moonlight, "I still have them out of the blue, usually when I've had a rough day."

He chuckled softly. "Hence, why you haven't fallen asleep tonight."

She shook her head. "Nope." Ava stuck her thumb out. "That's all *Thomas* over there."

Elliot liked Ava. She wasn't what he initially thought she was. Ava had handled all of this remarkably well. It made him want to ask her about it—her ability to stay so composed—but he decided that she'd tell him, if and when there was something to say.

**"Where is she?"** Osiris shouted, throwing a priceless artifact across the room. The historical significance of the squat, wide-mouthed vase was something very few knew about. The beautifully painted vessel was one that had once held the Cradle, its hiding place before it went missing from the Middle East.

To the Prophets, it was irreplaceable.

To Osiris, everything was replaceable, everything except his seat as their leader. That was the only thing that truly mattered. Not even his daughter's life was worth that. The only way he'd give up his station was if he was to meet Zeus in Olympus. But his time on this planet wasn't finished. Osiris still had much to do before he was content with the direction his life had taken him.

Izanami, the only other person in the secret room, didn't so much as slink back in fear. She'd seen him react violently to lousy news several times before. While not a good quality to have as a powerful leader, Osiris' mean streak served him well at certain times. It made him a feared man. No one knew when he'd snap and lash out.

"She is gone," Izanami said, her voice soft and direct.

Osiris stood, hunched, nearly frothing at the mouth. He pictured it in his mind's eye, saw himself looking like a rabid beast. He liked it. He loved the adrenaline rush.

"Has she deceived us?" he asked, feeling his heart rate begin to drop.

"Possibly," she replied. "I suggest you give her some more time to turn up. It is also possible that she is only out of communication and unable to respond."

Osiris toweled himself off and turned, half-dressed in an expensive suit. He only wore the very best Italy had to offer. He'd gotten his pants and shoes on before being notified of Hel's potential betrayal. Slipping into his dress shirt, he looked Izanami deep in the eyes.

"You care for her too much."

Izanami returned his look with one of her own. "And you don't care for her enough."

He rushed to her position across the room but stopped when she reached into the sleeve of her kimono. Osiris knew what hid within. She had used the ceremonial dagger several times in the past, and since he was unarmed, Osiris halted his aggressive display and came to a stop only feet from her.

"Remember your place," he said, stepping up to her.

Now, face to face, she grinned. "And you must remember it too, master."

Osiris smirked. "I'll have to watch my back."

Izanami's grin faded. "Yes, you will."

Now fully clothed except for his silk necktie, Osiris unconsciously tied it as he waited for his private elevator to arrive. When it did, he stepped into it and blew out a long breath. When he eventually arrived at his destination, some sixty feet above his head, he'd no longer be the head of one of the oldest secret societies in the world.

Years ago, the Prophets spurred rumors of another similar group. Years ago, one of their agents had turned against them. He spoke of a clandestine organization buried within the governments of the world.

*They* were the real-life Illuminati.

The Prophets were that and so much more. Their rumored rise was a lie. They didn't begin inside the Freemasons during the dawn of America. No, the Prophets had been around long before that, formally originating at the same time as Prometheus. Once Khufu's tomb had been completed, and following its Grand Architect's death, as well as the pharaoh's, the architect's successor stole away the Cradle and claimed it as his own.

Nearly two thousand years later, after changing hands countless times due to open war or covert operations, it turned up again in what would become modern-day Iraq. This time, a member of Prometheus held the Cradle in his hands, and with it, he built an impressive underground garden complex. Five decades after that, another erected a temple dedicated to the goddess, Artemis, in Greece.

Osiris smiled.

In 466 B.C., his direct ancestor began construction on the only ancient wonder to be erected by the Prophets, the Statue of Zeus. Except for the Great Pyramid, all the other Wonders were razed by the enemy to gain control of the Cradle. None, however, possessed the courage to enact what needed to be done. Every leader of the Prophets before Osiris was a coward in the end, including his father.

The true Prophets yearned for this to occur. It must work for them to reach their deity in deep space. Few believed it as much as Osiris, House Representative Michael Towns, Chairman of the Armed Services Committee.

*If only Hel were as devout.*

He didn't want to terminate her, but he would if it meant being reunited with Zeus on Mars' outer moon of Phobos. In 1958, Russian astrophysicist Iosif Samuilovich Shklovsky stated that the moon might, in fact, be hollow. Osiris smiled at the reflection of himself within the elevator car.

*Shklovsky was so close. If only he knew what I do.*

Not only was the moon hollow and inhabited—it wasn't even a moon at all—not anymore. Eons ago, Phobos had been mined and emptied, becoming the gods' orbital research station. Currently, it held the cryogenically frozen forms of the gods of old. All of the gods, except for Zeus and Prometheus, were frozen in time, unable to emerge from their slumber without the might of a core. Prometheus had been cast out after he defied Zeus and stole one of his people's cores, the Cradle.

Phobos, the city-sized, camouflaged station, needed to be activated, and its builders awakened. Then, Olympus, also known as Mars, could be rebuilt and recolonized. Long ago, war had ravaged the landscape, eventually burning away the planet's atmosphere.

Osiris' eyes opened, and his hands twitched. "The Cradle must be found!" He punched the inner wall of the elevator car, nearly breaking his hand.

He didn't rub it as he stepped out of the car and into a dusty closet. Before him, on the other side of the utility door, was the hallway to his office in Washington, D.C. He knew what he had to do, but his life in the Congressional spotlight was too chaotic just to get up and walk away. First, he needed to figure out a way to disappear. Then, Michael Towns would focus on what mattered most.

*Destiny awaits.*

But that ending would only happen if everyone worked together. Distractions, like Hel, needed to be taken care of. Pulling out his phone, he texted his full-time bodyguard in both the political world and his private life, instead of Izanami. He required absolute dedication to the cause, and none were more dedicated than Hades.

The brute would, in turn, find the right men to do the job.

*The target?* Hades texted back.

Osiris stopped halfway to his office and frowned. He didn't want to murder Hel, but he would if it meant getting what he desired most.

So, he sent the kill order.

*Your target is my daughter, Ava.*

# 13

Ava Towns, Hel, the Goddess of Death, stalked toward the Cradle and a sleeping Elliot Oxley. She had waited all night for the man to fall asleep, and when he did, she quietly sat up from her false slumber and eyed her prize. She would've made her acting coach proud of her performance. Her natural skills had paid off big time. Here she was, in the good graces of a Prometheus agent and their "Chosen One" friend.

It was her ticket back to her father's side. With her success here, Ava would be catapulted up the Prophets hierarchy. The fanatic members of the organization, her Congressman father mostly, would see her as their savior. Some of their more deep-seated beliefs were ridiculous. Ava was nothing more than a professionally trained assassin looking for a significant pay increase.

She found it hard to believe that the ancient beings that had created the energy core were, in reality, Martian aliens. They weren't little green men either. At least, that's what her father believed. They were an advanced race of humanoid creatures whose actions here on Earth embedded their influence as "godly." Then, the human imagination and psychosis took over.

The gods of Greece, Egypt, Asia, Scandinavia… She knew that what was taught in present day was not true. Then again, Ava didn't believe in most of it, to begin with. Her outlook on it all was that it was just nonsense. She did everything in her power not to roll her eyes when her father spoke of them—the gods.

Were there aliens out there? Sure, why not?

Did they come to her planet and become our ancestors' great teachers? No, Ava didn't think so, but her father did, and like most entrenched zealots, you didn't cross Michael Towns' core beliefs unless you wanted a violent response in return. Her father's past was an ugly one, and he had the best people in the world helping him cover it up. No one within the government knew of it, not even the heads of the various security agencies. If it did ever come to light, the person who discovered the truth had always been quickly silenced.

*Accidents happen all the time,* Ava thought.

She'd personally been responsible for a number of them. She recalled, in detail, a Senator that died of an "accidental" drug overdose when she was sixteen. He liked his girls young, and he had a big mouth. Ava did what she had to do. She seduced the whistleblower to get close to him, before slipping him a lethal dose of oxycodone.

The encased Cradle sat on the table next to Elliot. He'd fallen asleep in the same chair as she had found him, though now his feet were propped up on a second chair. She had covered him before returning to the couch. Something inside of her liked Elliot. He was a true "man." He was honorable and straight-shooting. He was emotional when he needed to be and felt no need to hide it from anyone. But he was also tough as nails and a fighter.

She'd hate to have to kill him.

Elijah's snores paused her stealthy advance. She was only a step away from being in arm's reach of the Cradle. Cursing the man's soft palate, she glanced over her shoulder and waited for him to quiet. After an agonizing long ten seconds, he finally stopped. Ava breathed a sigh of relief and returned to the task at hand.

Stepping lightly, she reached out for the Cradle and made contact with it. Slowly, she flipped open the magnet lid and gazed upon the artifact's glow…just as Elliot awoke.

Each of them tried to stop the other from touching the artifact, but instead, both grabbed it at the same time and were whisked away into the past. Ava was stunned when she discovered that it wasn't Elliot who was controlling them this time. It was her. Her father told her that she had ancient blood within her, but, to this day, she never believed him. He'd promised to personally watch over her after she was orphaned, because she was "meant to do great things."

Flashes into the Prophets' past horrified both Ava and Elliot. They were brutal replays of war and assassinations. The killings she saw were both ones she had completed and ones of other shadowy figures. She couldn't see any of their faces, but she knew the identity of at least one of them.

Her father, the Congressman, Michael Towns.

Osiris stood over a pleading couple, and in their arms, a blonde-haired baby.

She didn't know how, but Ava knew she was looking at herself. She felt it in her heart. It hurt to watch her adoptive father snuff out her biological mom and dad's existence with a pair of bullets. Then, he picked up the blood-splattered infant and smiled.

"You are meant to do great things."

After watching what must have been thousands of deaths, each of them at the hands of her and the Prophets, Ava dug deep into her alien bloodline, as Elliot had done hours earlier, and tapped into a power she didn't know she had until now.

Sobbing, Ava yelled, "Enough!"

She and Elliot were violently thrown back into Lincoln's apartment. Ava crashed into the wall just inside the front door, denting the drywall with her hip. Elliot fell from eight feet in the air, crushing the kitchen table beneath him. He quickly sat up and looked wide-eyed at his murderous assistant.

Ava, for her part, curled into a ball, sitting knees-to-chest, tears streaming down her face. She didn't know what to think. She'd been trained her entire life to be a killer, all for a cause she didn't believe in. The visions had broken something inside her.

*You are meant for great things.*

Osiris' words echoed in her head, banging around like a hammer on an anvil. She savagely clawed at her skull, but to no avail. The cerebral overload was too much, and her breath caught, and she passed out into Elliot's awaiting arms. Even after what he'd seen, he still showed concern for her, a woman that was supposed to end his life.

**"Wakey-wakey..." Lincoln** said, poking at Ava's temple with the muzzle of his sound-suppressed pistol. The long, thick cylinder attached at the end of the gun's barrel would turn the typically loud report into a mere cough.

Elliot sat across from the bound killer—a woman he'd thought he could trust. The visions he just experienced had spooked him. He couldn't imagine the effect they were having on Ava. She was a seasoned assassin, that much he now knew. She was also still very young. He was more than twenty-five years older than her, and he could barely hold it together now. All the death Elliot had witnessed at the hands of this...child.

He blinked away the horrible memories and waited for her to awaken.

"Wuh—what happened?" Ava asked, drowsy.

Elliot leaned forward on his knees, eyeballing her hard. "You touched the Cradle."

The killer's eyes snapped open, and she attempted to wrench her arms and legs free. After she passed out, Lincoln had come bolting out of his room with nothing more than his boxers on, and his gun gripped tightly in his hands. Elliot quickly relayed what he saw and who he suspected that Ava really was. Lincoln couldn't believe it.

"You're shitting me, right?" He pointed at the unmoving Ava. "Her?"

Now, Ava had her wrists and ankles zip-tied to one of the kitchen chairs, the one she had sat in only a few hours prior. She calmed down when Lincoln raised his pistol, aiming it at her temple. Her face was flushed, and her breathing was incredibly guttural. Elliot wasn't sure if she was going to slip into unconsciousness again, or not. Happily, Ava got her breathing under control and sat still.

"I saw what you did," Elliot said, keeping his voice soft.

Ava's attention jerked from Lincoln to him. She looked mortified. Her privacy had been ripped away and set alight. She had no idea what to say.

So, like the well-trained operative that she was, Ava said nothing. The only thing that spoke were her eyes. Elliot thought they'd be sharper, as fierce as a wolf. Instead, she looked frightened and vulnerable. Ava had been mentally broken by what she had seen.

*Just like me.*

Elliot continued. "I know what you are and what happened to you when you were a baby."

"Shut up!"

"Ava, I—"

Tears rolled down her face. "Shut the fuck up!"

Lincoln placed the gun's muzzle against her head. "Be nice, Hel."

"Hel?" Elliot asked.

"That's your callsign, isn't it?" He leaned in close and dug the gun in deeper. "You're the infamous Hel, the 'Goddess of Death.'"

"Prometheus swine!" she snarled.

Elliot kept his cool and waited for Ava—Hel—to calm. "Do you really believe that, Ava?"

"Of course I do. Look at him!"

Elliot sat back. "Based on what I just saw, I don't think you've ever believed it."

"You saw nothing!"

Elliot smiled, but it wasn't a happy one. He felt sorry for her. "I saw enough to know that you don't believe what your father has taught you. What I saw was someone who was biding their time until they could disappear and start over without having to look over their shoulder constantly."

Ava's eyes filled with liquid again. She didn't lash out at Elliot, though. She quietly waited and listened to him, blinking hard as the tears became too much to contain.

"The baby," Elliot said, sad.

Ava growled.

"That was you, wasn't it?"

"What baby?" Lincoln asked.

When Ava didn't explain, Elliot did.

"Her father killed her real parents when she was just an infant."

"What—why?" Lincoln asked, stunned.

"I…" Ava replied, her voice shaky. "I don't know."

They sat in silence for a moment before Elliot started up again. So far, Elijah sat at the table, never once looking Ava in the eye. If he were going to say something, he'd yet to come up with anything that hadn't been covered.

"I've done a lot of things I'm not proud of," Elliot said, sounding tired.

"I was trained to do them—believed in all of it for a time." He glanced at Lincoln. "Then, one day, I got tired of it all—tired of the killing and the bureaucratic bullshit that came with the job. I was sick of being just another number in a book to some asshole back in Washington."

"How…" Ava said, sniffing back another round of tears, "How did you move past it?"

Elliot smiled. This time it was out of happiness.

"First, you turn around and walk away. You force yourself to move on." He again looked at his friend. "You forgive and forget."

Ava laughed. "No one in their right mind would forgive me."

"You're right you son of a bi—"

Elliot held up a hand and stopped Lincoln.

The two agents stared each other down for a moment until Elliot started talking again.

"I don't pretend to know what your people's histories are with one another, but what I can tell you is that everyone deserves another chance." Elliot turned and faced Lincoln. Then, he met eyes with Ava. "Everyone deserves a chance to make things right."

He stood and walked to the window. "We saw what would happen if your father gets his hands on the Cradle. The entire world is at stake." Elliot turned and faced Ava. "Do you prefer that ending or one that involves the globe continuing to spin?"

Ava laughed softly. "It's pretty obvious which one I want." She nodded her head at Lincoln. "If I wanted him dead, I would've offed him at the hospital."

"I'm honored," Lincoln said, stepping away from Ava's side and out in front of her. He lowered the gun. "Why didn't you?"

She looked ashamed to answer him, but she did anyway. "My father…"

"The Congressman?" Elliot asked, knowing he was dangerous of what he'd just seen through Ava's memories. Still… "What about him?"

Tears flowed freely. "He terrifies me. Who do you think trained me to be who I am? Michael Towns is one of the most dangerous men I've ever met."

Hearing her say the man's name out loud sounded strange, but Elliot knew, without a shadow of a doubt, that he was the man in charge. A member of Congress was the head of the Prophets. That in itself was insane. The fact that it was Elliot's assistant's dad was even crazier.

"Why were you assigned to me?" Elliot asked, figuring it wasn't by accident that she was sent to Qumran.

"He believed that the Cradle was lost in this area hundreds of years ago. I was the only American of age that could pass for a college student, so, here I am."

“Plus, uh,” Lincoln said, his voice faltering, “your looks certainly help the cause.”

Ava rolled her eyes. “Yes, they do…” She looked at Elliot. “Would you have taken me with you if I had been a big strapping man?”

Elliot would’ve liked to think he would’ve, but he knew what she was saying. The fact that she was a woman would bring his honor to the forefront. He needed to protect her because that’s what he was trained to do. It was also the right thing to do.

“So,” Lincoln said, “the Cradle.”

Ava shook her head. “Keep it. I don’t give a shit about it.”

“What about your fa—” Elliot stopped himself. It didn’t feel right calling him that. “What about Osiris?”

Ava’s face turned predatory. She didn’t look afraid anymore. If anything, Elliot thought she looked vengeful. What she said next, confirmed as much.

“I want that bastard’s head.”

# 14

Ava knew something had happened to her when she contacted the Cradle. Something inside of her shattered. But she also felt like that same something was released—set free. The deep sense of hate she'd grown up with was gone. A weight had been eradicated from her psyche and shoulders. She pictured the baby again in her mind. Little Ava, what would she do now?

*She'd help Elliot,* Ava decided.

She trusted him, but that meant she'd also have to help Lincoln, a man she'd probably never learn to trust. Even now, still bound to Lincoln's kitchen chair, she chuckled. It was ridiculous to think that she'd be welcomed into their fold with open arms. Only a few hours ago, she'd been close to killing all three men, Elliot, Lincoln, and Elijah. Part of her had been playing Elijah, but part of her did like the guy. She respected him.

"What do we do with her?" Lincoln asked.

It was a rhetorical question, of course. In a situation like this, Lincoln was in charge here, not Elliot, who, despite his abilities, was a civilian. He wasn't looking for an answer from Elliot. He sought out someone else's opinion.

So, before the archaeologist could reply, she provided her opinion.

"You let me go."

The Prometheus agent laughed so aggressively that he spit a mouthful of water all over the table. While he wiped his mouth and blew his nose, Elliot remained silent and watched her. He was studying her. He wanted to see what she was up to.

"Yeah, fucking right!" Lincoln sat back in his chair. "Then you'd slaughter us all."

Ava smiled. She liked it when people openly feared her—who she was and who she represented. But in a time like this, with who was in the room, Ava needed to convince them that she meant them no harm. She needed to stop her murderous father's plans for Armageddon.

"Why should we trust you?" Lincoln asked. "You're an imposter and a murderer." He pointed a finger at her. "I know three good men that died at Hel's hands. If I had known that was you from the get-go…" He ground his teeth. "No one in their right mind should ever trust you!"

He had her there. Ava couldn't argue against his logic. She brought them nothing of value besides a magical change of heart. She'd been successfully subdued by her enemy. Now, she'd be seen as a liar, someone who'd say anything to get out of being killed. Even worse, they could turn her over to the authorities where she'd be rightfully labeled as a terrorist.

She dipped her head, tears flowing freely again. She couldn't stop them lately. "Osiris can't win." She looked up at Elliot. "We have to save the world." Next, she looked at Lincoln. "You don't have to trust me, but at least hear me out before you make your final judgment."

"Final judgment?" Elliot asked.

She tipped her chin at Lincoln. "Once I'm captured, he's supposed to interrogate me, by any means possible. Then, he's supposed to silence me forever."

Lincoln shrugged. "You'd do the same."

Ava shook her. "No, well, yes, but not now!" She pleaded with them to let her help. "I never aspired to be like my fa—like Osiris. I never planned on following him down this road." She grew angry, stunned by what she was thinking. "The end of the road for Osiris was never going to be Olympus!" She gritted her teeth. "It was always going to be in a body bag—by my hand!" She broke again. "That bastard murdered my parents and stole me!" She shook violently. "He stole me!"

Elliot got up and stood before Ava. Then, he knelt. Now, he was right in front of her, face-to-face. She sobbed twice more before sniffing back the next set of tears. Looking up, she didn't see someone that was angry with her. Ava saw someone who felt sorry for her. She was being given a gift that she had not received in a very long time.

Compassion.

"Do you think we can succeed?" he asked, holding up his hand before Lincoln could argue.

Ava took a deep breath and answered truthfully. "I…I don't know, but I want to try."

"I'm sure you would," Lincoln said, scoffing at the idea. "How 'bout you tell us what we need to know, then, maybe, we'll release you."

Ava sighed. "Not a chance."

"Uh," Lincoln said, "I don't think you understand the gravity of your predicament?"

She frowned, knowing what was going to happen. "Either way, I'm a goner."

"Why do you say that?" Elliot asked. He didn't understand the game these two were playing. He was a soldier, after all, not a spy.

"If I keep quiet, he'll either shoot me or call it in. Either way, I'll only be alive long enough to be of value." She looked over at Lincoln. "I know what they do to people like me."

"Only that which you've done yourself."

Ava was ashamed. She couldn't argue with him, because he was right. She'd done some terrible things.

"If we let you go—" Elliot started to say.

"I'll do whatever has to be done for this world to keep spinning."

"All because of that?" Elliot asked, motioning to the artifact sitting on the kitchen counter.

Ava knew she had to throw them a bone before they'd trust her in any capacity. So, she did just that.

"If the Cradle isn't charged soon, the containment system that houses Zeus' fire will fail." She looked hard into Elliot's eyes. "What Lincoln hasn't told you is that you may have already sealed our fates by undocking the Cradle from its station." She sighed. "The end, as they say, is nigh."

**Elliot reacted to** Ava's statement by standing and facing Lincoln. Not only didn't he fully trust his excavation assistant, but apparently, he couldn't rely on his close friend either. If Lincoln did, in fact, know that the Cradle's housing was failing, why hadn't he told him?

"Did you know this?" Elliot asked him.

Still seated, Lincoln crossed his arms and replied with a single nod of his head.

"And you didn't find it necessary to tell me I was transporting an active nuclear weapon—that happened to be mid-countdown?"

"I—"

"Dammit, Linc!" Elliot exploded. "You're as bad as her!" He jabbed a finger at Ava. "But, at least she wasn't my friend before all this." Elliot laughed. "You used me like a mule. Why?"

Lincoln stood and cleared his throat. "Because you can activate the Cradle."

"That's it? That's the only reason you haven't left me in the dust?"

Raising his hands in a calming gesture, Lincoln stepped forward. "Woah, woah, woah… No, not at all. Well, maybe a part of the reason. Regardless of *why*, I also knew that you weren't going to blow up the planet willfully—"

"And you knew me—my past as a SEAL," Elliot was pissed. "Once a soldier, always a soldier, right? You knew I'd jump right back into the fire."

"Ox," Lincoln said, "you were the best all those years ago because you never gave up, and you were loyal to a fault." Lincoln frowned. "I don't have that out here. I can't even trust most of my own people."

Elliot's eyes squinted. *What does that mean?*

"You recently asked me about whether or not I can trust the people making the tough decisions inside the Prometheus hierarchy. Well, no, I can't, okay? Happy now?" He looked at Ava. "I'm sure you're tickled to hear that there's some real drama within my arm of the Company."

"No, that doesn't make me happy," Ava said, "but it doesn't surprise me, either." She opened her hands the best she could. "Look at me. I never thought I'd be in this position, but here I am."

"But you just said—"

Ava interrupted Elliot. "That I'd end Osiris' life myself, not that I'd be doing so while also helping my sworn enemy."

Elliot glanced back and forth between the two agents. He shrugged. "Okay, fair enough. But if this is going to work, I need you two to behave."

They both laughed, and Elliot wasn't having any of it.

"I don't care if you trust one another—because I don't trust either one of you." That quieted them. "The only thing you need to do is trust me. I don't have any skin in this game except for that." He pointed at the Cradle. "Your personal war… I don't give a shit about it."

He looked at Ava. "I'm assuming it needs to be redocked?"

Ava didn't answer. She stayed silent, her eyes going from Elliot to Lincoln.

Lincoln growled and threw up his hands. "Dammit, fine, you win," he produced a switchblade and started cutting her bonds away, "but you're not getting a gun."

Ava eyed Elliot and gave him a smirk. "I don't need one."

Once Ava's left ankle was freed, Lincoln stood and backed away from her, looking very wary. Elliot didn't fear her, though. He'd seen what Ava was on the inside. He knew what she was going through mentally. He knew she had changed. The only thing he couldn't guarantee was to what extent she had changed.

"So," Ava said, rubbing her wrists, "Egypt?"

"No."

Elijah stood up from the table, speaking for the first time since this episode started with Ava. He confidently stepped up in front of one of the most dangerous people on Earth and looked her in the eye.

"I'm sorry," he looked hurt, "but I can't be involved in this…with you." He turned away from Ava and faced Elliot. "I think it's better for everyone if I sit this part of our adventure out." His eyes met Lincoln's. "I will stay here and keep my ear to the ground and look out for trouble."

"You sure about this?" Elliot asked, holding out his hand.

Before taking it, Elijah gave Ava one last look. "Yes, I'm sure."

**With the sun** rising, Elijah's departure went quick and quiet. He said his "goodbyes" and "good lucks" to everyone, even Ava. She liked that about him. Ava had openly lied to him—to them all—and yet, Elijah still wished her well. He could've just as quickly thrown her to the ground, stoned her, and kicked dirt on her face. She wouldn't have blamed him for doing any of it.

With their foursome down to three, they all took a few minutes to clean up and eat. Ava wasn't sure how they'd be traveling. Her contacts were a bust. By now, every agent within the Prophets knew she had forsaken their master. She just painted a huge, blood-red target on the back of her head. Ava didn't care, though. She knew she was doing the right thing.

Stepping out of the small square bathroom, Ava stopped short and held the doorknob in one hand. Both Elliot and Lincoln were waiting for her. If she needed to, she could leap back into the room and lock the door. After that, Ava had no idea. They'd eventually break in and overpower her, but until then, she could wait and bide her time.

"We need to talk," Elliot said, crossing his arms.

Lincoln carried a pistol, but it was tucked into the front of his jeans. That, in itself, told her that they meant her no immediate harm. Still, she needed to be cautious.

"About what?" she replied, stepping out of the room. She left the door open, just in case.

"Everything," Lincoln replied, eyes serious. "It's time to keep your end of the bargain and fill in the missing pieces. With what we both know, we might be able to stop Daddy from killing us all."

Ava didn't appreciate the jab, but she knew that if she wanted to earn their trust, then she needed to play ball.

She kept her head and stepped around them. "Fine, but we should sit." Ava crossed the room and sat at the kitchen table, acting as confident as possible.

"This is going to take a while."

**The early wake** up and lack of sleep because of the late-night festivities were quickly catching up with them all. It got so bad that Lincoln had to get up and start on a pot of dark roast coffee. The aroma alone seemed to help Lincoln, especially.

*I can't believe I have Hel in my apartment!*

Osiris' stunning assassin was legendary, even given her age. She also happened to be none other than Elliot's number two, Ava Towns. Her dad being a high-profile member of Congress threw a monkey wrench into everything. It wasn't like Lincoln could call up his bosses and start accusing a person like Michael Towns when he had connections. He was pretty sure that Osiris was publicly friends with one of Prometheus' higher-ups.

Politicians were the worst.

Relationships were too.

Once Lincoln brought everyone their blissful java, they got started. Ava took a long pull from the mug with her eyes closed. Lincoln couldn't deny her beauty. It was hard not to stare at her. He couldn't deny that her ability as a killer was a huge turn on too.

She set down the drink and opened her eyes. "Giza, we have a problem with that."

Lincoln glanced at Elliot.

"What kind of problem?" Elliot asked.

"The capstone is gone," Ava replied.

Lincoln didn't understand, but Elliot did.

"Which means…so is the docking system."

*Oh,* Lincoln thought, *well, that sucks.*

It wasn't the end, however. There were other docking systems around the globe. Unfortunately, most of them were out of reach, or under heavy security, like the one at the Area 51 site in New Mexico, or the one Prometheus had in their possession in Washington. Neither locations were an option at the moment. Lincoln couldn't trust anyone back home until he knew for sure who was secretly plotting against him.

Prometheus was on hand when the famed 1947 flying saucer crash took place. Lincoln knew that much, everyone in his organization did. It was one of the selling points recruiters used to sign up new agents.

After preliminary tests were done on the spacecraft, Prometheus scientists came up with very little because of the lack of technology humanity wielded at the time. But as the years went by, they learned a lot about the beings that operated the saucers. He wasn't sure how the craft was controlled, but it had been done from afar. The UFO that the government uncovered was remotely piloted from someplace else—somewhere in space.

As far as the "greys" were concerned…

The tall, gangly, classically built extraterrestrial was nothing, just a rumor that had been spread by Prometheus. They preferred to keep the impressive technology to themselves, including what would become modern-day autopilot systems. The original intent had been that none of it would ever come to light. As far as Lincoln knew, there had never been physical "aliens" on Earth. Ever.

*The gods, on the other hand.*

Lincoln still didn't know what to make of them. Prometheus believed in their namesake, as did most of the people that worked for them. Lincoln was still a soldier at heart. Alien tech influencing everything he had known and loved over the generations seemed to be a tale.

There had been no probing over the years either, thank God.

The UFOs had one primary purpose. The gods used them to run tests on the planet which involved measuring the Earth's natural, raw power. They gathered the energy, much like how they were shown beaming people and cows up.

The tractor beam collected the energy that was churning beneath a hot spot, totally unlike the movies when the light beamed up people and cows. The gathered energy was transferred into units, known as cores. These cores were in the same place as the docking systems. And, when the energy was introduced into Earth's atmosphere, it turned green, for whatever reason. Lincoln wondered how much of this Ava knew, but he always figured that everyone in either of the groups shared this common knowledge.

"Back to the capstone," Lincoln said, having zoned out for a moment.

"What about it?" Elliot asked. "She's right. It doesn't exist."

Lincoln shifted in his seat. The small movement got both Elliot and Ava's attention. What he said wasn't entirely true.

"What do you know?" Ava asked.

The Prometheus agent smiled wide and sat forward. "Wait a second! So, let me get this straight. You, *the* Hel, don't know this?"

"Know what, Linc?" Elliot asked, sounding tired.

Lincoln sat back, very happy with himself. "The capstone." He crossed his arms in triumph. "It exists."

# 15

Lincoln turned on the local news before they headed out. Luckily, all three of them were fluent in Arabic, so could follow along. They could plainly see that the policeman being interviewed was very upset. The assassins' bodies had been discovered in the park only an hour earlier. A park ranger had been making his rounds when he "stumbled" across the horrific scene.

Elliot was proud of Elijah for keeping his word. He'd done as he promised and had kept his ear to the ground. In this case, he played innocent and told the police nothing. Elijah knew all the cops in the area too. It seemed that Elijah was a trusted person within the community. Elliot was grateful to have met him and was also thankful to continue to be in the man's good graces.

Getting to Ben Gurion Airport took longer than it should've considering it was only thirty-five miles away. The handful of checkpoints that had been placed following the incident slowed them down, as did the ultra-tight security at the terminal. Luckily for them, Lincoln knew someone that dealt in American comic books, oddly enough, and all it took for him to help was a sizeable donation from Lincoln's private collection to get them into the airport unseen.

"How much did that cost you?" Ava asked, honestly curious.

Lincoln held back a laugh. "Forty-eight bucks."

Whenever Lincoln needed to track down someone flying into the area, he contacted a man named Omar, the superhero geek. Elliot didn't know the security guard's last name—and he didn't want to know it. Back home in the States, or just about anywhere else in the world, it would've taken ten, twenty, or even fifty times as much to pull it off.

"The dude just really loves Tony Stark," Lincoln said, snorting.

Dressed to work on the tarmac, Lincoln led Elliot and Ava around to the rear entrance. According to Omar, there weren't many women, if any, that worked in the backend of Ben Gurion Airport. So, Ava slipped into a loose-fitting jumpsuit. She was forced to remove all her makeup and tuck her hair into a baseball cap. Then, for good measure, she fit a medical mask over her nose and mouth. She looked ridiculous, but the ruse seemed to work. No one looked their way as they entered.

Hiding her identity was a good idea, even if no one was officially checking them out. A major airport would be an excellent place for either an agent of Prometheus or the Prophets to be lying in wait, maybe both. No one would recognize Elliot. Lincoln didn't look the part either. His face was hidden behind a pair of aviator sunglasses, and his heavy five o'clock shadow made him look like a sleep-deprived, hungover tourist, not a dangerous CIA agent.

Under the circumstances, Elliot would've preferred not to fly. Too many things could go wrong at an airport, especially when you were carrying around a bomb that could swiftly decimate the entire city—and then some!

He wasn't entirely sure if the Cradle was truthfully a planet killer, though he didn't plan on testing that theory any time soon. If they weren't in such a hurry, he would've suggested that they drive to Cairo to see Maggy. Just the thought of seeing her again sent a chill up his spine, though. Then, the cold AC of the terminal hit him. His partners noticed his reaction to the double chill.

"Easy, buddy," Lincoln said. "We're almost home free."

"Don't jinx it," Ava said, her voice muffled by the mask.

Elliot knew she was itching to rip it off. Plus, it appeared as if the mask did, in fact, itch her. The main reason they had disguised themselves as employees was to slip past security. Once safely on the other side, they'd ditch the getups and swiftly board their flight to Cairo International. Lincoln had quickly purchased three separate coach seats. To the untrained eye, the trio was traveling independently of one another.

Lincoln led them forward. It was impressive that he'd remembered Omar's directions so effortlessly. But also, Elliot knew the man's mind was like a steel trap with certain things, and Lincoln had used the airport several times before. He could recall anything if it mattered to him, or at least, his subconscious held onto things of that nature.

They stopped just inside a third non-descript door. There, Lincoln put a hand to it. Then, his ear. He closed his eyes and listened, earning a groan of displeasure from Ava. Elliot did have to admit that he looked ridiculous. He was taking the sneaky spy thing a little too seriously for their liking.

"Any day, Johnny English," Ava said, annoyed.

Elliot shifted the saddlebag he carried beneath his jumpsuit. It was challenging to keep it in place, tucked in his armpit. For one, it chafed something fierce. Still, he kept his left arm tucked into his side to keep it steady. Once they liberated themselves of their false personas, he'd strap it back onto his hip where it belonged.

"Hey!"

They spun away from the door. Ava was the closest to the technician and reacted accordingly. She turned, snapped her right leg up, and delivered a near-fatal blow to the side of the man's head with the bridge of her booted foot. Both men stood there, locked in place, in awe at how promptly Ava had taken the man down. Elliot wasn't pleased that she'd almost killed the unsuspecting airport employee, but she kept him from sounding the alarm, nevertheless.

Elliot and Lincoln quickly stuffed the unconscious man into a trash bin and then proceeded to strip out of their jumpsuits. Ava followed suit under the watchful eye of her former boss, Elliot.

"Uh, good work," he said, looking back toward the oversized garbage can.

A smirk formed on her face. "Thanks."

"Don't compliment her," Lincoln warned. "It'll just go to her head."

Ava didn't find the comment funny. She was about to respond but halted her response when Lincoln pushed open the door into the terminal. They'd need to move fast and slip away from one another. Their flight left in twenty-five minutes, and hopefully, no one would check the garbage until they were safely in the air. The word "safely" didn't feel right to Elliot. He knew Lincoln and Ava would agree. They weren't going to be safe until the Cradle was gone and the planet left in one piece.

**"You boys behave,"** Ava said, not turning around.

"Yeah," Lincoln said, "you too."

Just then, Ava stopped and opened her small purse. She pulled out a mirror and pretended to dab at the makeup that didn't exist. Instead, she angled it so she could see Elliot. He smiled and nodded at her. In return, she gave him a wink and snapped it shut, disappearing into the crowd.

"Think she'll keep her word?" Lincoln asked, sitting.

Elliot rounded the double-sided row of seats and plopped down hard. They still had a few minutes until they were called to board. Their ramp was up ahead, and Elliot needed to take a moment to collect himself before being alone on a flight for three hours. Flying wasn't the issue. Being alone with his thoughts was. He was going to see Maggy later that day, and it petrified him.

"Ox?" Lincoln asked, still staring the other way.

"Sorry, yeah, I think she will."

"It was that bad, huh?" Lincoln asked.

"What was?"

"Her vision."

Elliot bit his lip. There were things that he saw that no one outside of Ava herself should've seen. They didn't talk about it back at Lincoln's place in Jericho, but Osiris' main man, Hades, the head of his private security, was allowed, by Osiris as some sick reward for his service, to rape Ava repeatedly when she was in her teens. The sorrow and self-hate that burned through Ava were heartbreaking.

"Yeah," Elliot replied, "it was that bad."

It was another couple of minutes before Elliot spoke again. When he did, it was because he heard his row being called. Standing, he said his goodbyes to Lincoln but was startled when a voice, other than Lincoln, answered. It came from an older local woman who said goodbye instead. Caught off guard, and on edge, he spun and lifted his balled right fist. Luckily, he saw the woman out of the corner of his eye and didn't deliver the knockout blow.

Lincoln, as it were, was already gone. He had no idea where his partner had gone, Ava either, for that matter. He just hoped that the two agents weren't getting into any trouble. Elliot couldn't do this on his own.

*No, idiot, you can't see Maggy on your own.*

He'd have preferred to just get it over with, but that wasn't on the cards. He still had most of the afternoon to think about it. Trapped in a flying soda can filled with untamable anxiety didn't sound like a fun way to travel. Like Ava, something cracked inside of him too after he had first grasped the Cradle. His past wasn't as terrible as Ava's, quite the opposite. Elliot had a good life, for the most part.

But then there was his failure with Maggy. Until recently, he didn't know how much it had negatively affected him. Since then, he'd steered clear of any, and all, commitments that weren't directly related to his job. Traveling the world and living abroad saw to it that Elliot never had enough time for a relationship. He had friends, but nothing more intimate than that.

Elliot made his way through the jet bridge. He found it funny that with everything humanity had come up with technology-wise, that this was still the best way to board an aircraft: a foldable, loud, non-airconditioned accordion. Stepping into the plane with no issues, he was relieved to see that the flight was only half full. His group was the last to board too.

He sighed. *Going to be a quiet ride.*

Elliot needed some more rest anyways. His head was swimming from the blitzkrieg of information. His best friend was a CIA agent that secretly represented the followers of an alien god-king, and his project assistant was a lethally trained assassin who opposed his friend's organization.

*Can't get any worse, I suppose.*

With nothing more than the clothes on his back and a satchel filled with instant death, Elliot made his way to the rear of the plane. His seat was in the back, just in front of the bathrooms. He didn't care, though. It still beat flying around in a c-130 transport while back in the military.

He audibly groaned and all but fell into his seat. It squeaked in protest and got the attention of the person sitting across the narrow aisle to his left. He sat up and turned to apologize but stopped when he saw her.

*Ava?*

She was there, staring at him. Then, she smiled and stuck out her hand.

Elliot didn't respond immediately, but when he did, he introduced himself as if he was a stranger. He was in a way. Neither of them really did know the other.

Clearing his throat, he said, "I'm Elliot." He clutched her hand and pumped it twice. "And you are?"

Ava laughed, looking so at ease. "I'm, well," she grinned, "I'm…complicated."

# 16

Lincoln Ryan was a jealous man by nature. When he and Elliot fought side by side, he had hated it when his superior, Elliot, got all the credit, not that SEALs got much of it at all. In reality, they didn't need it. They knew what they did, even if most of the world was left in the dark.

Even now, he turned and peered down the aisle. There, laughing it up, was Lincoln's friend…and his enemy. Ava may have turned over a new leaf after gazing into the past, but that didn't mean she should be completely absolved of her crimes. She was a killer, and he felt that those she had put in the ground needed to be avenged.

Hel was relatively new on the scene from what Lincoln knew, and with how young Ava was, it didn't surprise him at all. But, even with her youthfulness, the Prophets assassin had been responsible for a lot of sorrow. She was known to be especially brutal up close. Ava preferred an intimate, face-to-face kill.

*Friggin witch…*

He glanced over his shoulder again. They sat ten rows behind him. He sighed. Even a man with Lincoln's training and paranoia couldn't explain it. Ava Towns—Hel—seemed entirely harmless at the moment. She wasn't pretending to get along with Elliot. He could tell that she was enjoying their conversation. Lincoln needed to have confidence in his friend's decision to trust Ava. Elliot wasn't some slouch trying to lay by some pretty coed. He had been known as the best for a reason when he'd been in the service.

Elliot was even more paranoid than Lincoln. If he suspected that Ava was going to betray them, he'd be able to handle her. But Lincoln's jealousy was climbing to a new height as he watched them talk. It gnawed at Lincoln that the attractive blonde wasn't eyeing him instead.

*God, she's hot!*

Lincoln turned and dug out his phone to check the time. They still had another two hours of flight time left. He wished he had his earbuds, but their quick exit had forced him to leave non-essentials behind in Jericho. So, instead of watching reruns of *The Office*, Lincoln did what he knew he should do.

He texted his boss.

His phone was as secure as it got. Everything he did, call or text, was encrypted. There was only one number saved to his contacts list too. There was no name or number listed, though. The only thing that was there was a series of gibberish which included four asterisks and two exclamation points.

Opening a new text message, Lincoln paused, contemplating whether or not to stay underground until they landed. He needed to see what the Cradle showed them next—if it showed them anything else at all. Having the Cradle so close to his grasp gave him pause in contacting his superiors. Elliot didn't trust them. Lincoln understood his concerns too. An object as powerful as the Cradle couldn't fall into the wrong hands, even if those hands were that of Prometheus' brass.

"Shit," he mumbled, getting a look from his neighbor.

The older man had been enjoying a book the size of two bricks. Just the girth of the thing gave Lincoln a headache. Angling the screen away from the passenger's eyes, Lincoln decided to give an update but keep it vague.

*Egypt inbound,* he typed.

A series of thought bubbles instantly popped up, telling him that his direct superior, Mark Conners, was texting him back. Mark was the closest thing Lincoln had to a friend inside Prometheus. Mark had taken the former SEAL under his wing and given him a new purpose in life.

*News?* Mark replied.

A smirk formed on Lincoln's face. He could've started anywhere, but he kept to his plan and stayed vague. He'd only tell Mark what the man needed to hear.

*Possible Prophets in range.*

Mark got right to it with his next reply.

*You know what to do. Report back when you have verification.*

As a field agent with Prometheus, Lincoln was supposed to detain, interrogate, and eliminate all Prophet operatives. Ava Towns was one of those operatives—but she was also the daughter of a United States Congressman and someone he needed to play ball with for the foreseeable future.

He gave Elliot and Ava one more look and pocketed his phone, stopping his movements when he found Ava staring him down. Elliot had closed his eyes, but not the assassin. She was staring daggers right into Lincoln.

He must've looked for too long because other people were beginning to take notice. Giving Ava one last, long look, Lincoln turned, his mind racing. He wasn't sure if she was playing them both for fools, or did she just not trust him? Lincoln figured it was probably a little of both. He didn't trust her, and Elliot didn't have faith in either of them.

It was quite literally the worst team in the history of the spy game. A trio that was "skilled" that didn't see eye to eye.

*What could go wrong?*

Lincoln knew Ava wouldn't act out in public now, especially since they were on a plane, of all places. So, Lincoln took Elliot's lead and decided to get some sleep. He gratefully closed his eyes. Any rest was good rest. After they landed, he didn't know when he would get another chance at some z's.

**Deputy Director of** Prometheus, Mark Conners, set down his phone and closed his eyes. Being the man in charge of all field operations had aged the fifty-five-year-old man considerably. He'd buried more agents than he'd like to admit, and he was hoping Lincoln Ryan wasn't going to be the next.

Lincoln's encounter with a member of the Prophets didn't shock him given that he was overseas. If anything, it slightly soothed his already stinging ulcer. It had been months since a Prophets member had been spotted. If his man's text was correct, and he had new information, it would also soothe the director's rising temper. Even Mark had to lay low when "the boss" was in one of his moods.

Either way, no one in Prometheus was in danger of losing their jobs because of their lack of movement. They were playing the long game, and they had what added up to be an infinite amount of funding. Still, Mark hoped Lincoln's lead came to fruition. It wasn't their employment that depended on it. It was possibly their lives that did—everyone's lives.

It had been confirmed that the Prophets were limiting recruiting. But even before the Prophets went underground, they found that their leader, Osiris, a man whose identity was still unknown, even after all these years, had a plan set in motion.

There were also rumors that the Cradle had been found.

Mark grinned at the possibilities they had in store for such a thing. If they could gain access to its power, the war against the Prophets would be all but over, and the world would finally be at peace. Plus, the people at DARPA, the Defense Advanced Research Projects Agency, would kill to get their hands on a device with an unlimited energy source.

He picked up his phone and dialed. His assistant picked up after only one ring.

"Sir?" Wanda asked.

"Tell Vincent to get him and his team to Giza International within the hour." Mark squeezed his fist tight. "I want confirmation of Lincoln Ryan's account."

**Elliott dropped as** he woke but he didn't physically fall. He'd been startled from a deep, much-needed nap. Opening his eyes, he realized he was one of a handful of passengers that weren't on their feet. While in his slumber, he missed the plane's landing, its taxiing to the terminal, and just about missed disembarking. Knowing what was involved in a plane's arrival, he couldn't believe he'd slept through it. That's how 'dead to the world' he'd been.

"Hey, Ava, what—"

He turned and looked across the aisle, finding no one staring back at him. Ava was gone. She must've hurried forward as soon as the "Fasten Seatbelt Light" was extinguished. It made sense too. They were supposed to be flying to Egypt as individual passengers, not a trio of lightly packed American agents.

Elliot was still thinking about how Lincoln roped him back into this life. He thought he'd made it pretty clear when he retired that he was done with military service. Standing, Elliot made eye-contact with Lincoln and mouthed a question.

"Ava?"

Lincoln's eyes widened, and he pushed his way through the onrushing horde. Elliot didn't know why he was freaking out. Ava was smart, she…

*Shit,* he thought, realizing there may have been another reason for her quick exit.

Ava was going to sell them out.

If he didn't hate being in the spy game before, he certainly did now. Someone he thought he connected with was about to turn them over to the police, or worse, possibly meet up with a team already on the ground in Egypt to terminate Lincoln and him. And it's not like they'd be able to fight back. Yes, they were all armed, but there was no way he or Lincoln would be stupid enough to engage in a firefight while inside Cairo International.

*I've done some dumb things in my life,* Elliot thought, hurrying forward, *and this would absolutely shoot to the top of the list. Armed Americans with military training in an Egyptian airport, what could possibly go wrong?*

By the time Elliot arrived in the terminal, Lincoln was already pulling out his cellphone. He didn't hear much of what was said, but he had heard enough. Prior to their landing, Lincoln had alerted his superiors to Ava's arrival.

*No wonder she bolted!*

Ava must've come to the conclusion that Lincoln was going to flip on her. And here Elliot thought it was Ava that was going to go rogue.

Elliot latched onto Lincoln's left triceps and squeezed, pulling his friend along like a child. No matter how hard Lincoln tried, he couldn't break free of Elliot's viselike grip without making a show of it—and that was something nobody, especially Lincoln, wanted. A foreign government agent getting in a fistfight with a civilian wouldn't look good.

A set of eyes found Elliot's. They were cold and calculating. The man was Caucasian, probably American, and he was watching them. He was studying them as if he were trained to do so.

Snarling, Elliot practically threw Lincoln through the restroom door, charging in after the man, fists balled. He didn't know what he was going to do, but he knew just about anything was on the table after the stunt Lincoln had just pulled.

"What the hell, Ox?" Lincoln yelled after he was released. Elliot quickly checked the stalls and confirmed that they were alone. Lincoln didn't budge. "What the hell's gotten into you?"

Elliot laughed, reaching behind him and locking the door. No one would be interrupting them.

"What's gotten into *me*?" Elliot laughed again. "You're asking me that question? Really?"

Lincoln's eyebrow raised. "Uh, well, you did just lock us in the shitter."

Elliot grinned, but not at Lincoln. He smiled at himself. At the foolishness of his actions. He was a pawn on the Prometheus chessboard. Lincoln Ryan was the knight about to lead Elliot and Ava, the pawns, to the king for their slaughter.

Holding out his hand, Elliot said, "Give me your phone."

Now, it was Lincoln's turn to snicker. "Not on your life."

"Last chance, Linc."

"Or what?" he asked, smirking. "You gonna take it from me?"

Elliot swiftly cracked his neck without the use of his hands and sighed, feeling the pressure in the vertebrae release. Standing tall, he stepped forward. He held out his hand once more.

Through a clenched jaw, he repeated his request one more time. "Give me…your phone."

Lincoln pulled his phone out of his pocket and set it on the counter behind him. Then, he removed his jacket and pulled free his gun, setting them both down next to it. Not wearing a coat of any kind, Elliot did nothing else except unbuckle the travel bag from his waist. Both the Cradle and his gun were inside, snuggly pressed against one another.

After setting it down, Elliot balled his fists and turned…just as his head was nearly taken off.

# 17

Ava didn't trust Lincoln. Not at all. Elliot, however, was more dependable, mostly because she knew he didn't trust the Prometheus agent either. Plus, there was no reason for her not to have confidence in him. Yes, he was a former SEAL, but as of now, she saw him as more archaeologist than a soldier. So, watching Elliot strongarm Lincoln into the men's room wasn't a big deal to her. It did, however, get the attention of someone else.

Four someones, actually.

Ava was sitting across the central aisle of the terminal, watching the scene unfold behind her sunglasses. Elbow propped up on her armrest, Ava's head was tilted to the right, leaning on her hand. She was pretending to be an exhausted passenger taking a break in between flights. She had barely slept a wink in days and was starting to pay for it in spades, so she didn't have to *act* tired.

She sighed and blinked herself back awake, struggling hard.

Ava didn't know if the newcomers were a part of Lincoln's outfit, or hers, so she needed to treat them as one and the same, especially since she had defied Osiris' orders and gone underground. Both sides would want her dead.

One of the men was dressed as a janitor, wearing an off-white jumpsuit with the word "STAFF" printed across his back. He made his way to the bathroom door and pushed, but luckily, he had no success. It looked like Elliot or Lincoln had locked it, and since she placed her faith more in Elliot than Lincoln, she figured it was Lincoln that was responsible, which meant that something bad was happening on the other side. If it were her in his shoes, she'd be trying to take the Cradle by force.

*Would Lincoln do that to his friend?* She'd seen Elliot in action. *'Could' he even do that to Elliot?*

Three of the four men had looked her way, obviously surveilling the area. No one knew who she was, thankfully. If they had, their reactions would have been immediate. They would've at least called it in since they wouldn't want a violet scene to unfold here at the airport, in public.

Ava refrained from grinning. She needed her ruse to remain in place until Elliot and Lincoln finished their business with one another. Then, if necessary, she'd make her move to intervene and assist her new associates. Whatever the two men were *discussing*, they needed to hurry. Those that sought an audience with them were getting impatient. Soon, the foursome outside would throw caution to the wind and force their way inside.

The thought of leaping chairs and getting into a brawl aside Elliot and Lincoln caused the corner of her mouth to twitch. Working side-by-side with a duo of their background was refreshing. She had worked with former military personnel in the past. It was refreshing to know that her training was on par with some of the world's best. But she had never teamed up with two SEALs before. Most of the men and women she teamed up with over the years had been regular military washouts.

Now, she was starting to beg for something to happen.

The man wearing the janitorial jumpsuit dropped an "Out of Order" sign in front of the restroom. Ava's expectation that these men would eventually get fed up and bull rush the door was wrong. It seemed that they were prepared to wait it out. Sooner or later, someone that actually worked for the airport would notice the bright orange sign and take a look. Businesses with a lot of foot traffic, like an airport, rarely closed bathrooms for long, if at all.

*Come on, guys,* Ava thought, getting worried. *What the hell are you doing in there?*

**Lincoln blocked Elliot's** left jab but didn't see his right leg twitch as he lashed out at his knee. Weakening your opponent's base was always the best thing to do when given the opportunity. The Prometheus agent grimaced and limped away, but never took his eyes off his larger adversary.

Elliot didn't want to fight Lincoln, but he would if it meant destroying the man's phone and cutting off his communication with his offices back in the States. They needed to move in secrecy if they wanted to succeed. Funny enough, Elliot was still fuzzy with the goal of the mission. All he knew was that the Cradle was pushing him to Giza. The revelation that the capstone, specifically the docking mechanism hidden within, still existed, was the period on the end of the sentence.

The Cradle wanted to go there. There was no other explanation.

"You betrayed us, Linc."

Lincoln shook his left leg and gritted his teeth.

"I did my job!" Lincoln roared, face flushed. "You remember what that was like, right? We don't befriend known terrorists."

Elliot laughed. "You mean, like you?"

"You don't believe that."

Elliot shrugged. "I'm not sure what I believe anymore. Both sides of every conflict I've ever been a part of were in the wrong, one way or the other." His eyes narrowed. "But what you did back there was a dick move."

Lincoln raised his fists, but instead of throwing a punch, he dove at Elliot. In the close quarters of the six-stall, rectangular restroom, he impacted Elliot in no time, and the two men slammed into the door leading back out into the terminal. As soon as they hit the door, a voice picked up on the other side, berating them for locking it.

Their time was running out.

Lincoln had him pinned against the door. His hands were strong, digging into his shirt, pushing into his shoulders. Elliot had a hold of Lincoln's shirt, too, but didn't have the leverage he needed. In a flash, Lincoln released his right hand, rocking it back to strike Elliot. Balling it into a fist, he was confused when Elliot didn't try to defend himself. If anything, he was going to let Lincoln hit him.

Confused, Lincoln stalled.

"Do it," Elliot said. "But, if you do, I'm done. You can take the Cradle back to Washington and give it to your bosses. After you do, watch what happens. Watch the most powerful device on the planet be weaponized by the most powerful people on the planet."

Lincoln squeezed his fist harder. "You don't know that's what'll happen."

Elliot lifted his head away from the door. "Neither do you, but at least I'm willing to see what's on the other side first."

He watched Lincoln's fist turn white from the strain. Then, finally, instead of punching him, he shoved Elliot in frustration and let go of him. Lincoln turned and stomped away, grumbling incoherently to himself. His inner struggle was all too familiar. Elliot knew what he was going through. The soldier inside never died. Sometimes duty reared its ugly head in certain situations, but so did common sense.

Lincoln was battling the two forces right now.

The agent spun, but before he could decide whether or not to re-engage his opponent, Elliot kicked him in the gut. Bending him at the waist, Elliot leapt forward and drove his knee into Lincoln's face, purposely laying off a bit. He didn't want to render him unconscious. He did, however, want to disable him enough to destroy his phone.

Dazed, Lincoln stumbled back.

Elliot grabbed his shirt and belt, snapped his hips to the left, lifted, and drove his slighter comrade into the mirror above the row of sinks. Lincoln's back crunched the smudged glass, spiderwebbing it in every direction. Large chunks fell away from the wall and shattered into smaller pieces, following Lincoln's downward trajectory. He hit the floor with a groan, landing hard on his back.

Elliot stepped over the wheezing man and pulled his pistol out of his bag. He used his gun as a hammer and pummeled the phone's screen multiple times. Satisfied, Elliot turned on the sink and tossed the broken device in, soaking its exposed innards with water.

"God, I hate you," Lincoln moaned, giving Elliot a feeble middle finger.

Elliot didn't reply until after he threw the busted, drenched phone into the garbage can near the door. When Elliot did answer him, he did it with an open hand. Lincoln took the offer, and gingerly got to his feet. Elliot brushed loose glass from his friend's shoulder.

"Ready to go?" Elliot asked.

Lincoln laughed, but stopped, prodding his ribs with his thumb. "Geez, man, you didn't pull any punches, did you?"

Elliot grinned. "You know I did. If I hadn't, you'd be dead."

Lincoln shrugged and nodded. "I'd like to think I could hold my own against you."

Elliot smiled and slapped Lincoln's shoulder. "Keep telling yourself that." Even at his best, Lincoln never could beat Elliot one on one.

"One of these days, Ox. One of these days…"

Even still, if Lincoln genuinely wanted to hurt Elliot, he would've done it without remorse. They'd both gone easy on each other. They were more than friends when they served together. They were brothers in arms, and brothers looked after one another.

Brothers didn't always have to agree on things, though.

They took a minute to clean themselves up and regain their composure. When they were somewhat put back together, Elliot flipped the deadbolt and threw open the door. They stepped out and found an Out of Order sign blocking the entrance. Did Ava put it there? Elliot wasn't sure.

A lone man stepped out of the growing crowd. Lincoln grabbed Elliot's arm and stopped him from advancing any further. Something about him being here spooked Lincoln.

"Vincent?" Lincoln asked, visibly shocked. "What the hell are you doing here?"

The newcomer smiled. "Mark sent us to give you a hand."

"Us?" Elliot asked. He scanned the immediate area. "Dammit, Linc…"

Lincoln was stewing, visibly angry with himself, but he wasn't thrilled with his bosses in Prometheus either. He stepped closer to the younger, clean-cut agent.

"Why wasn't I warned that you were inbound?" Lincoln asked.

Vincent didn't reply.

"Answer me!"

Lincoln's outburst got the attention of the three other men. All of them spun towards Lincoln and Elliot from various places around the terminal. One of them was dressed as a janitor. Elliot figured that's who they could thank for the "Out of Order" sign.

*Four against two,* Elliot thought, not liking the odds.

Something crashed to the floor behind Vincent. With everyone on edge, they all turned their attention to the origin of the noise. Across the main aisle, they found an old man struggling with his rolling suitcase. It had just fallen and startled them all. Elliot was hoping to see Ava but didn't. She was nowhere in sight.

He was confident that she hadn't betrayed them. She was, however, a wanted criminal. It wouldn't shock him if she were watching them from the shadows, patiently waiting to make her move, and…

*Do what exactly?*

What would Elliot allow a killer like Ava Towns to do to these four American agents that were just doing their jobs? How far would he go to finish the mission at hand?

Elliot didn't know what *he* would do either. What was his move going to be? Would he opt to save himself and Lincoln, or would he seal their fates and ruin their opportunity to get the Cradle to the Great Pyramid's hidden capstone, a location Lincoln still had yet to reveal?

Vincent's men casually closed in, tightening the invisible noose. The other Prometheus agents smiled like a trio of toothy carnivores.

Vincent's eyes burned. "Let's take a ride, shall we?"

# 18

As Elliot and Lincoln were escorted toward the front pickup curb, Lincoln leaned in and spoke under his breath.

"See, this is what I get… Now, I'm going to be brought in and removed from the case."

"I don't think they're here for you, Linc."

Lincoln glanced at Elliot. "What makes you say that?"

Elliot gripped his small duffel bag tighter. "They haven't stopped staring at me since we came out of the shitter."

His assessment was accurate too. The only agent that gave Lincoln the time of day was the man in charge, Vincent. The other three men, including the janitor who had since ditched the getup, only had eyes for Elliot. They knew what he possessed and who he was in reference to Lincoln and the Cradle. Lincoln was just the errand boy at this juncture. He was expendable as far as the mission went.

"Can we trust these guys?" Elliot asked.

Lincoln shrugged. "I only know Vincent."

"And…?"

"He's a straight-shooter—by-the-book in every way," Lincoln replied. "Honestly, it's really annoying. The guy needs to loosen up a little if he's going to last in this business."

"Or maybe you should tighten up."

Lincoln snorted. "If I had, you'd have been the one wallowing on the floor of a filthy bathroom."

Elliot grinned. "I went easy on you, Linc."

"Eat me, Ox."

"You done, Lincoln?" Vincent asked, turning on a dime, fire in his eyes.

If Elliot didn't know any better, it sure felt like they were being arrested. Their escort team had surrounded them in the shape of a diamond with Vincent leading the way. If Elliot tried to leave the confines of the diamond, he knew he'd be met with force.

*It might come to that,* he thought, gauging their options.

If they did make a run for it, Elliot knew that heading back into the airport would be the best option. They could lose their pursuers in the crowd and regroup somewhere else. The problem with openly defying the Prometheus agents was that A) They were the good guys, and B) Airport security was bound to notice. Elliott didn't want any of them to land in a Cairo prison. It was NOT high on his to do list.

The sextet of men strolled by a duo of armed police officers.

Thankfully, they were in deep conversation with one another and didn't give Elliot and the others a better look. Typically, six casually dressed people wouldn't have sent up a red flag, but these six, all solidly built with stern looks chiseled into their faces, stood out from the crowd. Most of them were locals, but not everyone.

They slipped past the cops with no issues, and Elliot let out a breath he didn't realize he was holding. He assumed everyone on Vincent's team was armed. Elliot himself was, but he also had what accounted for an atomic bomb in his small duffel. Worst case, he could call on a memory from the Cradle and distract everyone long enough for him and Lincoln to make a run for it.

Unconsciously, his right hand clutched the artifact through the bag. Even through its lead-lined casing, and the polyester bag, he could feel its smooth edges. He also felt the subtle vibrations as the energy within rolled and swirled.

The front sliding doors opened, startling Elliot. He hadn't been paying attention. Instead, he visualized what the Cradle would show him next. With his increased heart rate, the core reacted and pulsed, nearly knocking him off his feet. No one except Lincoln saw what happened. Vincent almost did when he turned, and Elliot's quick thinking saved him from any questions.

He stopped and looked down, inspecting a lump in the door's threshold that didn't exist. He swiped his foot over the metal track and shrugged, pretending that he tripped over it. For what it was worth, Vincent's reaction was one of annoyance, not suspicion. He was buying Elliot's act.

Seconds later, a large black SUV pulled up and stopped.

"I'll take the Cradle now, Mr. Oxley."

Lincoln stepped in front of Elliot. "Not a chance."

"Agent Ryan," Vincent said, serious, "I have orders to—"

"And I have my orders, Agent Recchie," Lincoln interrupted. He continued before Vincent could speak up again. "And I outrank you and your boyband." He grinned and got into Vincent's face. "Now, be a good little Prometheus do-boy and give us your truck. We have work to do, you know, saving the world and all."

Impressively, Vincent didn't back down.

"I'm sorry, Lincoln, but I can't do that. Your loyalty has been questioned, and you're out of your jurisdiction."

"Wait, my loyalty is in question?" Lincoln looked hurt.

"And you're outside of your jurisdiction… Mark doesn't think you should be involved in the case anymore. Your connection to Mr. Oxley has clouded your judgment."

"I'm trying to save us!" Lincoln seethed.

"By obliterating protocol," Vincent added.

The driver's side door popped open.

"Is there a problem, sir?"

Vincent shook his head and replied without looking back.

"None. Not unless Lincoln wants to make it one."

Elliot was so engrossed in the battle of wills he didn't notice that the driver was making his way around the front of the SUV. He stopped next to Vincent. The newest arrival was only a few inches shorter than Vincent but was far leaner.

His eyes locked onto the driver's. *Her* eyes were hidden behind a pair of aviator sunglasses. The Prometheus driver wasn't who Vincent expected it to be. Distracted, he turned to reprimand her, but stopped, confused.

That's when Ava made her move.

She drove her shin into Vincent's groin, pivoted, and slugged the next closest agent in the nose with the heel of her palm. Lincoln ducked when Ava let a kick fly, nearly taking off his head. Her boot whizzed over him and connected with the gun hand of the janitor agent. Then, she used Lincoln's crouched form as a pommel horse and shoved off of him to deliver a spinning back kick. Her foot connected with the third man's face, knocking him out cold.

The fourth member of Vincent's team grabbed Ava from behind, successfully pinning her arms down to her side with a strong bearhug. She countered it by slamming the back of her head into his face, connecting with his left eye socket. Stunned, he released her enough for her to backhand him in the crotch with her closed fist.

The former Prophets assassin snagged the man's wrist and performed a textbook hip toss, then used her momentum to leap atop Vincent's wobbling back. He stumbled forward and banged his head into the passenger side door and crumpled to the concrete.

Casually, she strode over to the only mobile agent. He was still breathing but was struggling to do so. Elliot was happy to see that she didn't break his windpipe. Ava delivered a wicked uppercut that rocked the man back. In one long, drawn-out arc, he fell to the ground.

In just a few seconds, Ava had taken down four, well-trained Prometheus agents with just her hands. No weapon had been needed, and none of Vincent's team even got a shot off. As impressed as Elliot was, Lincoln was that much more astounded. He had never trusted her, but the fact that she would risk everything to help them spoke volumes to her claim that she was on their side.

Without a moment wasted, they piled into the SUV and sped away, leaving the four agents to the wolves. Elliot could tell that Lincoln was down.

"Hey, you did the right thing."

Lincoln nodded, behind the wheel. "I know, but it still doesn't feel right." He looked into his mirror. "I feel like I betrayed my people."

Ava snorted out a laugh from the backseat. "Tell me about it…" She leaned forward, sticking her head between the two men. "So, Agent Ryan, did that change your opinion of me?"

"The fact that you just assaulted four of my colleagues all because they disagreed with me, I'm supposed to be impressed?"

Ava's face soured.

Lincoln smiled. "Well, I am."

Her face brightened.

Elliot turned around. "Thank you—and thanks for not killing any of them."

"Yeah," Lincoln chimed in, "that too."

Ava took her sunglasses off and sat back. "You're both welcome." She took a deep breath. "I'm not going to lie…it feels pretty good being on the right side of things for a change."

They sat quietly for a moment. Lincoln was the first to speak up.

"So, Maggy?"

Elliot sighed. "Yeah…Maggy."

**Congressman Michael Towns** successfully slipped away for a meeting in the Middle East. Theoretically, he was doing precisely what his schedule dictated. He was meeting with an allied dignitary. The untold truth about their meeting was that the politicians were loyal to the Prophets first, not to their countries.

The official meeting was professional and somewhat productive. The secret meeting was also fruitful, but much more intense. Osiris was livid that Ava had betrayed him, even more so when there were whispers that she'd done it to help Prometheus.

Very rarely did he get his hands dirty anymore. His high-profile position in Congress didn't allow it. But on occasion, he would; He'd schedule his undertaking to occur whenever he was out doing his duty on behalf of the president. Even now, Osiris had already adorned a wig and sunglasses. He changed out of his expensive suit and into a t-shirt and jeans. No one would recognize him now. Whenever he was undercover, he altered his speech too, not just his looks. Sometimes, like now, he'd use a convincing Australian accent.

His operatives had failed twice now, first at the hospital and then at the excavation site. He wasn't going to let another team fail. Osiris was going to lead the next strike team himself alongside his number two, Ardath Seif, callsign Hades. The imposing Iraqi-American never left his side except when he was in his private office.

Reports indicated that Ava and her companions flew to Cairo. Airport security footage that he'd purchased confirmed the claim. Ava was, indeed, assisting Prometheus and defying Osiris' direct orders. She openly defied the master of the Prophets. The only punishment acceptable was death. Whether it was by his hand or that of another agent, Ava was done for.

**Vincent Recchie barely** got away before airport security came down on them. He stumbled back into Cairo International and headed straight for his locker. Inside was a change of clothes and a spare phone. He grabbed it all and headed for the bathroom at the other end of the baggage check.

Being in a business suit felt awkward after having worn a t-shirt and jeans combination for the last few months. So did the phony spectacles. The lenses were glass but held no prescription. Satisfied with the quick-change, Vincent dumped his old clothes in the garbage and stepped back out into the gambit of world travelers. He walked slow, confident, texting on his phone as everyone else did.

The person he texted? Mark Connors.

*Ryan slipped away with Prophets agent and Oxley,* he typed.

He navigated the room and found a busy place to hide. Vincent needed to receive his new orders before getting back on the road. For now, he'd hide in plain sight and wait. He wasn't sure what to do about a new team. The others had been arrested but would eventually be cleared of any wrongdoing and released. It was a delay Vincent couldn't afford, though. He was lucky that the blow to his head had only stunned him and didn't render him unconscious.

Text bubbles appeared. Mark was getting back to him already.

*Please confirm,* Mark replied. *Ryan is working with Prophets?! Are you sure?*

Vincent couldn't believe it either. Lincoln Ryan had, until now, been an exemplary agent. He was seen as a troublemaker, but he nevertheless got the job done more often than not. Vincent wasn't a veteran like Lincoln was. He'd been with the CIA since graduating college and did as he was told without question.

Lincoln Ryan questioned everything.

Vincent texted Mark back.

*I believe so.* He thought about what to write back. The only common denominator was Oxley. *Oxley at fault for betrayal?*

More text bubbles.

*Possibly,* Mark replied. *Pursue with caution and report back.*

Vincent stood and made his way to his backup vehicle. He knew where they were going. An old friend of Lincoln's worked at the Egyptian Museum. She was listed in his contacts file back at HQ. Every agent had each other's contacts, just in case something drastic happened.

Vincent would visit Magdalen Bitar and see if he could get lucky and run into the liability that was Lincoln Ryan. Maybe he could even be fortunate enough to rid the world of the Prophets scum too.

# 19

Watching Elliot toil in misery was amusing, and not because of the unbalanced way people in Ava's line of business were forced to think to survive. It was as simple as watching a man of Elliot's age squirm while waiting to speak to a woman he still had feelings for. It was cute, but also kind of pathetic.

Ava had no idea what Maggy looked like, or what type of temperament she owned. She didn't know if the woman would be happy to see Elliot or not. From what Ava knew, Elliot ended things badly. Hopefully, for what they needed her for, she didn't hold grudges against men who personally wronged her. If she did, this was where their journey would've ended. Not even a person of Ava's ilk could get into the Great Pyramid unnoticed.

Elliot and Lincoln sat on a bench outside Maggy's office, impatiently waiting for her to finish a conference call. Not one to usually sit around and do nothing, Ava kept watch at the outside edge of the alcove holding said office and bench. Leaning against the wall, she studied everyone's faces, praying she didn't recognize anyone. If she did, they'd all be in serious trouble.

Ava was used to trouble. It found her everywhere she went. She sometimes preferred it over peace. That was a part of her irrational thought process. If things were "normal," then things were most likely wrong.

A handsome tourist with striking blue eyes walked by her. His hard gaze never left her body. She was used to people ogling her, and she never found it flattering. Usually, she'd tell the person off, but in this case, she just ignored him and turned away. She'd never forgive herself if she blew their cover because someone was staring at her chest.

When she turned, she found another man eyeing her from across the rotunda. He was looking at her through a glass display case housing the remains of an Egyptian noble she'd never heard of. His name was Zadmarr Something Something. Supposedly, he was responsible for building the Great Pyramid. Even with all her knowledge on the subject, she'd never heard of the man. But she did remember the architect that had been in Elliot's vision—he had died after he raised the capstone. Was that Zadmarr?

*I guess anything's possible.*

Ava noticed the stranger she caught staring at her was gone. She pushed away from the wall and scanned the room again and couldn't find him. He had a mop top of black hair, and thick, black-rimmed eyeglasses. She didn't get a good look at his face, but she was sure she didn't know him.

Like Elliot, now it was her turn to feel nervous. She thought about leaving the recess and searching for the man, but she decided that splitting up wasn't the right move. They needed to stay together. She and Lincoln together would be an unstoppable force when it came to the Cradle's history. And Elliot was too important to leave behind. Ava still couldn't believe that she, of all people, had activated the artifact. She didn't trust herself with that kind of power. Elliot, however, could control it.

"Mr. Ryan. Ms. Bitar will see you now."

Ava peered over her shoulder and found a short, heavyset man guiding Elliot and Lincoln into Maggy's office. Quickly, Ava turned and followed them in. She gave the stout man a wink and stepped inside.

Like you'd expect, the office to the Associate Director of the Egyptian Museum was in itself, a small gallery. It held artifacts from all over the world—a private collection of sorts. A female of average height stood behind the desk, head down as she scanned a stack of papers. Even from the awkward angle, Ava could see that Maggy was beautiful. She'd yet to look up and formally greet her guests. When she did, the look on her face was priceless.

"Lincoln, hi, good to see y—" She looked behind him and stopped the pleasantries when Elliot entered.

"Oh, Elliot. Wow…" She was instantly flustered. "I had no idea you were…" Her hand went to her mouth. "Um, okay, wow."

"Good to see you too, Maggy," Elliot said. "It's been a while."

"Yes, it has." Maggy looked Ava's way. "And who's this?"

"Oh, right, sorry," Elliot replied, waving Ava forward. "This is Ava. She's helping me at the dig site."

"Right," Maggy replied, "the thirteenth Dead Sea Cave. How exciting," her face soured, "especially with all the extracurriculars and all."

Elliot shrugged. "Nothing I can't handle."

"I bet…" Maggy glanced at Lincoln. "Still getting into trouble, is he?"

Lincoln chuckled. "You know Ox. The man never stays out of it long enough to know what he's stepped in. He's also terrible at realizing what he has before it's gone."

Ava rolled her eyes at the last comment. Lincoln was baiting Elliot and Maggy into a tiff. He enjoyed watching his two, long-time friends bicker back and forth.

Elliot stepped forward. "Look, Maggy, I didn't come here to argue over the past. We need your help, okay?"

Ava could see that Maggy was pissed that Elliot had shown up unannounced. It also proved that she still held feelings for him. The only problem was trying to decipher which of the feelings she had was more dominant—love or anger?

"Please," Ava said, coming to Elliot's side. She stood next to him. "It's vital that you hear what we have to say."

Maggy looked at Lincoln. He nodded. She took a deep breath and sat, motioning for them to do the same. No one spoke, so Ava started, and she decided to be frank with the Egyptologist.

"I'm not really who they say I am, Ms. Bitar."

Maggy's left eyebrow rose. "Oh really?"

Ava nodded. "I'm actually—"

"Ox's bodyguard!" Lincoln finished, sounding nervous. "She's his bodyguard."

"And why does Elliot need to be protected?"

"Because of what I found in Qumran," Elliot replied, being serious. He didn't like hiding Ava's true identity from Maggy, but nor did he want to ruin any hope of her agreeing to help them.

"And that is?" Maggy asked, looking suspicious.

Elliot dug into his bag, uncovered the Cradle, and set it on Maggy's desk.

"This."

Maggy stood and backed away from the swirling plasma cube. It snapped and popped angrily, but it was also soothing to look at, like a lava lamp.

Wide-eyed, her eyes darted to Elliot. "You found this in a Dead Sea Cave?"

Elliot nodded, but then shook his head. "Actually, no. Under it."

"Yeah," Lincoln added, "Ox took a tumble down an undiscovered rabbit hole. He found an ultra-modern room filled with pictographs and a docking station complete with the Cradle."

Maggy sat and held up her hand. "Woah, back it up. The *Cradle*?"

Ava leaned forward. "You know it by another name… Pandora's Box."

Maggy burst into laughter, holding her chest with one hand while the other gripped the edge of the desk. Tears formed in her eyes as she snorted and guffawed. Elliot looked irate. So, he did the only thing he could think of to tell their story. He showed her.

He reached out and took hold of the artifact and told it what he wanted Maggy to see. "Show me destruction."

The room lit up in the same green as what was inside the Cradle. Then, like before, the people within the object's aura were mentally whisked away to a time of great sorrow and death. Elliot had never asked to see such devastation. It was a moment in time that he'd never studied. He had never heard of it happening at all.

He knew the Sahara Desert was once a part of what would eventually be dubbed the "Mediterranean Sea," but no one knew, for sure, how it became what it was today. Most people thought it had been a result of a natural shift in regional temperature. The scene before them told them something completely different.

**A robed man**—a king—stood in the middle of a windstorm the likes of which Elliot had never seen. It was a massive tornado that had a green glow from deep within it. Elliot wasn't sure how the Cradle could be directed to do such a thing, but this person was doing it. Elliot knew who the man was, he didn't comprehend how he knew, but he knew. This person's role in the world below had come to him as the scene developed. Regardless, thousands of people were about to die.

Elliot's mind translated the ancient language effortlessly. He understood what was happening. The man, the kingdom's leader, had gone mad with power and was trying to force the Cradle to abide by his will. Their island sanctuary was about to fall because he attempted to abuse the gifts the artifact could bestow. Now, he and his people were experiencing the other side of raw power—a planet killer.

*It really does respond to your intent,* Elliot thought.

If you wanted to be progressive with it, and build beautiful monuments, or feed your people for generations, the Cradle did as asked and acted on your behalf. But it also responded if you wanted to use it as a weapon of war.

High above the island, Elliot and the others witnessed dozens of seafaring vessels sailing toward the epicenter of the green tornado. Below the eye of the storm, the king was trying to wipe the invading force off the map. Instead, he may have doomed everyone he ruled over. With the knowledge he now had, Elliot knew everyone was about to die. The tumultuous event he was witnessing right now had never been confirmed, but now he knew.

*No one survived to tell the tale.*

Yet, through the vortex beneath his feet, Elliot saw something he recognized. It wasn't quite what the conspiracy theorists described, but it did have the three rings the legendary island empire was known for.

"Atlantis."

"What?" Maggy said, her eyes wide. "You're kidding?"

Lincoln laughed nervously. "Uh, I've learned to just go with it."

Ava stepped forward. "Ditto," she added. "We're looking into a past that no one has seen." She leaned around Elliot and Maggy and confirmed her supposition. "Lincoln?"

He shook his head. "Nope. We've never heard of this either."

"Then that means...Atlantis was real?" Maggy asked, watching intently as the massive storm tore into the gorgeously erected structures.

The structures reflected those of every ancient culture known to mankind.

Egypt, Mesoamerica, Sumer, Asia—they were all there.

*Makes sense,* Elliot thought. *Atlantis was supposedly the inspiration behind them all.*

"So, the alien gods started here?" Lincoln asked.

"Aliens?" Maggy asked.

"It's a long story, but yes," Elliot replied, "the gods of ancient history were real, and they were beings from another world." Maggy looked up at him. He gave her a soft smile. "Trust me."

"I don't know if the gods started here," Ava continued, "but I'd say it's safe to think that this is one of Prometheus' first attempts at advancing our species."

"And boy, did we screw that up," Lincoln said, shaking his head.

Maggy looked confused, but she was smart enough to put it together. Elliot planned on filling her in on everything as soon as they were done here.

Now, the island was all but gone, broken, and engulfed by the sea. Then, the world switched to fast-forward, and the water surrounding it was swept away, exposing a barren seabed. The plateau that had held Atlantis quickly crumbled and collapsed in on itself, erasing its existence forever. Move ahead thousands of years later. Sandstorms drove in the dunes that are in the present day, completely burying all traces of the city.

That's when the myth was born. The few people that survived and made it out alive told their tale, but eventually, it got lost to time.

Maggy was freaking out, so Elliot decided to show her the construction of her beloved Great Pyramid. He replayed what the rest of them had already seen, and with it, Maggy's tears transformed from ones of terror to those of joy. Her hand unconsciously found Elliot's shoulder, and she gasped when the technologically advanced capstone was hefted into the sky with the grace of an angel—by the same Cradle Elliot held, no less.

"Incredible…" Maggy was awestruck. Her eyes darted around, taking in everything they could.

With the scene playing out in front of them, Elliot turned and faced Maggy, feeling the strain in his gut. He'd only be able to hold it for a little longer. He reached out and turned her face toward him.

"We need your help."

# 20

"What do you need from me?" Maggy asked, back behind her desk now.

She sat, lowball glass in hand. Occasionally, she'd enjoy a delicious Single Malt. This one was eighteen years old and finished in a sherry cask. It offered a slightly creamy mouthfeel with hints of dried fruit and soft spice. Everyone was indulging. Even the blonde with the most intense eyes Maggy had ever seen was sipping on the scotch like a pro.

"Let's start from the beginning," Elliot said, eyeing Lincoln and Ava. "She deserves to know what she's getting herself into."

Lincoln and the younger woman didn't look comfortable being asked to share whatever information they had, but they both nodded and began. Maggy was immediately thrust into a story she had a hard time believing…at first. They told her of an ancient war between two sects of followers. Some of them were even direct blood descendants to what they described as the "gods of old." She was shocked to hear that Elliot was one of them. It's how he activated the "Cradle."

"May I?" Maggy asked, motioning to the Cradle.

Elliot shrugged and handed it to her.

It was much heavier than she thought it'd be. The casing was a strange combination of metallic and synthetic materials. Honestly, she didn't know what it was. As interesting as the housing was, it was what was inside of it that was infinitely more incredible.

"So," she said, watching the goop roll over itself while it crackled and popped with pure energy, "this is what all the fuss is about?" She looked up from the Cradle to the three people sitting across from her. "This is the most dangerous object in the world?"

Elliot and the others nodded as one. They weren't playing a cruel joke of some kind. The trio were dead serious, each displaying a different level of concern.

Maggy turned her attention to Ava. "And you can activate it too?"

The female agent shifted in her seat, uncomfortable. "Yes, but I have no intention of doing it again."

"Why not?"

"Because," Ava explained, "it shows you things—painful things—terrible things…"

"But," Elliot interrupted, "it can also do good. You saw Khufu being built with your own eyes."

Maggy grinned. "It felt like I was really there."

Elliot leaned forward. "You were there, Maggy." He tipped his chin at her. "Look at your shoulder."

Confused, Maggy did as he asked, and she peered at her right shoulder. Strangely, it had a light layer of sand on it. It wasn't much, and she knew it hadn't been there before their jaunt through time.

She picked up a couple of grains off her jacket with her thumb and forefinger. Her hand shook. Maggy couldn't process what she was holding or how it had gotten there.

What she said next, stumped them all. "We traveled back in time?"

Elliot was about to answer but didn't. His mouth opened and stayed agape, like a fish. No one replied, actually, not even the government agent or the trained assassin. Their lack of explanation didn't confirm anything, but it also didn't deny her claim.

They sat quietly for a moment, silently sipping on their drinks. The only sound came from the clinking of ice. Maggy tipped her head back and drained the rest of the scotch. Slamming the heavy glass down hard, but not hard enough to break it, Maggy sat back and crossed her arms.

"Well, what do you need from me?"

Elliot leaned forward on his knees. "Private access."

"To what?" Maggy asked.

"To Khufu."

Maggy blew out a long breath and rubbed her face.

"That's a tall order," she replied.

"Why's that?" Ava asked.

Maggy stood and moved to a window behind her desk. She peered out of it and closed her eyes as her face was bathed in sunlight.

"Well," she explained, "for one, I don't work for the Giza complex. Also, it's a protected UNESCO site, and they don't take too kindly to unscheduled excursions."

That seemed to deflate them. Maggy felt terrible, but it was the truth. She held no authority over the site. She sighed, knowing she was going to hate suggesting what she was about to say.

"But..." she said, biting her lip.

"*But* what?" Elliot asked.

"But..." Maggy rubbed her arms. She didn't want to make the call she knew she needed to make. "I may know someone that can get us in." They waited silently for her to explain further. Her eyes flicked to Elliot and then quickly away from him. "He's an ex of mine."

Lincoln whistled softly. "Well," he slapped Elliot on the shoulder, "this won't be weird."

**While Maggy made** the arrangements, Elliot, Lincoln, and Ava sat and waited. They did their best to give the woman some privacy. They had offered to leave her alone, but she had insisted on letting them stay, stating that it wasn't a big deal if they were in the room.

It shouldn't have been an issue, but Elliot couldn't deny his rising jealousy. It was juvenile to think that she hadn't dated anyone in the last decade-plus—downright stupid. He'd seen other women since they'd been together, but none that could even compare to the woman that Maggy was.

Her ex-boyfriend was a man named Alexander Dukaras. He worked directly with UNESCO, overseeing things in Egypt for them. He lived here in Cairo and could get them a private tour of the innards of the tomb.

"Thank you, Alexander," Maggy said, finishing up. "I appreciate the help. You have no idea how important this is." She rolled her eyes at whatever he was saying. "Yes, of course. See you tonight."

She ended the call and set down her phone, looking like she had just made a deal with the devil.

"Is everything okay?" Elliot asked.

She nodded. "Yeah, we're good. Alexander is an interesting individual to deal with."

Elliot could tell that she wanted to say something else. She was trying to paint the man in the best light possible. He had zero knowledge of him and had no idea what to prepare for. Regardless, he was giving them what they wanted. A VIP tour of the pyramid was an infrequent occurrence, especially after the park closed. That had been Ava's idea. The fewer people around to possibly ID them, the better off they'd be.

Elliot was having a hard time remembering that Ava was a wanted killer. She had morphed into a completely different person since their trip down her memory lane. Before he knew who she was, he thought she was pretentious and uninteresting. She'd been acting, of course, but still… Then, there was her manic mentality as a member of the Prophets. Now, she was soft and inviting to speak to. She wanted to be included as an equal, and Elliot was happy to give her that.

Even Lincoln was warming up to her.

"What do we do until tonight?" Lincoln asked.

They had five hours to kill—an eternity considering they were *this close* to the end. At least, that's what Elliot hoped. Unfortunately, there wasn't any end in sight. As far as any of them knew, once they arrived on location, they might be sent to another place, and then another.

Elliot knew what they needed next.

He turned to Lincoln. "Tell us where the capstone is." The Prometheus agent had been uncooperative in providing them with its location. If they were to move forward, everyone, including Maggy, needed to know everything he did. "No more secrets, Linc."

All eyes were on Lincoln now. Maggy had stood to collect her belongings but stopped and was now waiting for him to answer Elliot.

"See," he said, "here's the thing..."

"Lincoln..." Maggy said, crossing her arms.

Ava stayed quiet, but her eyes screamed for answers.

"Okay, look," Lincoln said, getting up and pacing the room, "I *think* I know where it is."

Elliot sat back and looked at the ceiling. "You *think* you know?"

Lincoln got on the defensive. "Yeah, that's what I said. At least we have that." He pointed at Ava. "That's more than she's had to offer."

Ava leapt to her feet but bit her tongue and stayed quiet. She balled her fist but kept it by her side.

Lincoln stepped back to a safer distance.

Ava matched the stride. "I've done more than you could ever do! I turned my back on everything I know—my family, my life."

"Ava," Elliot said softly.

She took a deep breath and relaxed, sitting back down. Still, everyone stared at the Prometheus agent, waiting for more details.

"Well, Lincoln," Maggy said, "tell us what you *think* you know."

"Fine, look...a lot of what I have to go on is hearsay and hypotheses. I put together a lot of it myself over the last couple of years." He took a breath and leaned against the inside of the door. "After the Great Pyramid was finished, and after its architect died, that man's apprentice took over and wielded the Cradle for evil."

"I thought only a member of the gods' bloodline could operate the Cradle?" Maggy asked.

Lincoln nodded. "Very true. This man, Mankesh, was selected to study under the architect *because* he was the only other person that could activate it. The problem with him was that he came from a more evil, warring background."

"He was a soldier?" Elliot asked.

"Yep, just like you and me, bud. Only Mankesh saw the Cradle as a way to destroy his enemies, not as a way to advance humanity. *That's* where we differ from him."

"And about five thousand years," Ava added, grinning.

"Yes," Lincoln agreed, "and that."

"What does this have to do with the capstone, though?" Maggy asked.

"Hold your horses, Maggs. I'm getting there." Lincoln continued, "The only people that were let in on the deepest, darkest secrets surrounding the Cradle were the king and his architect. That's it. One of those secrets was a prophecy of sorts." He looked at Ava. "One that a certain group of people is still trying to make come true."

Ava leaned forward, placing her elbows on her knees. "That's where the Prophets come into play."

"They existed back then?" Maggy asked.

Ava shook her head. "Not as we know them now. The organization has had many names over the years. They've been known by their current moniker for the longest of times."

"And their prophecy?" Maggy asked, steering the conversation.

Ava sighed. "To rejoin the gods in heaven, or in this case, space."

Maggy laughed aloud but saw that Ava hadn't joined in.

"Oh, you're serious?"

She nodded. "We—I mean, the Prophets—believe that Zeus and the other gods are still alive on an enormous space station inside Phobos."

Elliot's eyebrows rose. "Mars' moon?" Even he didn't know that.

"Yes," her eyes were tense, "Phobos isn't what it seems."

"How is that possible?" Maggy asked. "There's so much evidence to the contrary."

Ava looked away.

"Tell them," Lincoln said, pushing away from the door. "Tell them what Prometheus has suspected for decades." His eyes were locked in on the assassin.

She dipped her head as she spoke. "The space program—anything to do with the tech involved—was invented by deep-state Prophets agents. Their original goal was to send a manned mission to Phobos."

Ava looked up at Elliot with sorrowful eyes. "There's so much out there that people don't know—things hidden for the benefit of one sect of ancient followers. It's not right…"

"And Mars itself?" Elliot asked.

Ava sat up. "Most of the Prophets believe it to be Olympus—a kingdom in the heavens, as it were. Once a thriving world, it's since believed to have been destroyed during a civil war between those loyal to Zeus and those loyal to a covert rebellion leader, Prometheus. They called the devastation, the 'Burning.'"

"Let me guess," Maggy said, pointing to the Cradle, "that's what annihilated the planet."

Ava shrugged. "Possibly. But I think it was probably another core of a similar ability. They are said to be highly unstable."

"The capstone," Elliot said, interjecting, "is a docking station of some kind. The casing will eventually fail if it's not plugged in and charged."

Maggy's eyes widened. "How long do we have?"

Lincoln shook his head. "No idea, but I'd rather not dawdle."

Maggy stood. "Agreed. So, Lincoln, where is the capstone?"

"That's where it gets a little hazy," he replied. "My research tells me that after a battle, the capstone was removed—obviously by someone using the energy from within the Cradle. There's a legend that we uncovered eons ago, about a "mighty mechanism" being returned to the 'horizon.'"

Maggy cleared her throat. "Hmm, well, 'Khufu's Horizon' is the ancient translation for the pyramid. But I'm not sure what it refers to in this case. How do you return something to a place that it already is?"

Lincoln nodded. "That's what I thought."

"Unless it's inside the pyramid," Elliot said, thinking aloud. "What if they found it on-site before the pyramid was erected?" He sat back with a look of disbelief on his face. "What if Giza was selected for Khufu's tomb because of what sits beneath it?"

Ava's eyes scrunched, deep in thought. "A cover-up?"

"Exactly!" Elliot said, standing and pacing the room. "What if they built the pyramids in that exact spot to erase evidence of something else?" He turned to Maggy. "Any chance we can meet your guy sooner?"

# 21

Ava was impressed with the BS excuse that Maggy came up with on a whim. Alexander bought it hook, line, and sinker too. This time, the Egyptologist put the man on speakerphone. Instantly, Ava could tell that the guy was full of himself and that he still had feelings for Maggy.

Sadly, she could only squeeze another hour out of him. Now, instead of five hours to kill, it was down to four. It was an eternity to someone like Ava—someone that was used to operating on her own schedule. She was also very familiar with the practice of patience. She'd routinely have to wait hours for a target to get into position to strike, or sometimes her downtime could last days before they even showed themselves, let alone presented her with a viable target.

This was different, though. Ending someone's life wasn't as strenuous as saving one.

"You okay?" Lincoln asked, opening the door. He'd noticed that she was having an inner struggle.

"I'm fine," she lied, stepping around him.

He laughed.

"What?" she asked, annoyed.

"You were a better liar when you were a bitch."

She couldn't help but smile. As the minutes turned to hours, she started to like Lincoln more and more. The man found a way to lighten the load by doing little else than muttering a few words. Elliot was always so intense, but incredibly thoughtful and caring of others. Lincoln was a laxer and, for the most part, looked out for himself.

Ava was more like Lincoln than Elliot, though her connection to Elliot was more profound than just their personalities. He knew her on an intimate level now. He also knew more about her than anyone; even her murderous, adoptive father. She could never be anything more to Elliot than a close friend or mentor.

Lincoln, on the other hand.

*Geez,* she thought, rolling her eyes at the idea, *get over it and focus.*

When she stepped around Lincoln, her foot caught his, and they both stumbled slightly. The shift their bodies made ended up saving both of their lives. A bullet tore through the air directly between their heads. When it did, both agents dove for cover and yanked their weapons free. She saw Elliot draw his weapon too as he shoved Maggy low and out of sight behind a statue of someone she didn't recognize.

The half-moon shaped alcove took up a portion of the eastern wall of the main hall which now swarmed with shrieking museum patrons.

"See anyone?" Lincoln shouted, scanning the room.

Ava shook her head. "No! Elliot?"

"Negative!" he yelled back. "All I see is chaos!"

*Same here,* Ava thought, taking it all in one person at a time.

Situations like this were when she was the most patient. She never ran into a firefight if she could help it. She always did her best to calculate what her opponents were up to first. In this case, she was attempting to ID the shooter and count the aggressors' numbers.

Someone was shoved through a display case over near the front door, smashing it to pieces. Ava didn't want to see the look on Maggy's face. It was her museum, after all. Security officers were, no doubt, on their way. If the attack didn't get pushed any further inside, they could each swiftly holster their weapons and play the part of a frightened tourist and head for the nearest exit.

Just as she was about to sound the all-clear, someone to her left caught her eye. He wasn't moving toward the entrance, nor was he part of the museum security team. She didn't recognize him in any way. Still, he moved with purpose, hunched low while sliding around box-shaped, glass display cases.

On one knee, she pivoted her weight and turned her hips to face the man of interest. Lincoln must've seen him too, because he moved as she moved, like a well-oiled machine. She grinned and stood up at the same time as the newcomer. His gun came up a split second after both of hers and Lincoln's. Together, they took down the shooter with one quick twitch of their forefingers. Both projectiles hit their mark and took the man off his feet.

*That's one,* she thought, keeping track of the fallen.

Streams of bullets tore into their cover. They'd given away their positions after springing to their feet. Now, the other gunmen had a lock on them. She counted four more—five in total if you counted the one they'd already shot.

"Time to go to work," Lincoln grunted, scampering to his left.

Ava went right and slid across the marble floor. She yelled back to Elliot, "Keep Maggy and the Cradle safe!"

Elliot shouted after her. "Safe, right!"

The pops of Lincoln's pistol were followed by a succession of automatic fire. Their pursuers were using military-grade rifles of some kind. She'd yet to be fired upon, and she knew why. Lincoln had drawn their attention first, which meant that Ava could go about doing her part of the job uninterrupted.

She crept up behind a case with a scroll in it. It, like everything around her, looked like it was priceless. Regrettably, a significant portion of the main hall's displays were now ruined. Hopefully, for Maggy's sake, the archaeological finds held within them survived the day.

Staying low, Ava darted out into the center aisle and got a good look at the closest assailant. He was wearing plain clothes and gripped a compact submachine gun. The stock was foldable, making it easy to conceal beneath a coat. Raising her sidearm, she pumped three rounds into his back and moved off, not watching him fall. In doing so, she was able to slip away undetected.

*Two down.*

Now, she and Lincoln only had three more to silence.

It took her another thirty seconds to maneuver into position. She edged out from behind a tall, upright display case. Inside was another sarcophagus. This one was propped up on its end, so museum patrons could see what was inside. She used its positioning to her advantage and stood.

Bullets roared from behind her, pummeling the case one round after the other. One of the gunmen must've spotted her. With their attention now on her, Lincoln's pistol erupted to life. One of the assassins shouted in pain and slammed into a four-foot-tall case that lined the central walkway. The butt of his rifle smashed through the glass partition and got wedged in tight within the collection's framework as the shooter flopped to the floor.

Ava turned and was bowled into. One of the men circled around the rear of her hiding place, timing his assault perfectly. The two combatants exchanged blows, eventually breaking away from one another. The combatants raised their guns into the other's faces, as they backed into the base of the tall display case. Squatting next to one another, Ava and her attacker held pistols to the other's throat. Thankfully, neither fired.

"You!" Ava was shocked to see Vincent, the Prometheus agent from the airport. "What the hell are you doing here?"

"Stopping you!" Vincent yelled, digging his sidearm in deeper.

Ava did the same thing, and growled, "I'm trying to help Lincoln!"

"The hell you are!" Vincent's aggression cracked just a bit. He had no way of knowing that Ava, a wanted criminal, was on his side now. She needed to convince him. But how?

The opportunity arose seconds later. One of the last shooters alive rushed their position behind the upright sarcophagus. Ava saw him coming, but Vincent didn't. He was facing the wrong direction. In another life, she would've let the goon take him out, but she wasn't like that anymore.

All she had to do was aim a little to the left of Vincent's head. Quickly, she pulled the trigger. The bullet buzzed by Vincent's temple and impacted the incoming threat in the chest. The Prometheus agent reflexively dove to his left to avoid the shot. As he did, he got a look at the man Ava had just taken down. The surprised look on his face told Ava everything she needed to know. Vincent recognized that she had just saved his life. He turned around again and gazed at the dead man. Then, he looked back at Ava, who gave him a soft nod.

"Look," she said, checking her gun's ammo, "we can kill each other later, but for now, we need to find Lincoln and the others."

**Keeping a pack** of semi-well-trained mercenaries busy wasn't what Lincoln thought of when he described a "good time." It wasn't what he planned on doing at all. Initially, he figured he'd go on the offensive and take each of them out one by one. Ava had beaten him to the punch, which wasn't okay in his book. Lincoln wasn't being sexist. He just really didn't like to be shown up by anyone. Ever.

Occasionally, he'd poke his head out just long enough to get the attention of their foes. Then, he'd fire a shot near one of them to entice them to follow him further away from Elliot and Maggy deeper into the main hall. He zigged and zagged, taking inaccurate potshots as he moved within the maze of wood and glass display cases.

He figured that there was only one more of them left now. Lincoln would gladly take care of business himself, except that he lost track of him. For all he knew, the gunman had already said, "To hell with this!" and exited the museum. Keeping his head down, he listened for movement.

Nothing.

"Where are you?" he silently mouthed.

He crouched like a catcher, keeping all his weight on the balls of his feet. Gently, he leaned his back against the long, rectangular case, and came up with a stupid plan. It was bound to flush out his pursuer.

*Here we go…*

Lincoln turned and put his hand on the ground, getting into a classic "sprinter's pose." He sprang from his cover and took in the entire room. And just like he thought, the last of the assassins leaned out from behind his cover and depressed the trigger of his submachine gun.

Lincoln dove to the ground and scrambled up to the back of a vertical case. Inside was a department store mannequin dressed as a pharaoh, along with the king's crook and flail.

Glass rained down from above, blanketing Lincoln in hundreds of tiny, razor-sharp pieces. He covered his head and waited for the shooting to end. When it did, he planned on diving out to the side and unloading the rest of his magazine toward where the bullets originated. Hopefully, he'd get lucky and wing his attacker.

The gunfire ceased, and Lincoln made his move. Sliding across the glass as if it was a soapy waterslide, Lincoln raised his pistol to fire, but didn't. The shooter beat him to the punch and let loose a stream of bullets. Each one of the projectiles ate into the marble floor, tracing a line of death right toward him. Just before he was struck, the killer was taken down in a hail of gunfire.

*Huh?*

Ava stepped out from behind a thick column. That's not what perplexed Lincoln, though. Vincent joined her and kept his gun trained on the dead man and not the Prophets agent. *That* confused him!

Ava Towns, the helpful turncoat, had teamed up with the straight-shooting Prometheus agent, Vincent Recchie. They'd successfully put their differences behind them and saved Lincoln's life.

As Lincoln got to his feet, Vincent snapped his gun over to Ava. He didn't say anything, though. Lincoln holstered his sidearm and made his way to Vincent. Without saying anything, Lincoln slid his sore body in between Vincent's gun barrel, and Ava's chest.

"Move, Lincoln," Vincent said.

He smiled. "Giving me orders now, are you?"

"I said, move."

Lincoln shook his head. "Sorry, bud, that ain't happenin'. She's with me."

"You're a traitor." Vincent's burning eyes glared into Lincoln.

"No, I'm not," he countered. "I'm a realist. She's an ally, and we're lucky to have her," he grinned, "and her insight." Vincent's brow relaxed a bit. "She's given me a lot of intel on the Prophets and the Cradle."

At the mention of the Cradle, Vincent's face went from one of anger to one of intrigue. Lowering his pistol, he stepped back.

"You have the Cradle?"

Lincoln nodded. "We do."

"Where is it?"

Lincoln took in the main hall.

"Uh…" he replied, scratching his head, looking around, "I'm not sure."

# 22

As soon as the shooting started, Elliot, the quick thinker that he was, pulled Maggy back into her office and locked the door. He didn't mean to rip her shirt in the process, but the elegant, and no doubt expensive, silk blouse tore from her neckline down to her left shoulder.

They huddled behind her thick, wooden desk and listened, conversing quietly about what was happening. Elliot never took his eyes off the door. Nor did his aim waver from it. If anyone unfriendly made it through, he'd put a stop to them.

The buffeting of automatic gunfire made Maggy flinch, so did the singular pops of Ava and Lincoln's pistols. Elliot didn't twitch in the slightest. His nerves were immune to the sound. If anything, they comforted him. War was sometimes similar. Good versus evil, plain and simple. Real life was complicated.

"So, a thirteenth Dead Sea Cave…" Maggy said, nervously trying to make conversation. "That's pretty cool, right?"

"Yep," Elliot replied.

"Find anything interesting?"

He chuckled softly. "More interesting than an alien artifact that can destroy the world?"

Maggy smiled. "Touché."

It sounded like it was settling down. Elliot heard very little automatic fire, but there was still the occasional pop of handguns. It meant that Lincoln and Ava were winning.

In between gunshots, Elliot glanced over at her. Maggy was just as beautiful as he remembered. The only evidence of her aging ten years since he last saw her was a single wrinkle that had begun to form on her forehead.

"What about you?" he asked. "What has Magdalen Bitar been up to lately?"

She took a moment to think. "Hmm… Work has had me so engrossed that I haven't had much time for anything else."

"And this Alexander guy?"

She blushed. "Oh, he's nobody."

Elliot tipped his chin at her. "Those rosy cheeks say something different."

Maggy looked away but explained, "He's not just my ex-boyfriend. Alexander and I were engaged for almost two years. Even though we worked closely with one another, we still couldn't find time to be together. We both travel a lot, and it didn't feel right to commit to a relationship that didn't really exist."

Elliot nodded, thinking of the past. "I know how you feel."

Maggy's cheeks turned bright red this time. "I'm sure you do." She cleared her throat. "So, anyone special in your life?"

"No," Elliot replied, shaking his head, "just me and my work."

Maggy smiled slightly. "Two peas in a pod."

Bullets tore into the office wall. Two pierced the partition and impacted the wall behind them. One splintered a window, and the other was halted by a stud. They ducked beneath the desk, nearly headbutting one another in the process. Their faces were impossibly close. Maggy smelled of lavender. She'd worn the same perfume every day back when they had dated. She loved the soothing aspect of it. Elliot liked it too, mostly because it helped him sleep.

She noticed that his breathing had changed. He was taking in the fragrance one deep inhalation after the other. Elliot caught himself, but it was too late. Now, it was his turn to be embarrassed.

Luckily for him, the doorknob shook. Someone was trying to get in. Elliot climbed to his feet and then knelt behind the desk for a second time. Locking in, he waited.

Oddly, the potential intruder didn't try to kick in the door. They knocked, and it was to a rhythm.

*Shave and a haircut?* Elliot rolled his eyes. *Linc…*

Slowly, he gave his bag to Maggy, stood and crept toward the door, staying off to one side. If the knocker wasn't Linc, and they decided to shoot through the door, he'd be out of their direct line of fire. He glanced over his shoulder and waved for Maggy to get back under the desk. She nodded and disappeared.

Approaching the door, the knock repeated a second time. This time it was louder and at a more fervent pace. Its owner wanted in, now! He slid up against it and quickly peered through the peephole. He saw Linc and Ava. Strangely, he also saw the Prometheus agent from the airport, the one that had tried to arrest them.

Elliot tried to look around them to see if there was a squad of agents waiting for him to open the door or not. Unfortunately, he couldn't see much past the trio.

*Dammit,* he thought, not liking the situation at all.

Readying his gun, he leveled it to where he last saw Vincent. Then, with a lightning-quick flick of his wrist, he snapped the deadbolt to the left and threw open the door. He was about to shoot the surprised agent but was yelled at to stop.

"Woah, big fella!" Linc shouted.

"Elliot, no!" Ava yelled.

Vincent brought his gun up too but had it pushed back down by Lincoln. Ava gently laid her hand atop Elliot's pistol and likewise applied a small amount of downward pressure. At first, Elliot resisted, but Ava's eyes told him to trust her. If she was okay with Vincent's presence, then Elliot needed to hear them out at least.

He stepped out and scanned the surrounding hall. Nothing jumped out and shot him, so that was good. Still, he didn't like Vincent being here.

"You guys okay?" he asked, looking at Lincoln and Ava.

They both nodded.

"Yeah," Ava replied, "I think Vincent gets it."

"And that is?" he asked.

Vincent replied. "That the Cradle is more important than any transgressions made before now."

"And Ava?" Elliot asked.

Vincent didn't look happy, but he nodded. "She saved my life. I owe her the benefit of the doubt." He peeked inside the office. "Everyone alright?"

Elliot nodded. "Maggy, it's safe."

The Egyptologist climbed out from beneath her desk, looking flushed and a little spooked. Her silky shirt was torn at the shoulder, exposing the left strap of her black bra. Lincoln smiled and was about to say something.

Elliot ended it before he could. "Linc, don't…"

Lincoln's mouth shut, but he and Ava shared a look. They were both thinking the same thing. Lincoln wiggled his eyebrows, getting a laugh out of the former Prophets assassin. Clearly, Vincent didn't think any of this was humorous. He looked back and forth between the three of them like they were off their rockers.

"We need to leave," Vincent said, looking flustered.

"He's right," Ava agreed. "Police will be here any minute."

"What about the security cameras?" Maggy asked. "We can't just walk away from this. That's a crime."

Vincent smiled. "Leave that to me."

With that, the trio transformed into a quintet. They were joined by another civilian—an Egyptologist—as well as a second Prometheus agent. Vincent assured them that he wouldn't divulge their part in everything as long as he got the credit. No one argued with him, not even Lincoln.

For now, they'd split up and rendezvous at the edge of town. Naturally, Elliot stayed with Maggy. Lincoln forced Vincent toward the nearest watering hole. The only one that was left alone was Ava. She was used to operating in a solo capacity, though. In fact, she preferred it whenever she was attempting to stay off the grid. She'd done the same thing back at the airport and returned precisely at the right moment. Elliot felt like they had a guardian angel watching over them.

"See you all soon," Elliot said before they headed off.

Everyone nodded and dispersed.

As expected, Maggy received a phone call inquiring about the mishap at the museum. She didn't answer it, though. She let it go to voicemail, playing it back on speakerphone so Elliot could hear it.

"What are you going to say?" Elliot asked, walking next to her.

She shrugged. "I don't know." She looked sad. "I guess it all depends on what we find tonight."

"Why do you say that?"

"Because," she smiled, "if it's as big as we think it is, then maybe I'll get that promotion I've been looking for."

**Osiris witnessed the** entire firefight via body cameras. In fact, he'd just missed the fiery conflict by minutes as he arrived on the scene at the same time as the local authorities. Sitting quietly in the back of a parked, unmarked SUV, he gripped his iPad hard, eyes locked onto its screen. The only other person in the vehicle with him was his driver and head of his private security force.

Hades, named after the Greek king of the underworld, was both a member of Osiris' public staff as well as the top man in his clandestine organization. He was also the man that was the most responsible for Ava's physical training. There was only one person out there that could best Ava and that was her Iraqi-American instructor, Hades, Ardath Seif.

The video was playing back on silent. Osiris didn't need to hear anything to watch his people fail—again. He had seen all that he needed to see. The proof that his daughter betrayed him was right in front of him. It was the evidence he needed to warrant the kill order he sent out on her. There were still rumblings within the Prophets voicing against his directive. Some thought she could be *retrained.* Osiris knew otherwise. Ava was a free spirit. Her mind was made up for good.

He didn't outwardly show it, but he had desperately needed something to make him feel better about doing it. He was far from happy about sentencing her to death. Osiris had spent the better part of two decades grooming Ava to be who he believed she was meant to be.

Yet, here he was, willingly sacrificing her life to retrieve the Cradle.

Watching Ava in action was a thing to behold. She moved like a ghost, at the speed of a cheetah. It was like playing chess while others played checkers. She was herding his men into position and attacking from behind. Once the first gunman went down, Osiris knew it was over. The combination of Ava and the Prometheus agent was too much. She alone could've succeeded.

He frowned. "Such a waste of talent."

# 23

Elliot and Maggy were stuffed. With time to kill time, they decided to double back to the museum and get her car. Then, they grabbed dinner at her favorite local place. They didn't specialize in anything, per se, but everything they did was always topnotch. Elliot had never had such good *shawarma* in his life. The chicken was prepared perfectly—like everything else they ate.

But his favorite part of the meal was just them quietly enjoying each other's company over a small cup of coffee. The drink, much like its cousin from Cuba, was potent and would guarantee a much-needed boost. Maggy looked exhausted too.

Her greatest strength was her work habits, but Elliot also knew it was her greatest downfall. She put her work before everything else in her life. It was one of the reasons he had preemptively called off their relationship all those years ago. They didn't have time for one another. Unfortunately, at the time, Elliot was the only one who had noticed it.

"So," Maggy said, "besides all this, how is everything?"

The lighting was dim, relaxing. A candle sat in the center of the table, shining on Maggy's face like a flickering spotlight. It took everything Elliot had to not get lost in those dark eyes.

"Uh," he blinked, "fine, I guess. The British Museum sure does love sending me everywhere. Peru, Norway, Japan, South Africa, New Zealand…"

Maggy smiled. "Sounds amazing."

He shrugged. "Depends on your definition of a good time."

"True… Still…"

He leaned forward, his face directly over his glass. The aromas wafting off his drink were incredible. His body and mind were craving it—his "go-go juice."

"*Still*, what?" he asked. "You've got everything you've ever wanted."

Her eyes darted away from his. She didn't want to make eye-contact with him. It took him a second to realize that *he* wasn't a part of that *everything*.

"Look, Maggy, I'm sorry how things ended. I really am."

"Don't apologize, Elliot," she said. "We both moved on to great careers. We are rarities in today's world. We fulfilled our dreams with nothing more than hard work and—"

"Hard heads?" Elliot finished.

Both laughed.

"Quite true," Maggy agreed. "We sure did butt heads a lot, didn't we?"

Elliot leaned back, relaxing. "Yes and no. I don't think we argued any more than any other couple." He smiled. "But when we did, it was epic!"

They laughed again and, just for a moment, their eyes locked onto one another. The world went silent as they did nothing but stare. They would've been there all night if it wasn't for their waiter. Ghadir slipped into their periphery and poured them another small glass of coffee. His presence broke their concentration, and they each became embarrassed, sheepishly smiling like school kids.

Maggy glanced at her watch. "It's getting late. We should leave now if we're going to be on time."

Elliot had been so lost in their dinner, and Maggy, that he completely forgot about their meeting with Alexander, the UNESCO representative. He was also Maggy's ex-husband-to-be. Maggy paid for dinner. Elliot would've gladly paid, but it's not like he had much on him. Their departure from the West Bank had been *slightly* rushed.

Egyptian nights were chilly. The sun had set almost an hour ago. The temperature was dropping quickly as the minutes went by. Exiting the warm, family-owned eatery, they were buffeted by a crisp breeze. It sent chills down Elliot's spine, Maggy's too. Unconsciously, they huddled together and headed for her car. Feeling Maggy cling to his right biceps felt right. Elliot missed her deeply.

He opened her door and helped her in. Swiftly, he rounded the front of the vehicle and climbed into the passenger side.

Leaning to his left, he cleared his right hip to close the door. He did so under someone's gaze. Turning, he found Maggy staring at him. Like the starting gun of a horse race, the door clunked shut, and they were off! Elliot and Maggy's lips locked. It was quick but significant. Elliot felt, through her, the same thing he'd felt since he last saw her. A longing.

Separating, Maggy apologized for her behavior.

Elliot smiled.

"Oh, god..." she said, flustered. "Okay, then... Maybe we should, you know, get going?"

Elliot stayed quiet, enjoying her teenage bumbling. He loved the fact that he could still make her lose her words. Usually, it was she who did it to him.

"So, this Alexander guy?"

Her eyes flicked to his. "Shut it, *Ox*." She smiled and started her car. They were scheduled to meet Lincoln, Vincent, and Ava at the edge of town, just before crossing over the Qasr al-Nil bridge. The two Prometheus agents were headed for a bar on Nile Corniche. Ava was headed nowhere in particular, stating that she'd meet them there when they needed her.

With most of Elliot's attention back on the mission, he felt anxious about their next step. The Giza Necropolis was so close. They needed to be extra careful just in case anyone had discovered their ultimate destination. He figured that the Prophets would pop up again soon enough. The only place that he knew of in connection to the Cradle was the Great Pyramid. It's not like they were looking for a needle in a haystack. At one point in time, Khufu's tomb was the tallest man-made structure in the world for almost four thousand years, after all.

Elliot checked his gun over as Maggy pulled away.

**It annoyed Lincoln** that Vincent refused to have an adult beverage with him. He could've at least had a local brew, a beer that translated as "the King's Coffin." He had no idea what style it was, but it was robust and bitter. He figured it was the brewer's take on a Double IPA or something.

"I still don't trust her," Vincent said, twiddling his thumbs.

Lincoln sat back in the worn booth and watched the front door. He enjoyed another long pull from his bottle before entering into a conversation that he wasn't sure he could win. Nothing he said was going to change Vincent's mind.

"She saved your life, man. Isn't that enough?"

"How many of our men has she killed?" Vincent retorted.

Lincoln jabbed back. "How many of her people have we killed? Look," Lincoln quickly added, cutting off Vincent before he could reply, "we all have blood on our hands."

"That still doesn't make it right."

"True," Lincoln agreed, "but that doesn't mean we can't get along for the interim. The Cradle is all that matters."

"What about your friend?" Vincent said, crossing his arms. "He's just as important if he can access the core."

Lincoln quickly shook his head. "He's not a part of my mission. He's a civilian that happens to have some in-depth knowledge."

"He's a SEAL!" Vincent countered, getting too loud.

Lincoln gave him a look that said, "Shut up, bro!" He cleared his throat and leaned across the small, round table.

"Yes, he *was* a SEAL—so was I. And I know what Ox can do if he gets...*annoyed*...with someone." Elliot had already bested Lincoln in the airport bathroom. "Do yourself a favor and stay in his good graces." He shifted in his seat. "Your back will thank you."

The threat was clear.

Elliot would fight for his freedom if Vincent tried anything funny. It also meant that Elliot was right. There were people inside Prometheus with ulterior motives—darker ones. But would they imprison a man because of his abilities to activate the Cradle?

The fact that Vincent would even bring it up shook Lincoln. He needed to know.

"What exactly are your orders?" Lincoln asked.

"None of your business," Vincent replied. "You know how it goes, remember?"

"I do," he replied, "and it blows donkey dick."

Prometheus didn't trust anyone. They compartmentalized everything in case an agent was captured and interrogated. The truth would never be found out. The captor only ever got a piece of the intel, not all of it. While it was a smart approach, it was also incredibly frustrating.

So, Lincoln would throw Vincent off and lead him on.

"I was told to confiscate the Cradle and anything relating to it."

Vincent's eyes opened. "So you *were* ordered to apprehend Oxley?"

That was a lie. Lincoln was only ordered to collect the Cradle and bring it home, not Elliot. But he needed to get Vincent on his side so he could get him to admit that his orders were more reprehensible. Then, when Lincoln got back to Washington, he'd have a word with his boss, Mark Conners.

"So," Vincent said, smiling like a shark, "how do you want to do this?"

Lincoln mirrored his smile. "Do what, exactly?"

"You know…"

"Detain Ox?" Lincoln asked.

Vincent nodded. "And the blonde psycho."

Vincent was hit from behind. Lincoln winced when the man's forehead slammed into the tabletop. Following the blow, Vincent clumsily flopped onto the bench like a drunken *Gumby*. Lincoln watched as Ava, AKA, the "blonde psycho," casually took Vincent's place across from him.

She just pistol-whipped a government agent. Lincoln should've been pissed, but he knew that having Vincent down for the count would prove to be helpful. They needed to operate as a copasetic sleeper cell—no contact with anyone outside of their team. Ava was ruthless, but she wasn't heartless. She had demonstrated it multiple times when she saved their asses, first at the airport, and then again, at the museum.

"Thought I'd let you know that Elliot and Maggy are pulling in."

Lincoln nodded and tossed down triple the amount that he owed. The bar owner, who also happened to be their waiter, noticed that Vincent was lying face down on the bench seat. Then, the man's eyes shifted to the money.

Slipping into Arabic, Lincoln said, "Let him sleep it off for a while, okay?"

The owner grinned greedily, snagged the cash from the table and walked away. Lincoln winked at Ava, and the duo headed for the front door. They emerged into the brisk night air just as Maggy pulled up. Without skipping a beat, the agents hopped into the backseat, and they took off for Giza.

"No Vincent?" Elliot asked.

Lincoln looked at Ava and then back to Elliot. "He decided to stay put. He was complaining about a headache or something."

Ava shared a smile with him.

"What's that all about?" Elliot asked, motioning to her mouth.

Ava answered, "Nothing. Vincent really does have a bad headache."

"At least, he will when he wakes up," Lincoln added, mumbling under his breath.

Elliot and Maggy exchanged looks but didn't question Lincoln or Ava. They had a job to do: Find the capstone and dock the Cradle.

*If only that were it,* Lincoln thought. He knew better than most people that just when things started to look good, they crashed back down to earth in a hurry.

"Ava," Elliot said, "what can we expect from Osiris as far as a response?"

She leaned forward. "We know all about the pyramid and its connection to the Cradle. But we don't know that the capstone might still be on location. Like the rest of the world, we are under the presumption that it, along with the pyramid's casing stones, were pillaged and sold off."

"That's what we wanted you to think," Lincoln added. "We had the Cradle in our possession at the time, and our ancestors decided that the capstone was too important to keep out in the open."

"Khufu's Horizon?" Maggy asked, glancing in the rearview mirror.

"Yep," Lincoln replied, "whatever the hell that means."

**Osiris had eyes** everywhere in the United States. He also had eyes in most European nations. If his organization had a weak spot, it was the Middle East and Northern Africa. The gap in his web was currently showing. Only as a last resort would he reach out to the Egyptian government for help. The leaders in the Middle East weren't the easiest to negotiate with. Osiris avoided them whenever possible.

*I might have no choice*, he thought, sighing. No one had seen Ava or the others in her party since the failed assault on the museum.

Publicly, Associate Director of the Egyptian Museum, Magdalen Bitar, had been reported as missing. A faulty drive was blamed for the lack of security footage. Either way, the Prometheus agents wouldn't have been ID'd, along with Ava. None of them officially existed.

The only footage he had of the missing persons was that of a traffic camera. The Egyptologist was on screen with someone Osiris knew.

"Elliot Oxley," he said through a clenched jaw.

He was still in the spotlight after his daring defeat of armed terrorists back in Qumran. If Elliot resurfaced, Osiris was confident that his people would eventually apprehend him. And if local PD got to him first, Osiris would use his underground connections and have Elliot forcefully thrown at his feet. Worst case, he'd use his deep political contacts and have them do it.

"Where are they going?" he asked, speaking into his phone.

"I'm not sure," Izanami replied. "All of our research says that there's nothing in the area except the Great Pyramid."

"The capstone?" he asked, scratching his chin.

"Doubtful," she replied. "There are no reports of it still existing, let alone it still being in the area." She sighed. "We have nothing."

Osiris growled. "Don't tell me that!" He took a moment to calm down. "Cast a wider net and catch these insects before I decide to clean house and start over."

Izanami was silent. When she spoke up, her words were soft and shaky. "Yes, my master. We will not fail."

The call ended. Osiris threw his phone into the inside passenger window of his SUV. Up in the front seat, Hades sat still, waiting for his next set of orders. They had nothing. Plus, there was only a handful of men left in the area, though, another dozen or so could be here inside twenty-four hours.

*We might not have twenty-four hours.*

"Call Kalma," he said. "Tell her and the twins to meet us in Giza." Osiris wasn't sure where else to go. "We'll have a look around and see what we can find."

Hades was already dialing out. It rang once before it was picked up. The person on the other end didn't speak—she never did. All the assassin did was answer the order with a touch of the pound symbol. The pound symbol meant she accepted the contract. If she keyed the star symbol, she refused the job.

She *never* refused a job.

Kalma, the Finnish goddess of death and decay—properly translated as the *stench of corpses*—was a brutal killer. She had no problem getting her hands dirty, regardless of who the target was. The twins, on the other hand, a brother and sister with the callsigns of Mantus and Mania, were more reserved in their methods, but still very capable, in their own right. They always traveled together. The trio would speedily zero in on Hades' signal and meet Osiris and him there.

For now, a group of five was tasked with determining whether or not the Prophets brought about their group's long-awaited prophecy.

*I can taste it,* Osiris thought, picturing the end of the world.

He liked how it tasted.

# 24

Alexander Dukaras was a handsome man. He was also older than Elliot would've thought. Easily in his early to mid-fifties, the UNESCO representative supposedly knew everything there was to know about the Great Pyramid, Khufu's Horizon. Elliot wanted nothing more than to show the man up by revealing exactly how the tomb was constructed, something no one, except for a chosen few, knew.

Maggy flashed Elliot a stern look, one that said, "Be nice." As long as their tour guide did his part, Elliot would do as he was told. And honestly, they didn't need anyone else crashing their fight against Osiris and the rest of the Prophets. So far, they had involved a limited number of civilians.

*So far...*

Elliot didn't like their luck. They had too much of the good kind lately. The other side of that coin was bound to show itself sooner or later. Luckily, Elliot had two of the best strolling along behind him. The trio of warriors was as unstoppable a force as he'd ever been a part of. He was pretty confident that the good guys would win the day.

But how many of them would survive it?

It was dark, really dark. Even with very little in the way of light to guide their way, Elliot could still see reasonably well. The clear sky and amazingly bright stars above their heads gave them enough to see by. Alexander had a flashlight as well. Alas, his hands were so incredibly animated while he spoke that its beam spent most of its time in the air and not on the ground.

"So, Doc," Lincoln said, "anything spooky you can tell us about this rock?"

Alexander glanced at Maggy, who shrugged. "Excuse Mr. Ryan," she said. "He suffers from an enormous case of *thinks-he's-a-comic.*"

"Ah, well, Mr. Ryan, no, I do not know of anything that qualifies as...spooky. Not even in the Subterranean Chamber you've requested to explore. What I do know is the facts, and they are much more interesting than anything a writer of fiction could drum up."

"I highly doubt that," Lincoln muttered, his voice low.

"Excuse me?" Alexander asked.

Lincoln eyed Elliot and grinned. "Nothing, nothing. Please, Dr. Dukaras, continue."

Maggy had made it very clear that Alexander preferred to be called by his professional name. He was, as Lincoln had commented, an "incredibly uptight prick." Elliot couldn't fathom what a woman like Maggy saw in him.

*He's stable,* Elliot thought. That's a lot more than he could say about himself. Even in his good days, Elliot was all over the place. He'd lived in more places than he could count, staying away from home for weeks at a time. There were some months where Elliot found himself at home for only two days before heading back to the airport.

He groaned as they climbed a low rise in the sand directly in front of the base of the Great Pyramid of Giza. Elliot had never been so close, and he was taken aback by its volume.

Elliot was also an "expert" on the topic but quietly listened as Alexander spoke of the same facts that he already knew. Ancient Egyptian history was the first subject he dove into when he retired and made the move to what had become his current profession. He lived the subject. Alexander… He spoke of it as if he were giving a lecture—all business and no passion.

After he was through going over the height and weight of the structure, Lincoln asked the question that Elliot was dying to ask him.

"What did you do before this, Doc?"

Alexander turned and proudly said, "I was a professor at Cambridge."

Elliot rolled his eyes.

There were, no doubt, some wonderful people teaching there. Elliot knew of a couple of them. A lot of them, however, came across as excessively snooty—downright pompous even. Alexander exemplified in both.

Standing before them were the two entrances into the Great Pyramid. The uppermost entry point was the original access point built by Khufu's architect. The path they were about to take was cut later by those serving under the Islamic state leadership of Caliph al-Ma'mun early in the ninth century A.D.

Alexander stopped the group within feet of the nearest stone block. It was easily six-feet-tall and weighed at least two tons. Even though Elliot now knew exactly how the pyramid was built, it was still an incredible sight to behold in person. The Grand Architect literally died from the years of stress of directing the blocks into place. Elliot recalled the pull he felt on his stomach during the few times he had activated the Cradle. He could only imagine the strain the architect had felt.

Another man appeared from above, crisscrossing his way down a few of the smaller stones to the group's right. He stepped up next to the UNESCO representative and was introduced.

"This is Hassam. He will be joining us on our excursion."

Elliot didn't like that. Why hadn't they been warned about another person being here? What else were they in the dark about?

"No offense, Doctor," Elliot said, "but who is this man?"

"He is in charge of security during operation hours," Alexander replied. Hassam held up a keyring. "And…he has the keys to the gate."

Elliot felt ridiculous. He had been so quick to jump to the wrong conclusion.

"Here. You take," Hassam said in barely understandable English. He slipped out of a backpack, and it opened, quickly handing everyone numbered flashlights. "Very dark."

Elliot figured they were numbered because they regularly got stolen. That was his guess, anyways.

"Come," Hassam said, waving them onward. "Careful."

The security guard turned and headed back the way he had come. There, in the shadows to the right, a set of stairs were cut right into the base of the pyramid.

Even with the easier access, Elliot's lower back wept in protest.

He took up position right behind Maggy with Lincoln and Ava bringing up the rear. Hassam and Alexander, being the on-premise experts on the pyramid, naturally took the lead. Elliot knew a lot about Khufu before he came across the Cradle. He'd never had the pleasure of exploring it, though. The thought made his exposed skin break out in goosebumps.

Maggy glanced over her shoulder, smiling ear to ear. She was loving it too. Even though it was a mission of insane proportions, the significance of where they were was still so much to take in and enjoy. Lincoln audibly cursed with every six inches he traveled. He was definitely not having as good of a time as Elliot or Maggy.

Elliot looked up from the stone steps beneath his feet and saw that Maggy's butt was only a couple of feet from his face. His view was undeniably better than Lincoln's was. It was his ass that his friend was staring at.

He knew from various *YouTube* videos that they'd travel up a handful of stairs, then cut across a short expanse of flat rock. Next, they'd climb up another short flight of steps, and another flat section of stone, and so on until they made it up to the entrance gate.

Elliot's right foot slipped off the edge of one of the stairs, kicking a poof of sand into Lincoln's face. The Prometheus agent growled in frustration, but also voiced his displeasure.

"Seriously, Ox, get your eyes off the prize and back on the damned pyramid!"

Elliot stopped in his tracks when he reached the first expanse. Standing there, with the slightest of smiles, was Maggy. She was trying not to laugh. She had heard the entire exchange.

Slightly embarrassed, Elliot huffed away from Lincoln, who casually slapped him on the butt before he could get far enough ahead. Next, he whistled at Elliot like he was an attractive woman that was passing by a group of construction workers.

"Are you about done?" Alexander asked from nearly twenty feet ahead. He and Hassam were already at the next set of stairs. Both men looked eager to get moving again.

Lincoln gave him a mock-salute. "Yes, sir, Professor Alexander—I mean, Doctor. Just waiting for Romeo to get further ahead, and I'll be up in a jiffy."

"Hey, Lincoln?" Ava asked from below.

"Yeah?" he replied, turning around. Ava was stuck behind him. The stairs were too narrow for her to slip past him.

She tipped her chin up toward the entry. "Shut up and climb, will ya?"

**Adjusting the brightness** level of her infrared binoculars, Prophets assassin, Kalma, watched as their quarry successfully made it inside the Great Pyramid one at a time. Her orders were to wait until Osiris, in the flesh, arrived. Her associates, Mantus and Mania, were also laying down atop a nearby dune. Like her, they were spying on their prey, but unlike the siblings, Kalma enjoyed the slow hunt.

It made the kill all the more enjoyable.

The brother and sister team were classic mercenaries. They did what they did because Osiris paid them handsomely for their services. Kalma was paid well too, but she got off on stalking her targets, like some kind of murderous pervert. It was euphoric for her. She lived for it and never stopped "working" because of it. Wherever she was needed, she went without hesitation. She packed as if she was never going home, because sometimes, she didn't. Forcing to start over was nothing new.

"And now, we wait," Mantus complained. He did that a lot.

"Yep," Mania agreed. "We should've offed them when they were out in the open."

"We have our orders," Kalma quietly reminded them. "Besides, it's not like they aren't going anywhere we can't easily follow."

They grumbled some more, agitating the stoic killer. "And remember, Hades is coming too."

That shut the siblings up. What Kalma lacked in size, Hades had in bunches. He did as Osiris said, but unlike Kalma, he heard it in person around the clock. She envied his position within the organization. The reason he had the job was because of both his abilities and his beliefs. Hades was a die-hard truther in the way of the Prophets.

Kalma, Mantus, and Mania weren't. They were hired hitmen but on Osiris' full-time bankroll. They were even given callsigns after they joined. Kalma loved her moniker.

She grinned. *I am the goddess of death and decay.*

Kalma especially loved it because she was mostly of Finnish blood. Osiris had done his homework and named all of his operatives after the death gods of their bloodline's origin. Even being an American citizen, and having never lived in Finland, Kalma felt an immense sense of pride to carry the name.

She'd never met Osiris in person—never seen his face. Most of the people that worked for him never discovered his real identity. There were rumors, of course. The most popular one was that he was a prominent government figure of some kind.

Her phone vibrated, and she eagerly answered.

"Be there in five," Hades said, swiftly hanging up.

Kalma looked behind them, lifting her night binoculars to her face. She couldn't see anyone and had no idea which direction they were coming from. Still, whenever Osiris and his right-hand man did show up, Kalma would prove to them that she fully embodied her namesake.

*Death and decay.*

# 25

The Robbers' Tunnel was cold, dark, and unbelievably cramped—very claustrophobic. Ava wasn't afraid of the dark at all, nor was she uncomfortable with tight spaces. But when you have eighty-one million cubic feet of stone above your head, well, that can make even a hardened killer like Ava feel a little unsettled.

*At least it's mostly flat,* she thought, keeping her mind on the positive things around her. There weren't a lot of options.

Ava didn't prefer her position in line. She was still behind Lincoln and was tasked, by Elliot, with making sure they weren't followed. Ava appreciated the offer. It meant that Elliot trusted her with their safety.

She expected trouble to show itself soon, too—it always did. So far, so good, though. The only negative thing she was experiencing since entering the pyramid was a pain in the back. Literally. Most of the tunnels inside Khufu were barely over four feet in height.

*How short were these people?*

Appreciatively, they popped out into a taller chamber, and everyone immediately went about stretching their lower backs. Alexander and Hassam stopped on either side of a dark opening in the rock. They turned and faced the rest of the group.

"This is the Descending Passage," Alexander explained, not hiding his annoyance, "and it will lead us to our destination, the unfinished Subterranean Chamber."

Ava knew that most people would quickly make the arduous, but rewarding, climb up to the King's Chamber while also taking in the beautiful Grand Gallery on the way. Ava thought it was an odd name, the Grand Gallery, considering there weren't any pictures to view in the twenty-eight-foot high, 153-foot long passageway. The construction, she knew, was an incredible feat of ingenuity. But besides that impressive display of excavating skills, there wasn't much else to see.

The same could be said for the Subterranean Chamber too.

Ava hoped that wasn't the case, though. They all did. If there wasn't anything significant, even a hint at where to go next, then they had wasted a lot of precious time for nothing. The Cradle could go nuclear at any moment. As far as she and Lincoln knew, there was no way to tell when the time was coming, until it was too late.

She wondered if she'd even feel being torn to shreds at the molecular level. She understood that people closest to a blast would be vaporized in the blink of an eye. Maybe even less than a blink.

"Prepare yourselves for an *uncomfortable* journey," Alexander warned.

"Why?" Lincoln asked.

"Because," the UNSECO representative replied, "the passage is 345 feet long and averages only three feet in height." He patted his lower back. "Not the easiest of treks."

Lincoln audibly groaned in response. Ava kept her displeasure to herself but agreed with her Prometheus counterpart. The descent wasn't going to be a pleasant one.

*Unless the cheese at the end is worth it,* she thought.

Hassam ducked inside and shuffled deeper into the bowels of Khufu's pyramid. Alexander didn't follow him, however.

"You're not coming?" Maggy asked.

Alexander shook his head. "My back will not make the return trip. I will be spending my time in the Grand Gallery. It is—"

"Grand?" Lincoln asked, ducking in after Hassam.

Alexander rolled his eyes. "I was going to say that it is a marvelous place to collect one's thoughts."

"Suit yourself, Al," Lincoln called out, his voice muffled by the tight stone surroundings.

Maggy looked disappointed. Ava caught up with her and slipped in behind her into the square-cut tunnel. Elliot was the last to enter, nodding at Ava as she passed. He'd take up the rear now.

The stone floor of the Descending Passage had been reinforced with wood planks and makeshift steps, helping the explorers with their footing.

"You okay?" Ava asked.

Maggy quickly replied. "Me? Yes, I'm…fine."

"You don't sound fine."

The Egyptologist chuckled softly. "I am, actually. It's Alexander. As a lover of history, I'd do anything to make this trip, even if I'd done it a hundred times."

"What, you don't think he loves it?"

Behind Maggy, Ava saw the woman's slouched shoulders lift and drop a little. It was the best she could do to shrug.

"He used to," Maggy finally replied, "but now, he thinks of it as a business." She sighed. "I hope I don't turn into him."

Ava wished she had the passion of something that Elliot and Maggy had. Even Lincoln had something to live for. He loved what he did for Prometheus. Ava didn't love anything. She frowned. Ava didn't love anyone, and no one cared for her either, not even her adoptive father. He only saw her as a tool—a machine. She was just a means to the end of a centuries-old dilemma. Simply, Ava was nothing more than a period at the end of a sentence to the Prophets leadership.

Elliot's grunts got her attention off her self-pity. She glanced over her shoulder and saw his sweaty face in the aura of his flashlight. If the man wasn't so madly in love with the woman in front of her, Ava might've put it out there that she liked him.

But she respected Elliot too much to do anything to harm his potential relationship with someone she knew he loved deeply.

When no one else did, Elliot welcomed her with open arms after he realized the depths of her emotionally scarring past. He hadn't blamed her for anything she'd done. He'd never once called her out, not as Lincoln had. From the moment they watched Osiris kill her parents, their relationship had started over. The present form of Ava Towns is all he cared about.

*So*, she thought, *it's all I'll care about too.*

Ava felt something inside her stir. She didn't know how to describe it. It was like she'd just been given a desperate mission, but this one was personal. She came up with it on her own, and it felt firm and steadfast.

"The Cradle," she whispered.

She knew what she was.

Ava, the former assassin, would proudly watch over the Cradle and the man that carried it. She was now their protector, and if she was forced to—Ava's vision narrowed, locking in on her new purpose—she'd die for them both.

**Fifteen minutes later**, Osiris and Hades led the way with the stocks of their assault rifles tucked into their shoulders. They each had on fully outfitted backpacks and pistols holstered on their thighs. Inside their packs, they each had enough resources to last a week, including military-style MREs, medical supplies, and climbing gear.

Kalma, Mantus, and Mania were following them closely, moving fast. All five of them wore black masks over their noses and mouths. They'd help filter out the sand and dust, but they'd also veil their identities, specifically the Congressman and Hades. They were regularly in the spotlight and needed to keep their public images intact.

Hades arrived at the pyramid first and quickly charged up the steps to the first landing. He didn't wait for the others to catch up either. He took them two at a time and sprinted his hulking frame to the next set, taking them two at a time as well.

Osiris was right on his heels, though he intentionally hung back a little in case Hades drew enemy fire. Dead or alive, a US Congressman discovered in black military garb and armed to the teeth would be a bad look. It's the reason Osiris usually remained in Washington DC. He was typically his people's puppet master, not the commander of a strike team.

This was different, however. With the Cradle discovered and so close, he was willing to risk it all to acquire it. He'd even personally put a bullet in his daughter's head just to hold it. But he had more reprehensible plans for it than that. Not only would he sacrifice Ava's life to obtain the Cradle, but he'd also sacrifice the lives of every human being on Earth to get what he wanted.

He WOULD see Zeus and the other gods. He'd wake them with the power inside the Cradle. Then, he'd gladly kneel in their presence and worship them. Osiris pictured himself standing at their right hand, killing in their name as they laid waste to whatever civilization crossed them. Together, they'd rebuild Olympus—and it would be erected atop the ruins of his home world's wastelands.

Osiris' obsession almost got the better of him, but he refocused and fell in line behind Hades. They ducked inside the low opening into the Great Pyramid. Kalma, Mantus, and Mania entered behind them, breathing hard.

The Prophets leader heard one of them complaining about the pace they were moving at but paid no real attention to it. He was zeroed in on the prospects of finally having the Cradle. He'd dreamed of it since he was a young boy, ever since his grandfather and father romanticized about it. Politics and technology ruled all. Michael Towns excelled in public speaking and big-picture thinking, not science. So, he went into the world of government with a little help from his family and friends.

At six-four, Hades was forced to take the entry slow and steady. There would be no running in, guns blazing. If anything, they'd be limping into battle, whining about pulled muscles and slipped disks. Even in peak condition, especially at his age, Osiris' back was screaming at him to stop and rest.

*No.* He willed himself forward.

A chamber greeted them seconds later, so did the face of a surprised man. He was a local too. He was somewhere around Osiris' age, but nowhere near the same physical shape.

"Who…who are you?" he asked. His English was flawless. It told Osiris that the man had studied abroad. His region's accent was still prominent, but nor did he stumble to find the correct words.

"No one of your concern, mate," Osiris replied, augmenting his natural speaking voice. He used an Australian accent tonight, one he frequented if, and when, he was forced into unsanctioned missions, such as tonight.

"The weapons say something different."

Osiris stepped forward, just as the other three assassins joined him and Hades. He grinned behind his mask.

"Let me start over… We're of no concern to you, if you tell us where the Cradle is."

"Cradle?" the man asked. "What is this 'Cradle?'"

*They didn't tell him?*

Osiris changed his line of questioning. "Where's Elliot Oxley?"

**Everyone took thirty** seconds to unkink their spines once they reached the Subterranean Chamber. Elliot took a little longer than that. He was exhausted from both the romp and the life-draining ability of the alien energy core. Based on what he witnessed in his visions of the past and what he felt now, Elliot understood what the Cradle did to its user.

Inadvertent or not, it depleted your strength to feed its own.

It was like a parasite in a way.

He didn't think its creators intended that to happen. It was evident to him that it was a side effect of a human using it. The "gods" must've been able to handle the pull. He imagined that a human body was exponentially more fragile than the beings that designed the device.

"Elliot," Lincoln said from across the room, "it's time."

He pushed away from the southern wall, at least, he thought it was the southern wall. It was always impossible to tell when you were this deep underground. It made it even harder with no natural light, either. If he were outdoors, he'd be able to figure it out by the position of the sun or stars. He learned long ago not to become utterly dependent on technology to survive.

The chamber opened up to Elliot's right. In the middle of the space was a circular, fenced-in depression. Ava pointed her flashlight out over the square-cut shaft in the floor, inspecting it as thoroughly as possible. The right half of the room featured two waist-high plateaus. Cut down the middle of them was a walkway to the eastern wall. Lincoln was currently investigating that area. Maggy stayed with Elliot, and Hassam, who had presumably seen the chamber dozens of times, hung out by the entrance and waited.

"It's over ten feet deep," Maggy explained to Ava.

"What were they trying to do?" she asked. "I can't think of a reason to dig straight down, unless…" Her voice sounded far off.

Elliot finished. "Unless they were looking for something."

Maggy laughed nervously. "Come on, guys, really? There have been several theories as to what the Subterranean Chamber was designed for. I believe that it was a water pump." She explained further. "In the 1960s, a gentleman by the name of John Cadman experimented with a water pump copied directly from this room, down to every minuscule detail. What he found was incredible, though, this," she motioned to the space around them, "never fulfilled its purpose."

"A water pump," Lincoln said, eyebrow raised, "in the desert?"

"Miles away from a water source," Ava added.

Maggy turned to Elliot but didn't say anything. She wanted to hear his opinion, though, she wasn't going to force it out of him. He had one and voiced it.

"What if both are true?"

"What do you mean?" Maggy asked.

Elliot gripped the railing around the pit and inspected the hole below while he spoke. "What if the chamber was designed as some sort of ingenious pump, *but* it never came to fruition because someone else came along and put a stop to the construction. Maybe they got too close to something that wasn't meant to be found?" He looked at Lincoln. "We know the Cradle changed hands between the ancestors of Prometheus and the Prophets many times over the centuries."

Lincoln rubbed his chin. "Hmm, maybe. There are rumors that Khufu's Grand Architect only finished the main structure, including setting the capstone, before he died." He scratched his head. "I guess his replacement could've been on the wrong side of things and sought what his predecessor swore to protect."

"The Horizon?" Elliot asked.

"Yes," Hassam said, smiling ear to ear, "Horizon." It seemed that the man's English was only so good and that he didn't understand the majority of what they said.

Lincoln rolled his eyes.

"So," Elliot said, working it out, "the new architect built the chamber while also searching for what his old boss hid. That's what we're going with?"

Ava spoke up next. "A coverup within a coverup?" She laughed. "As someone who has lived this kind of thing out in real life…even I'm having a hard time following along."

Lincoln raised his hand. "Ditto."

The next thing that happened wasn't a deeper dive into what they, as a group, believed; it was a series of muffled *clunks* and a trio of explosions of gas. Elliot recognized them immediately. Someone had just sent three smoke grenades down the Descending Passage. If the chamber filled with smoke, they'd be forced to evacuate and most likely be mowed down from above.

Elliot pulled the Cradle out of his bag. "Against the wall, now!"

# 26

Elliot nearly threw Hassam from one side of the room to the other. He followed the others and also moved to the northern wall, away from the smoking projectiles. He recognized them too. Riot police used them for crowd control. Someone up top was either armed with a Milkor MGL-140 revolving grenade launcher, or more than likely, whoever had tracked them was using a lesser barrel-mounted variety. Elliot had used the compact version several times while in the military.

"We need to find a way out of here!" Lincoln shouted.

"What about the passage?" Maggy asked.

"Not a chance," Ava replied, drawing her pistol. She aimed it at the entry point. "We'll be cut to ribbons."

"Well," Lincoln said, coughing, looking at Elliot, "looks like it's up to you, Ox."

Elliot scrambled all over the Subterranean Chamber, even peeking inside the thirty-inch-wide dead-end shaft. None of them could fit in there with enough room to move, so that was a no-go. He scanned the hazy area, stunned to see two more grenades berthed into the room from above. He needed to act now.

*Right...*

The only thing he could think of doing was to have the Cradle guide him. He held it up. It felt comfortable in his hands now. He was confident in what he could do with it. He felt he could handle the load, and he understood his limitations. But he still had no idea what *it* could do.

"Here we go," he said, focusing on the energy within.

The Cradle pulsed and hummed, but nothing else happened. The smoke was beginning to choke off the oxygen in the room. He coughed, and got to his knees to find fresher air, but didn't lose his concentration. He didn't know how, but Elliot knew there was nothing along the raised, eastern half of the room.

The Descending Passage was off-limits, so the only other place was the pit in the center of the chamber. Elliot kept his head below the smoke-filled ceiling and grabbed the safety railing surrounding the short, vertical shaft.

"Woah," he said, feeling something beneath his feet.

Something was down there, but he didn't know what. It was still masked from him. It's as if he could see through the rock like he was scanning for new, unexplored rooms. But there, hundreds of feet beneath him was an opening.

And it was enormous.

"We have to go down!" he shouted, opening his eyes. He wasn't even aware that he'd closed them.

"And how the hell are we supposed to do that?" Lincoln asked, crawling up next to him, squinting against the stinging smoke.

Elliot grinned. "Like this."

It had just come to him. He stood and held out the Cradle over the railing, not once flinching as a beam of light blasted straight down. As soon as it made contact with the stone at the bottom of the narrow cutout, it vaporized it. The only thing that was left was a wafting poof of dust and sand. Elliot smiled, realizing he was digging through solid limestone with a laser.

Wave after wave of crackling, green "fire" poured into the opening, and just when Elliot started to feel the tug on his stomach, it stopped—the tug and the beam. The shaft was complete, but now, instead of finishing at just over ten feet, it ended at over a thousand.

A *whoosh* of air was pulled down into the shaft, taking with it most of the deadly smoke. The chamber beneath them was pressuring. Until now, it didn't have breathable air, and it was sucking in all it could. Everyone held on to whatever they could. The current was so strong that Elliot's feet were thrown into the air. It happened several times, until, stillness returned.

Everyone climbed to their feet, astonished by what Elliot had just accomplished…except for their guide, Hassam. The man was terrified and acted as such. He bolted for the Descending Passage, not hearing the shouts from everyone to stop. All of them called out to him in Arabic, hoping he'd turn around.

He didn't.

Hassam disappeared, and, for a breath, all was quiet. Then, the gunfire started. No one saw Hassam get torn to shreds, but Elliot knew what happened.

"Everyone over the railing!" he yelled, spurring the group along. "Hurry, it's coming!"

"What's coming?" Ava asked, vaulting over the barrier like a cat.

Elliot, Maggy, Lincoln, and Ava all stepped up to the empty four-foot-square, flawlessly cut stone shaft. Then, the floor began to vibrate, and an uncomfortably loud purring sound picked up all around them.

Elliot explained as much as he knew.

"They hid it here so it would never be found," he said, eyes wide. He looked borderline maniacal at the moment. He needed to see it.

"Hid what?" Maggy shouted, holding her hands over her ears.

The sound and vibrations increased.

"Elliot?" Lincoln cried, closing his eyes.

Then, it ceased, and in an explosion of dust, the shaft now contained a floor. But it wasn't a floor. It was something else entirely. It was metal, not stone, and Elliot recognized the material. It was made of the same stuff as the Cradle's pedestal back in Qumran, as well as the interior of the capstone from his visions.

"It's an elevator?" Maggy asked, dirty eyebrow raised.

They were all filthy, caked in millennia-old dust and grime.

"Yep," Lincoln replied, hopping on. He looked more than ready to get out of Dodge.

Everyone joined him, squeezing in tight with their backs to the other. Holding the Cradle tight in both hands, Elliot closed his eyes and asked the lift to lower them.

It replied with a hum, and then, he opened his eyes in time to see the first evidence of Hassam's demise. A river of blood slowly crept into the Subterranean Chamber, and with what they'd found so far, Elliot doubted it was the first time someone had been killed here. The room was never finished because the guards of this place had silenced all of those who sought out what Elliot was now doing himself.

*Except, they didn't have the Cradle,* he thought.

"This goes on forever, huh?" Ava asked, her nervousness laced in her voice.

"God, I hope not," Maggy replied.

Lincoln didn't say anything, and neither did Elliot until they were almost to their destination. He was still piecing it together in his head. Even with the strange gift of foresight that he'd been given by the memories stored within the artifact, Elliot still wasn't able to picture what they'd find below. It had been purposely erased from his implanted *memories*—forgotten until found again.

After another three hundred feet of descension, something dawned on Elliot. The Cradle wasn't just a weapon, or even a battery, or a key.

"It's a computer," he said, more speaking to himself than anyone. "It's a portable hard drive that doesn't need to be plugged in to activate. All it needs is someone with the right genetic code to connect with."

"Like you," Maggy said.

He turned his head, seeing her worried face in the green glow of the Cradle. The tunnel shaft was filled with the rolling aura.

He gave her a soft smile, unsure of what he could say to make her feel better. Sometimes, words weren't necessary. Everything in the last day or two had changed Elliot's life forever. He honestly had nothing to say. Lately, he'd been given very little time to figure it all out. He was living in the moment.

His mind wandered back to the Grand Architect's death at the hands of the Cradle's pull. Would that be his fate? If so, when?

The Cradle buzzed and throbbed, almost knocking Elliot off his feet. No one else seemed to be affected by the intense energy wave. But with it, more was revealed deep beneath their feet. The shaft ended, opening up into a perfectly cut, round room. It was as if someone had transplanted an arena-sized sphere into the foundation beneath Egypt.

"How?"

"What?" Maggy asked.

He shook his head, focusing on their destination.

"Almost there," he mumbled, sweating profusely.

To Elliot's left, Lincoln awkwardly raised his sidearm and checked it over. It sounded like Ava was doing the same thing, but Elliot couldn't see her. She was standing directly behind him, at the "southern" end of their compass, ever watchful of their backs.

"What do you see, Ox?"

Elliot looked within and described it.

"A cavern. Artificially built. Immense." He squinted his eyes, focusing deeper. "Something at its core. It's still veiled from my sight."

"Can you tell us more about the cavern itself?" Ava asked.

"Yes," Elliot replied. "It's a sphere. The same material as where I found the Cradle."

"The room beneath 13Q?" she asked. "Where I found you?"

"Yes, the same, only much, much bigger."

"How big are we talking?" Lincoln asked.

"Big…" Elliot replied.

His voice trailed off as the walls of the shaft disappeared. Now, they were standing on a tiny platform with nothing around them except air. Reflexively, they all leaned away from the precipice and into one another.

The space around them was pitch black except for a few feet around Elliot and the Cradle. It gave off enough light to see each other, but nowhere near enough to see anything else. With a resounding clunk, the elevator came to a stop. Even without being able to see the exact scope of the cavern, everyone could feel the breadth of it, the yawning emptiness.

Again, the artifact pulsed. Elliot knew it automatically responded to things of the same technology. Whoever built the Cradle had also somehow constructed the hollow here. Even with the intimate knowledge Elliot was afforded, there were still too many unanswered questions.

And one of them, specifically what the cavern held, was answered.

In an explosion of electricity, the voluminous spherical fissure bloomed to life. The foursome stumbled back from both the intense illumination assaulting their light-deprived eyes and the object resting at the room's center.

"Oh my god," Maggy said, bringing her hands to her mouth.

"Woah," Lincoln said, "didn't expect that."

Elliot and Ava remained quiet, taking it all in without voicing their reactions.

Docked in the middle of the enormous hollow in the Earth's crust was a spaceship. The vessel was magnificent, built of the same metallic material as the room itself.

Its shape was evident.

"It's a solar barge and—" Maggy said, tears running down her cheeks.

"It's the size of a fucking cruise liner," Lincoln finished.

They were both right. The modernized version was easily eight-to-nine *hundred* feet from bow to stern. From the keel to the craft's top deck must have been a hundred feet, ten stories tall, give or take. They were standing at the edge of the "hangar."

The *papyriform* design of the ship was typical of ancient Egypt. The high, bent ends were a signature of the region. This was no different, except exponentially grander in scale. They reached twice as high into the air as the hull was tall, another hundred feet if he had to guess. The style of construction had been used by other cultures throughout history. The age of the gods, when they were supposedly influencing humanity struck Elliot.

"It's the first one."

"What?" Maggy asked, placing a hand on his arm.

Even Elliot was overcome with emotion. He looked down at the shorter woman and smiled. "It's *the* solar barge—the original design. This was humanity's inspiration."

Maggy's mouth fell open. She turned back to the vessel in awe.

Ava stepped up next to Elliot. "Not to be a wet blanket, but we need to get moving."

"She's right," Lincoln said. "We gotta find that capstone."

The four set off but stopped almost as soon as they started. Elliot skidded to a halt, mumbling to himself.

"What is it?" Maggy asked.

"The name…"

"Uh," she said, eyebrow raised, "what name?"

"Look."

She followed his outstretched finger. It was pointing toward the rear of the ship. Like most modern-day varieties, they had names. In the American military, for instance, maritime vessels were named after historical figures in history. Former presidents and generals were common.

Inscribed into its rear right quarter panel of the ship was something that resembled a blend of Egyptian hieroglyphs and Latin text—a language

Elliot had never seen before, yet, he could read. Not only was he given a look into the future and the past, but he was also given the ability to understand their written language.

"The *Horizon*," Elliot whispered. He faced the others. "'Khufu's Horizon' isn't the name of the pyramid—it never was. It's the name of his ship!"

"If this belonged to the pharaoh," Lincoln said, working it out, "then that means..."

Elliot nodded and turned back to the barge. "Khufu was an alien."

Elliot's mind processed everything at lightning speed. He was smart and could sort out things quicker than most. With the help of the Cradle, he put it all together in the matter of a heartbeat.

He nearly dropped the Cradle when he came to his conclusion.

The barge—the alien craft—was buried eons ago, but by whom? The only explanation was that it was hidden by someone who didn't want it to ever be found. Who of the alien race didn't want to be found? The answer was simple, but nevertheless, astonishing. He had no idea how he—Khufu—had done it, but he did.

"Khufu wasn't just an alien," Elliot said, knowing he was right, "he was Prometheus in the flesh." Filled with overwhelming emotion, he closed his eyes. Tears fell freely. "The Horizon was the spacecraft he used to bring the Cradle to Earth."

# 27

"What did you do?" Alexander shouted, appalled. "You just killed a man in cold blood!" He shook. "And the others—Magdalen, Mr. Oxley… How could—"

The masked man with the bald head swiftly drew a pistol and, without pause, shot Alexander in the forehead. The bullet was fired at point-blank range, exiting through the back of Alexander's head with a splatter of dark crimson. Neither of the people accompanying Osiris flinched in response to the amplified discharge. The noisy death didn't bother Osiris either. While magnifying the report on the inside, the pyramid's dense layers acted like a gun's sound suppressor to anyone on the outside.

Osiris was already in motion as Alexander's body dropped to the floor. He followed Hades down the Descending Passage, moving as quickly as the path would let them.

"Mania, stay here," Kalma ordered.

She gave her brother, Mantus, a look, but did as requested.

When they neared the end, they were forced to navigate over a man's body. It saddened Osiris that it wasn't one of Elliot's team. Whoever the local was, he had unknowingly sacrificed himself by attempting an escape back up the entry corridor. The fresh blood made the last leg of the trek slick and cumbersome.

Hades unfolded his large frame from the three-foot-tall passage, rifle up. Osiris backed him up and was both stunned and confused by the fact that they weren't met with gunfire. He didn't see any bodies either.

"Mantus—" Kalma began.

"Yeah, yeah," he replied, "I'll watch the door…"

The man's tone was one of annoyance, but Osiris was too engrossed in the mystery of their vanished targets to care. He'd only care if the man's attitude cost them a chance at winning the day. Some people were a little rough around the edges. Those same people were some of the most successful people in this type of business. You couldn't be a sweetheart in a line of work such as this.

Osiris, Hades, and Kalma swept the room twice. Finding nothing both times, they met at the center of the chamber and leaned out over the hole in the ground. As leader of the Prophets, Osiris knew everything there was to know about the pyramid. The pit in the floor wasn't all that deep.

*It is now.*

"Give me your rope," Osiris said, eyes locked on the shaft, "all of it."

**"How old was** Khufu when he died?" Ava asked.

She was having a hard time believing a man in as such a publicly focused position as pharaoh could be anything other than what history told them. There were plenty of important—real—people from antiquity that humanity had very little information on. Why was Khufu any different than them? Just because they knew very little about the *man* didn't mean he was an alien.

"Early sixties, maybe?" Maggy replied. "No one knows for sure. There are no records of his birth, just his death." She bit her lip, thinking. "There are some in the scientific community that question whether Khufu was actually of royal blood." She snorted out a laugh. "It's not like they had paternity tests back then."

Ava was still trying to take in the scope of the room. For one, the walkway had a raised catwalk made from the same strange alien alloy as everything else. Whatever it was, the gods relied heavily on it. It rose over, what she decided was, a series of buildings, most of which, like the cavern, were spherical. A few were pyramidal, though.

"She's right," Lincoln said. "The primary reason people even believe Khufu was Sneferu's son was that it was customary to pass down the throne to your eldest son. Tradition, not fact, are our references here, and we all know how trustworthy that is. But, in this case, Khufu immediately followed Sneferu as king, so logically—"

"We assumed Khufu was Sneferu's son," Ava finished.

Lincoln snapped his fingers and pointed at her. "Bingo."

"Though, I guess it's possible that Prometheus somehow disguised himself as the pharaoh's son, and stole the throne," Lincoln added, laughing at his own words. "Maybe Sneferu secretly worshiped Prometheus and 'adopted' him, so to speak, and made it possible for him to take over?"

"He'd need to be a shapeshifter to pull that off," Ava countered. "Even now, that's a little too farfetched for me to believe."

"At this point," Elliot said, passing by his friend, "anything is possible." He took a handful of steps toward the ship and stopped. "They didn't find the pharaoh's body when the tomb was opened, you know. There was evidence that it had already been ransacked and reused by someone else."

"Perhaps it's another cover-up?" Maggy asked. "What if the body they found when they opened Khufu's tomb was put there on purpose and the poor condition of the room was staged?"

"Too many *what-ifs*," Ava said, interjecting. "Too many conspiracy theories."

"You think he's in there?" Elliot asked, lost. He was staring at the alien craft with a glazed-over look.

"Prometheus?" Lincoln asked, joining him. "No idea, but as you said, anything is possible."

Maggy stepped up next to Elliot.

"He might be," she added. "Solar barges were supposed to ferry the dead to heaven to meet Ra. It looks like they took that seriously here." She looked uncomfortable. "Though, this is a spaceship, so, who knows, right?"

"Transport to Ra?" Ava asked, joining the others. They all stood in a row, facing west.

Lincoln shrugged at Ava, who was on his right at the end of the row. "Ra…Zeus…whoever! Until proven otherwise, I'm operating under the impression they're the same damn person." He grinned. "Imagine the ratings *NatGeo* would get! *Prometheus: The Whore of the Ancient World.* His surviving DNA is the reason we're here, remember. He'd have to have done it with a load of women for that to happen."

Ava rolled her eyes and followed closely behind Elliot as he moved on. The opening around them was dizzying. She'd never seen anything, nor believed anything like it existed. Now, she didn't know what to think. Was everything true? Or, in a way, was it all a lie, to a degree?

She pushed aside the confusion and decided that the present conflict was the more pressing issue. If Osiris got his hands on the Cradle, everyone on Earth died. Plain and simple. He'd still have to be dealt with. Even if they successfully redocked the Cradle, and averted planetary disaster, they'd have another war to fight. Luckily, she knew the ins and outs of the Prophets.

*Prometheus Agent, Ava Towns?*

No. Ava wouldn't be joining up with Lincoln's people. After her mission to protect Elliot and the Cradle was over, she'd be moving on and disappearing with her small fortune. All she had to do was decide where to start her new life.

They were halfway across the catwalk. As they walked, their feet made no noise, which was weird. Typically, metal walkways were utilitarian and banged loudly. Each step usually sounded like a hammer connecting with an anvil. But here, they were soft, muted even. It was as if the material absorbed the sound rather than reflected it.

"I think it's a factory, you?" Lincoln asked Ava.

"Maybe? Could just be a storage facility."

"Well, that's…boring."

"History isn't always this fun," Maggy said.

Lincoln motioned back and forth between him and Ava. "It is for me."

Shaking her head, Ava sighed. "*Fun* isn't what I would've called it. The word I would've used was…*interesting*."

The ship was even more impressive the closer they got to it. Etched across the hull of the Horizon were hieroglyphs, amongst other patterns. Elliot eagerly translated them, happy to see that they were in the same language as the vessel's name.

"It speaks of their exodus from another world, Olympus. They wrote their story for all to see. They wanted everyone to know what happened."

"Kinda like a blimp advertising something," Lincoln said. "Think they planned on flying that thing around to show the world?"

Ava stopped. "Does it say anything about Phobos—about the other gods?"

"No, not that I can see. Not yet, anyway. There's still a lot of ship to inspect."

Ava wanted all the answers now. She needed to know if the lies Osiris fed her as a child were, in fact, truths.

*Not that it changes anything.*

Even if he was candid with her, except for the part where he killed her parents so he could steal her away, it didn't change anything about the man. He was a ruthless, cold-hearted killer with a one-track mind. He wanted his happy ending, regardless of who died along the way.

"War decimated Olympus," Elliot explained. "Those strong enough to survive did. They repaired a handful of vessels like this, as well as their forms. Then, they made the trip to their Phobos station."

"Forms?" Maggy asked. "What does that mean? Their bodies?"

No one knew.

"And?" Ava asked, a little too loud.

"*And* nothing," Elliot replied. "The story ends there." He stopped in front of what he presumed was the door even though there was no hinge or any other sign of one.

"The other side!" Ava said.

Lincoln gently grabbed her arm. "Hey, you okay?"

She yanked out of his grasp. "I'm fine, but I need to know!"

"And we will," Elliot said, smiling, holding up the Cradle, "inside an alien spacecraft."

He blinked his eyes.

A clunk on the other side of the ship's hull responded to the small, seemingly insignificant, physical movement. They all took a few steps back as a portion of the hull flickered and retracted into itself. Inch by inch, it melted away until a perfectly cut, triangular opening formed.

*More pyramids,* Ava thought.

"Has to be nanobots or something," Lincoln guessed. "Ox?"

Elliot shook his head, but not because he was disagreeing. It looked like he was fighting a bad headache—a migraine maybe.

He blinked hard. “Not…sure.”

“Really? The almighty oracle of everything cool, doesn’t know what it is?”

“The Cradle tells me whatever it deems necessary.”

Lincoln gave him a look that said, “uh?”

“It’s all I can figure,” Elliot explained, stepping in. “Each time it activates and does something, I’m given the knowledge we need to continue.”

Ava knew he was right.

First, Elliot was given a look into the future. Next, the past. Both events showed him what needed to be done. Next, he was given a much-needed ally in Ava after showing him her childhood. She was released from her bondage of hate and fear. The artifact brought Maggy into the fold as well. They wouldn’t have gotten into the pyramid without her. It then dug through the bedrock beneath the tomb and, just now, opened what would’ve been an impenetrable door.

Everything was given to Elliot at the moment he needed it. It begged the question…

“Why is it helping us?” Ava asked.

“What about the *how*?” Lincoln asked.

Ava patted his shoulder. “I think we’re past the *how*.”

The corridor beyond was nothing special—plain and uninspiring—the same as most military vessels. Ava guessed that the Horizon was a battleship. Elliot did say they were at war, and that the gods could only salvage a few of the spacecrafts before leaving for Phobos.

The hallway seemed to cut straight across the Horizon with several other passages crisscrossing it along the way. There were no doors in sight, either. Ava assumed they were invisible like the side door had been. The gods would’ve known where to go. The depth of their knowledge of the craft would’ve been second-to-none. Plus, like Elliot, they’d have the ability to open them without issue.

“Feel anything?” Maggy asked, clinging to Elliot’s left arm. In the crook of his right elbow was the Cradle.

He nodded, looking extremely uncomfortable. “Everything. It’s—it’s overwhelming.” The muscles in his face twitched. He tipped his chin to the right-hand wall. “Munitions of some kind in there.”

“Like the Cradle?” Ava asked.

“No,” Elliot replied, “they’re more primitive than it.”

“Anything we can use?” Lincoln asked, dragging his hand across the surface.

“No.”

Lincoln frowned. “Fine… Just tell me when you find something I can play with, okay?"

Ava wasn't surprised by the lackluster design of the ship's interior, though she was disappointed. Everything she knew about the gods was so dramatic and exciting. The bowels of the Horizon didn't paint them in that kind of light at all.

*Be patient.*

She knew being inside an alien spaceship should've been enough. It was fantastic to be there, for sure. Still, it gnawed at her that they had yet to find anything outrageous. Maybe the capstone would change that.

"Where are we going?" Maggy asked.

"This way," Elliot replied, turning down what Ava guessed was the central corridor running bow to stern.

"What's down there?" Lincoln asked, looking apprehensive. "I'm not scared or anything…but, if I'm honest, being on an alien ghost ship does kind of give me the heebie-jeebies."

"Ditto," Maggy agreed. "I'm not enjoying this as much as I thought I would."

"There's an elevator to the top deck," Elliot said, not commenting about the eeriness, "and no, I don't know what's up there."

"Not yet," Maggy said, smiling softly.

Elliot winced when the Cradle pulsed. He rapidly blinked just his left eye and moaned.

"Elliot?" Maggy asked, catching him as he fell into the left-hand wall.

"Woah there," Lincoln said, reaching out and grabbing him under his armpits. "We've got you, buddy."

"What's wrong?" Ava asked, helping Lincoln lower Elliot to the floor. Now, both of his eyelids were closed, but you could spot his eyeballs dancing underneath them.

"The Cradle," Elliot replied, grabbing his head. "It…hurts."

"Give it to me," Ava offered.

"No," Elliot said, gripping it tighter. "I…I can do this."

Ava knelt in front of him. She lovingly reached a hand up to his face and stroked it. It wasn't carnal in any way. She was showing him the love and concern she would for a family member.

Ava spoke softly. "But you don't have to." Elliot grabbed her hand and gripped it hard. "You said the Cradle has given you everything you've needed to get us this far." She smiled when his eyelids peeked open. It wasn't much, but he could see her and the tears welling in her eyes. "I'm part of that equation." She held up her hand and wiggled her fingers. "It gave you me to help."

Elliot hyperventilated, barely staying conscious. The pain must've been excruciating, and if there was one thing Ava was an expert at, it was dealing with pain.

"Elliot, please." She sniffed back tears. "We can't lose you."

Finally, he bit his lip and nodded. "Be careful."

"I will."

For the first time since seeing far into her past, Ava touched the Cradle. With it came an agony she'd never thought possible. Ava tilted her head back and roared in the air like a grizzly bear. Before falling over and blacking out, she halted her descent with her free hand and opened her eyes.

"I see it…" She looked around—through the walls and ceiling. Her mind was downloading the schematics of the Horizon. It's what Elliot had seen. "I see it *all.*"

# 28

Hades took point again, rappelling down the line without so much as a grunt of disapproval. Though, this time, Osiris wouldn't be going next. They had no idea how deep the shaft was. Luckily, they were prepared. They had tied off more than a thousand feet of rope. Similar in design to traditional paracord, their variation was thicker and superior in strength.

Kalma and Mantus were to descend next while Mania would stay put and guard the entry point into the pit. The park was due to open in a few hours. They needed to be long gone by then.

"So," Kalma said, watching Hades disappear, "what do you think is down there?" Osiris didn't look up or answer her. His eyes were locked onto the hole in the floor. She tried again. "Sir? What do you—"

"Destiny," Osiris replied.

"Destiny?"

Osiris had no time for her questions. Nor would she be the one to see their find as they had planned. He shoved Kalma aside and leapt over the guardrail, clipping onto the line with a hefty carabiner clip. Without looking back to his subordinate, he jumped into the shaft and began to freefall. He kept one gloved hand around his back, lightly clutching onto the cable. When his destination approached, he gently squeezed and slowed himself.

He fell for much longer than he anticipated. When he did finally exit the shaft, he applied pressure on the cable and slowed. Spotting his landing point, he arrived and dropped to one knee.

He calmed before he stood, letting the adrenaline dissipate. When he climbed to his feet, his eyes first found those of the unemotive Hades. The large man was locked onto something that was further away in the room. Unclipping, Osiris followed suit and turned to the middle of what was an enormous, well-lit chamber.

*Lights?*

Upon seeing the vessel, Osiris' legs turned to Jell-O, and he fell to his knees. He babbled on and on in his mysterious language, speaking of the gods and reuniting with them in heaven. Hades stood rigid, never taking his eyes off the alien spacecraft.

**Kalma touched down** a few feet to Osiris' right. Unlike her employer, she noticed the ship almost immediately, spotting it as soon as she fell. She had slowed earlier, giving herself more time to take it in. It truly was an incredible sight.

She stood and unclipped, rolling her eyes. Osiris was on his knees, babbling incoherently like an infant.

"Is he broken?" she asked, looking from Osiris to Hades.

The large Arab-American turned and forced the Congressman to his feet.

"Sir?" Kalma asked.

Osiris looked blankly at her, then back to the ship.

"Hello, Earth to Osiris…"

Blinking several times, he wiped the drool off of his chin and greedily took a half dozen deep lungfuls of air. The only parts of his face Kalma could see were his eyes and the upper portion of his head. His nose and mouth were still covered by his tactical mask, as were hers.

The man's eyes burned with psychosis. She knew Osiris was passionate, but she had no idea he was *this far* off the reservation. His beliefs—his religion—had been proven right, and his mind was lost in the euphoria of it.

"Let's…go," he said, his voice shaky.

"You okay, sir?" Kalma asked.

His cheekbones rose. He was smiling behind his mask.

"Never better."

**It had only** been a couple of minutes, but Elliot was already coming out of it. With his connection to the Cradle reduced, he was beginning to feel like his old self again. The link wasn't entirely gone, however. Everything Ava saw and felt, he also experienced it. Though, it was to a lesser degree.

It saddened him. He also felt down, sorrowful, alone even, like someone close to him had recently died. Most of all, he felt worn out. The Cradle was draining his life away with every moment he spent using it. If it were possible, Elliot felt years older than he did just days before.

*All the more reason to get it docked.*

That was still their plan, even though they had nothing to go on as to why. It had been whispered to Elliot and shown to him multiple times. The Cradle wanted to come here. It yearned to return to the Horizon, and with the potential threat of its casing failing, they had no choice but to abide by its will.

Ava now carried the Cradle over her shoulder, in Elliot's bag. She had accepted the responsibility of watching over it and protecting it with her life. She knew what was on the line—they all did. Under no circumstances could the Prophets gain control of the artifact's power.

"Under no circumstances," he mumbled.

His earliest vision was of a mushroom cloud rising into the sky. He knew full well what the devastating implications were. Osiris didn't want to destroy his enemies. He wanted to kill everyone.

When he was in the SEALs, Elliot's battles were usually contained within one specific location. This was a real-life global danger, not the ones that most dictators around the globe boasted about with empty threats. Elliot knew which world leaders could reduce Earth to ash. There were less than a handful of superpowers out there.

Elliot walked on his own but used the wall to support himself. He wasn't dizzy, just achy and weak. His mind was in the best shape of all, his body, however, wasn't. Everything below his neck hurt—it throbbed like crazy.

"Should be up here," he said, shining his flashlight ahead.

"It is," Ava confirmed, heading off.

Everyone held back and continued at a steady pace. Elliot wanted nothing more than to rush after her but knew what would happen if he overexerted himself. He needed to be patient and wait until he felt better. He had other people depending on him, not just himself.

A woman he never forgave himself for leaving.

A friend that always had his back.

And someone new in his life, but a person he had a deep, emotional connection to.

Ava stopped up ahead. She removed the Cradle from the bag and held it up. The wall in front of her wasn't a wall at all. Like the entrance in the hull, the wall faded away. Beyond it was a circular room twice the size of the underground elevator. Ava entered last and turned back toward the door. As quickly as before, the wall was whole again.

Elliot watched Ava closely. Even if he wasn't able to see the lights flashing wildly, he could feel the Cradle pulsing like crazy in his body, like he was standing next to a column of speakers at a concert. The floor beneath them rose, but the upward movement was barely discernible. Besides him, Ava was the only other one who felt it too. Her body shivered slightly.

"You okay?" Elliot asked.

She nodded. "Yeah… So far, so good."

Elliot knew she was lying. She was feeling the same strain he had experienced. It shouldn't have been as crippling as it appeared to be, though. Ava was barely keeping it together. He thought back to the first time he had used the Cradle. Uncomfortable, but not debilitating. It wasn't until he arrived in the pyramid's Subterranean Chamber that Elliot started to feel an increase in the "pull's" strength.

*The closer we get, the worse it'll be,* he decided.

And he just gave the Artifact to someone else. He needed to get it back before it was too late—before Ava paid the price for *his* poor judgment. What lay ahead, and above, was the end. He could feel the raw power emitting from the Cradle as they rose higher and higher toward the top deck. The artifact was like a dog about to see its owner. It eagerly *wagged.* It recognized its surroundings.

The energy within the Cradle was alive.

# 29

*But how?* Elliot asked himself. *How is the Cradle alive?*

The technology on display was way over his head. It went way beyond artificial intelligence and supercomputers too.

He didn't get an answer to his question, however. Instead, his thoughts traveled to the room around him when the roof above their heads opened. Their destination had always been the capstone, and there, at the center of the lengthy, rectangular hangar-sized space, was just that: the Great Pyramid of Giza's missing capstone.

"Holy shit," Lincoln said, voice low. "We found it." He laughed, smiling wide. "We found it!"

Maggy ran her hands through her hair. "Inside an alien spaceship buried one hundred stories beneath the Great Pyramid. Amazing…" Her forehead scrunched. "What exactly is the capstone, anyways?"

Elliot didn't know, and from Ava's blank expression, she didn't know either. The only thing they saw before they met up with Maggy was the Cradle being docked inside the capstone, and it sent a surge of energy into space.

The Cradle showed them *what* it wanted—*when* it wanted it. It acted as a person would in situations like this, carefully giving pertinent information to people he, or she, didn't trust entirely. The thing that bothered Elliot the most was that they had no idea what would happen next. In the last day and a half, he'd seen more than he could describe, both physically and mentally, and none of his visions showed him anything like this.

This was all new.

Ava stepped toward the capstone.

"Wait!" Elliot shouted. His voice echoed in the enormous room.

She stopped and turned around. "We need to finish the mission, Elliot."

He held up both hands. "I'm not so sure."

"What?" Lincoln and Maggy said in unison.

Lincoln stepped up next to Elliot. "You feeling okay, Ox?"

Elliot nodded. "I'm fine. It's just…none of this feels right."

"No shit?"

"That's not what I mean." Elliot looked back toward Ava. "You feel it, don't you?"

She looked nervous. "I…I feel something, sure."

"What is it, Elliot?" Maggy asked. Her presence was helping him focus.

"The Cradle only shows us what it wants when the time is right, correct? What if—and it's a big *what if*—but what if the Cradle isn't just some intergalactic battery. What if it's alive and getting us to do its dirty work?"

No one said anything.

Lincoln looked like he wanted to, but he couldn't formulate the correct words.

Maggy got it out, though.

"You think this *thing* is playing us?"

Elliot didn't know what to think. He did come up with a solution, however—an experiment. He came face to face with Ava and hovered his hand over the surface of the Cradle. She pulled the core away from him, ever so slightly, but stopped when he gave her a warm smile.

"I'm not taking it," he said. That relaxed the former assassin. "I need your help."

Ava's face brightened a little. "What do you need?"

He glanced down at the Cradle. "We do this together."

**Ava felt sick** to her stomach. The last time they had touched it together, she'd seen her "father" kill her real parents in cold blood. It was all because of what she might be able to do if she ever came into contact with the relic she held now. Osiris was right, but he shouldn't have made the decision for her parents. They'd been members of the Prophets as it was. She could sense as much. All her mother and father would've had to do was allow Ava to be trained. They'd have likely agreed to it too. Any family within the organization would've seen it as a great honor. Her mom and dad didn't have to die.

But Osiris had evil and greed in his heart. He wanted the Cradle, so he needed to have the source of its communication, Ava, all to himself. She knew that eliminating anything that could ruin his mission was the smart thing to do.

*But they were my parents!*

Ava held up the Cradle in between Elliot and her. She took a deep breath and nodded her head once. Elliot's body tensed as he laid his hand on top of the cause of so much grief. The duo was instantly transported back in time again. Now, it was to a private meeting between who they recognized as Khufu and his Grand Architect. They spoke of preparations, leaning against the railing of Khufu's upstairs palace balcony. It was seen as an immense privilege to be invited to the pharaoh's private quarters. The architect was, indeed, unique in the eyes of Khufu.

Ava overheard Khufu call the other man Zadmarr.

*The man inside the museum display?*

He was beginning construction on the pharaoh's pyramid at sunrise.

He, along with a thousand laborers, were to rise and start what would become the first of the legendary Ancient Wonders.

The two men finished, and Khufu dismissed his devout follower. Ava, and therefore Elliot, could feel the emotions that the two men had for each other. They cared for one another as Ava cared for Elliot.

*That's it!* But they needed to know for sure.

Zadmarr turned and headed off.

Elliot stepped forward. Khufu leaned on his elbows, over the railing, and inhaled a lungful of fresh desert air. The man mumbled something incoherently to himself, before turning around and stopping dead in his tracks.

"Oh," he said in a strange language, but Ava understood it, "I didn't see that I had visitors."

"You can see us?" Elliot asked, looking behind him. Ava also looked behind her and saw that they were alone with the pharaoh.

"I can, but then, this is just a vision. It's not real life."

Ava and Elliot exchanged glances.

"It's not?" she asked.

Khufu smiled. "You still have so much to learn…"

**"Like what?" Elliot** asked, crossing his arms. He realized, as soon as they arrived, that the Cradle was gone. It had stayed with them every other time they had traveled forward or, in this case, backward in time.

Khufu smiled. "That I," his form flickered, "am not what I seem."

The pharaoh's ceremonial garbs flickered and shifted, just as the doors to the ship and elevator had done. They then liquified and slithered around his body, turning into a full, midnight blue bodysuit. The bald man looked similar to how a deep-space astronaut was pictured in the movies.

"Prometheus…" Ava said, taken aback. "It's true!"

"Yes, it is I," he said, standing tall. The bodysuit tightened around his powerful, yet lean, physique. The only things that weren't wrapped within the uniform were his head and hands. He caught Elliot staring at his clothes.

"Impressive, yes?"

His wardrobe changed a second time. Now, he was dressed in traditional Greek robes.

"You're a con artist," Elliot said, stunned.

Prometheus didn't smile. He looked angry at being called a professional phony. His bodysuit reappeared, and his brow deepened.

"I am not a sham," he said. "I gave Earth more than it could've ever cooked up on its own."

Unbridled rage burned off Prometheus' form. The room around them got so hot that Elliot was forced to wipe sweat from his forehead. He needed to calm the god quickly before either of them was injured. Unlike a traditional dream, they could get hurt here.

"And we thank you for that," Elliot said, giving the man a curt bow.

The uncomfortable heat subsided, returning the palace bedroom back into its former comfortable self. Elliot relaxed and asked Prometheus a question. It was something that had been gnawing at him for a while now.

"What is this?"

"*This*?" Prometheus asked back.

"The communication and visions," Ava said. "How are we even doing this?"

Prometheus smiled and held up his hand. "With this."

The Cradle appeared above his open right hand. It just floated there, rotating slowly in the air.

"We figured as much," Elliot said, "but *how*?"

The ancient being looked sad. What he was about to say hurt to talk about. His eyes traveled from Elliot to the Cradle, then back to Elliot.

He sighed. "The Cradle is not *just* an energy source." He placed a hand on his chest. "It's me."

"What?" Ava was shocked, as was Elliot. Both didn't speak again. Instead, they patiently waited for Prometheus to explain.

"Our exodus from Phobos was taxing," he said. "I gave as much of myself to the capstone as I could."

"The capstone?" Elliot asked, picturing it.

Prometheus nodded. "The navigation computer. It knows every star system in the known galaxy." Before either of the humans could react to finding out what the capstone was, Prometheus continued. "The Horizon was low on power, and I was afraid that we'd be unsuccessful in our travels, so…I linked my life with the core at its center, something that we called—"

"The Cradle," Ava finished, eyes wide, which was a common reaction lately. Stunned, shocked expressions of all kinds, really.

"And," Elliot said, "a cradle holds things."

"Things that are precious," Prometheus added.

"Like someone's lifeforce…" Elliot felt crushed.

The god nodded. His eyes were sad.

"You call it your 'soul,'" he said. "It was everything we were while we were alive. It's *us*. Our lifeforce is everything we are as a unique individual. Without it, we are nothing except a speck of dust traveling throughout the cosmos with no goal. We'd be a horrible waste of space, no?"

"That's why we can see your history. You were showing us what you thought was the most significant events."

Prometheus shrugged. "I needed to be careful not to show you everything. Just because you are of my bloodline, doesn't mean you want the Cradle for constructive reasons."

"You were testing us."

He nodded. "To a degree, yes."

"How..." Ava started, "How did you do it?"

Prometheus sat on the stone railing overlooking a prototypical Egyptian city below. Elliot couldn't tell which city it was, or if they were even in a real place. This could've been a fictional location built by the god himself.

He looked beaten down by Ava's question. Prometheus didn't want to talk about it. It caused him pain. Elliot could feel it. It honestly felt like the man's heart had been ripped out of his chest and set ablaze.

"I killed myself," he said, looking down at his feet.

Elliot and Ava couldn't believe it.

"What?" Elliot said, unsure what else to say.

Prometheus shrugged and crossed his arms. His shoulders were slumped, looking even more defeated than before. "I destroyed myself, well, my body anyways..." He lifted his right hand. Elliot and Ava watched as his sleeve, skin, and muscle tissue peeled away to reveal a skeleton made of the same material as the Horizon.

He was made of metal.

Prometheus was a highly intelligent synthetic humanoid—an android, but with a soul.

"What?" Ava said, backing away at the sight.

"Does this bother you?" Prometheus asked.

She laughed. "A lot of things about this bother me."

Elliot stared intensely at the mechanical appendage. "Who made you?"

"No one," Prometheus replied. "We were grown the same as a human is, except that our womb was in a lab. My skeletal structure is metal, but it is also organic and grows as your bones do."

"And your lifeforce?" Ava asked. "How does an artificially created being have a soul?"

He explained. "There was an ancient sect of us that could harness the energy of the universe. Unfortunately, they were noncombative by nature and the first to perish in the Burning. Zeus refused to let another potential overthrower be born, and in doing so, condemned us." He closed his eyes. "That's when I left—how you humans say, 'it broke the camel's back.' But let's face it," he sighed, "if I didn't sneak around in the shadows and betray Zeus' rule, none of this would've ever happened. My people would still be here."

Elliot had so many questions. Prometheus was so incredibly hurt by the memory. Elliot decided to give him some room and avoided talking about the Burning. It sounded like he caused a lot of it, even though he'd done exactly what Elliot would've done.

He cleared his throat. "So, it's magic?"

Prometheus blinked out of the past. "In a way, yes."

"How do you have descendants if you aren't human?" Ava asked.

Elliot knew what she was getting at. Thankfully, Prometheus explained before either of them had to mention that he had procreated with human women.

"My genetic code is passed using my lifeforce."

"Right…" Elliot laughed, rubbing his forehead. "Immaculate conception."

Prometheus pushed the conversation forward. "Like our lifeforce, our bodies were powerful. They contain enough energy to power something large for a short while. I sacrificed my form to get us to Earth."

"And your lifeforce now?" Elliot asked, still staring at the god's robotic hand.

"It's still as strong as ever, merged within the pure energy of the Cradle. I ensured that my existence would be here until one of my descendants found me," he looked up at Elliot, "and resurrected me."

Elliot took a step away from the being. "I'm not a puppet."

"I didn't say you were." Prometheus slid off the railing, with his arm intact, and walked up to Elliot. "I can only ask you to do it. I'm not here, remember? I have no power over you." He looked hard into Elliot's eyes. "But if you want to find the other cores that my people hid around your planet, then I'd suggest you consider my offer."

"*Other* cores?" Ava asked. "There's more of them?"

Prometheus nodded. "I built dozens of them, though, only twelve have survived to date."

"You?"

"Yes, I was Zeus' lead scientist, which also meant I was his chief weapons developer too."

"Are there more of you guys trapped within those Cradles?" Elliot asked.

"No," Prometheus replied, "it's just me down here. As Ava can attest, the others are still on Phobos, awaiting my Cradle."

Elliot didn't understand. "Why your Cradle?"

The god scratched his head, looking very human with his expressions and mannerisms. It was no wonder he fit in with mankind so well. For all intents and purposes, he was one.

"Without getting too technical, I altered my core to hold my lifeforce indefinitely. The other Cradles are just regular cores. While they'd properly power up the Phobos station, my brethren still wouldn't be able to power up their ships."

"Why?" Ava asked.

Prometheus again put his hand on his chest. "They need me to do it." He grinned. "I locked them out of the computer systems before leaving for Earth in one of our research vessels. Then, I spent time with your people here and began to love them for who they were. Yes, I may have nudged them in certain directions, but never to cause them harm. That they did on their own."

"The Great Influencer," Ava said.

Prometheus turned toward her. "I *am not* the Devil." He frowned once more. "But, yes, by coming here, I may have condemned this world to Zeus' wrath. *He* is the worst of us all. He wants to conquer and then annihilate everything that isn't in his image." Prometheus looked terrified. "He's a monster."

# 30

"If he's such a monster," Ava said, "then why hide the capstone and your Cradle on Earth? Wouldn't destroying them have been better?"

"Perhaps, but at the time, no, I thought this was the better option, just in case you needed both of us down the road. And since you're here, I can only assume that I was right."

"A contingency plan against a violent ruler," Elliot said, understanding the being's logic.

Ava wasn't as understanding.

"We wouldn't be here," she growled, seething, "if you'd sacrificed yourself in the first place! The only reason we're in this mess is because you failed and put us, the people you *love*, in harm's way!"

Elliot thought Prometheus was going to light the room up with heat again. He didn't. Instead, it got cold.

Incredibly cold.

"The leader of a group called the Prophets wants to use the Cradle to destroy Earth and reunite with Zeus on Phobos," Elliot explained, shivering. Saying it out loud sounded ridiculous, yet here he was, talking to an alien android that wasn't really here.

Prometheus started to laugh but stopped. Something caught his attention.

He was worried.

"What's wrong?" Ava asked, calming some.

"This man… His plan might just be possible." He started pacing back and forth. "If he allows the Cradle to detonate while simultaneously placing it inside the capstone, it could technically send the matter that makes up his mind and body to Phobos." His eyes found Elliot's. "It's not a world-ending doomsday scenario, but the resulting surge would still vent downward and decimate a large portion of the planet."

Elliot crossed his arms, happy to feel the temperature righting itself. He was still cold, though. "It can teleport someone?"

Prometheus wiggled his hand. "Eh, sort of. It's more of a specialized transference of energy from one place to another. Then, he'd reform within the navigational capstone on the Phobos station and get his wish."

"Um," Ava said, "that's teleportation."

The god rubbed his smooth-shaven chin and shrugged. "So it is…"

"Can't you stop it from happening?" Elliot asked.

"If I have no connection with the person, no." Prometheus looked at Ava. "Can he activate the Cradle?"

Ava shook her head. "No, but I can. It's why he took me from my parents. I was his key to the lock. Only," she glanced at Elliot, "we didn't know the artifact was occupied."

"Some secrets have their own secrets," Prometheus said.

"So," Elliot said, "these other cores…"

"They are still very dangerous," Prometheus replied. "Even if they are undocked, they can cause limitless damage—or worse—be weaponized."

"Can someone do that?" Ava asked.

"It's possible as long as the person has the financial backing and technical wherewithal."

She nodded. "He does."

Prometheus' eye opened wide. "Then you must resurrect me so that we can destroy the other cores."

"You left them here!" Ava shouted, gritting her teeth. "You are responsible for—"

"And I regret it—all of it!" he cried back. "All I ever wanted was to share my knowledge and experiences with humanity. I wanted to make a difference in the lives of people that needed it the most. You were so close to advancing on your own, but I foresaw failure, and couldn't let it happen."

"And Zeus was near," Elliot added.

"Yes," Prometheus agreed.

"Then, you really did save us," Elliot said.

Prometheus shook his head. "No. I only delayed the inevitable because of my selfishness." He closed his eyes. Opening them again, he looked at Ava. "You were right. If I had just done the proper thing and completely terminated myself…"

"We'd be in even more trouble," she finished, smiling at him. She wasn't angry with him anymore. "You've given us something more valuable than power. You've given us knowledge." She stood tall, determined. "You don't have a body, but we do." She looked at Elliot. "We can do this." Her attention switched back to Prometheus. "We'll protect the capstone."

"And the Cradle," Elliot added. "Where are the other cores?"

"I don't know," Prometheus replied, thinking hard. "I must've erased their location from my memory before transferring my consciousness into the Cradle." His expression brightened moments later. "But I know what does!"

"What?" Ava asked.

"The capstone," he replied confidently. "Dock me, and I will tell you everything you need to know."

"Is that a good idea?" Ava asked Elliot. "We'd be at our most vulnerable with them together."

"Is there any other way?" Elliot asked Prometheus.

The being shook his head.

"How long will it take?"

"That is unknown," Prometheus replied, "but it *will* work."

Elliot mentally went through every plausible situation but found none that worked. Though, in his defense, he'd never been in a situation like this before.

He nodded, eyeing Prometheus. "Okay."

The room darkened, quietly turning to black. The world around them was hollow and void of noise. The sudden quietness ate at Elliot. Then, the room on the top deck of the Horizon came back into view.

Elliot was now standing directly in front of the beautiful capstone. It was exactly as it had been in his dream. The others, including Ava, were still over near where they had entered via the elevator. He'd somehow made it over to the navigation computer without remembering how he'd gotten there, and based on Lincoln and Maggy's faces, they didn't know either.

"Hey," Lincoln called out, "who are you, David Copperfield? How the hell did you get over there?"

Elliot knew how. Time didn't work the same inside the Cradle as it did in real life. No time had passed at all to Lincoln and Maggy. Elliot had just appeared in front of the capstone in the blink of an eye.

In Elliot's hands was the Cradle, and like it had so many times before, it was flashing and strobing excitedly…as if it were alive, because it was. Prometheus was inside, raring to go. He wanted to escape and do what he'd planned on doing centuries ago. His contingency plan was coming to fruition, but not against Zeus.

The man they were trying to stop was worse in Elliot's eyes. He was human and wanted nothing more than to wipe out his species from existence.

Zeus was genocidal, and a warmonger.

His original goal was to advance his own people's way of life, not end it. But then, something inside him snapped, and he decided that the future of his race was less important than his individual goals.

Yes, the human villain, Osiris, was infinitely worse.

Elliot raised the Cradle. A reply originated from somewhere deep within the room, a resounding *clunk.* Lights bloomed, blinding everyone for a moment, but within Elliot's blurred vision, he saw things begin to materialize around him.

At first, slowly. But as the chamber powered-up, the same nanobot-like technology got to work on what Elliot realized was the Horizon's command deck—the bridge. Chairs and screens formed, and then what must've been the helm. The capstone, the navigational computer, pulsed wildly. With each strobe, another piece of equipment was created out of nothing.

"Incredible," Elliot said, smiling.

The Cradle left his hands and floated into the air, doing the same thing it did when he was in ancient Egypt. Then, the twenty-foot-tall capstone separated with a hiss. The cap rose forty feet off the ground on a bed of pure energy. Locking into place, the Cradle moved off, migrating over to a simple pedestal built into the concealed base. It was the same dock as the one he discovered in Qumran.

When it came into contact with the dock, the inside walls of the floating cap lit up. So did the floor surrounding the pedestal. Like a holographic light show, star systems projected themselves around the Cradle, most of which Elliot had never heard of. But there, at the center, was a tiny swirling cloud.

*The Milky Way.*

Elliot stepped away as the cap lowered back into place, sealing the Cradle, and Prometheus inside. The floor around the capstone separated with a clunk, and a second pressurized hiss. Then, it rose into the air just as the cap had done. A hole in the ceiling above it materialized like everything within the advanced command deck.

A single burst of electric green energy surged from within the capstone and quickly made its way around the room. Elliot could feel it continue into every room within the Horizon, activating systems throughout. Not only did Elliot just help activate the capstone, but he also assisted in powering-up a deep-space research vessel.

The Horizon was fully operational.

**The four-person Prophets** team skidded to a halt halfway to the ship. When he saw the vessel, Osiris reacted the same way as he did when he first translated its name. His knees buckled, but instead of falling to them, Hades caught him.

"Horizon," he mumbled. He repeated the word several times, stopping only when the ship's hull lit up.

Circuitry within the matte black craft blinked to life. Bright LEDs seemed to chase one another from end to end, racing to see who could reach their destination first. And with each lap finished, another section of the Horizon illuminated.

Someone had turned it on.

Just seeing the enormous, space-aged solar barge was incredible, but seeing it up and running was something else. Once the activation lights reached the uppermost deck, the room around them rumbled. Leaning out over the edge of the elevated platform, Osiris watched as a trio of enormous docking clamps retreated into the floor. But the Horizon didn't fall.

It hovered in place by itself. The propulsion was deathly silent. The only viable way it could've achieved lift like that was with an abundant amount of force. It was something the military had been secretly trying to accomplish for years.

Electromagnetic thrusters.

The gods had technology that could tap into the Earth's natural magnetic field and then push against it with enough strength to elevate a vessel the size of an oil tanker. What was most surprising was that the force of the thrusters didn't seem to affect the ground beneath it. Theoretically, the thrusters should've crushed everything beneath them.

He thought about what he could so with such ingenuity at his fingertips. Also, the thrusters were nowhere to be seen. The only indication that the Horizon even had any were a series of slim, glowing openings along the craft's keel. They reminded him of long air vents.

"Incredible…"

"Sir," Hades said, speaking—something he didn't often do.

It was enough to get Osiris moving again.

"What's that?" Kalma asked, pointing at the top deck.

Slowly, a bright white, pyramidal object appeared from below. Osiris recognized it for what it was. It wasn't a pyramid, but rather, the Great Pyramid's missing capstone.

"It's part of what we seek," he replied, taking off at a sprint. "Do not stop," he shouted, entering the ship, "and kill anyone who gets in your way!"

# 31

When the surge rolled through the Horizon, Elliot and Ava's senses were sent into overdrive. Not having the Cradle in hand was strange. The only time either one of them felt an overload, such as this, was when they were holding it. The artifact, along with the capstone, was nowhere to be seen. Both had disappeared above their heads.

While Prometheus searched the Horizon's navigational systems for the locations of the other cores, Elliot, Lincoln, and Ava all decided to take up positions to head off against a possible infiltration. Happily, Lincoln offered to look after Maggy back near one of the consoles.

"I think I can make out parts of their language if I take it slow," Maggy said. "I might be able to, at least, update everyone on a timetable."

"I'll help," Lincoln offered. "I can watch her back too." He tilted his chin at Elliot and Ava. "You two go kick some ass."

They were given their targets seconds later.

"An armed team has entered the Horizon from below," Prometheus announced, startling Lincoln and Maggy. They had yet to hear the god speak. His voice boomed through the bridge. "And I don't think they mean well."

"Can you show us?" Ava asked, looking up to the ceiling.

"And turn down the volume a little," Lincoln said, rubbing his right ear.

One of the monitors blinked to life. It showed what Prometheus had detected. The camera angle was odd. It looked as if someone was running in front of them. The invaders didn't know they were being filmed.

"Osiris," Ava muttered, growling.

"How?" Maggy asked. "The angle, I mean."

Prometheus spoke up. "Another of our inventions. We do it by—"

"It doesn't matter!" Ava shouted, heading for the elevator. "Just keep us in the loop!"

"You're speaking English?" Elliot asked, following along with Ava.

"Yes," Prometheus replied, his voice quieter, and originating from the wall in front of them. "I analyzed your memory while you were connected to me."

"You downloaded our language in a matter of minutes?" Ava asked, glancing uncomfortably at Elliot as they stepped onto the lift.

Elliot knew what she was thinking.

*What else did he download?*

Ava pulled her sidearm from the back of her jeans. Elliot also figured it was as good a time as ever to check his ammunition supply. The gun was in perfect working order, but his ammo wasn't. He had one full magazine left, and it was currently loaded.

"Ten rounds left," he said, "how 'bout you?"

"Worse..." she replied. "I'm down to eight."

Elliot blew out a long breath. "Okay, so, eighteen bullets for four targets."

"We're not completely helpless without our guns..."

He agreed with her, but a fistfight only worked if there wasn't anyone around to shoot you. They needed to gain an advantage. Neither one had the Cradle anymore, but they did still have their connection to it. He could feel it, which meant that Ava could too.

"Prometheus?" Elliot asked.

"Yes?" he replied.

"Can you dim the lights below decks?"

"Of course, why?"

Elliot turned and faced Ava. "The energy flowing through the Horizon, you sense it?"

She nodded.

"Let's see if we can use it to our advantage."

"Close your eyes and concentrate," Elliot followed his own instructions, "what do you see?"

He searched for it, feeling it and then seeing it.

Ava's eyes snapped open. "The Horizon's blueprint!"

Elliot smiled. "...and the doors that only we can access."

There were hundreds of doors throughout the ship.

The elevator opened, and the lights dimmed. Elliot stepped out, pistol up at the ready. "You ready?'"

The corner of Ava's mouth curled into a small smile. "It would be my pleasure."

**Attempting to translate** an alien language on location, on the fly, wasn't easy. Luckily, Maggy could read Egyptian hieroglyphs with no issues. She also had Lincoln to aid with the Latin formations. His intimate knowledge of the gods was a big help.

Maggy kept track of the locations in her phone.

"Uh, so," Lincoln said, leaning over her shoulder, "I think that says something about a Mayan pyramid."

"Chichen Itza?" Maggy asked.

On another monitor was the weird camera feeds. They were still tracking the Prophets team. Osiris and a hulking man led the charge. They hit the same juncture they had earlier, and Lincoln tried desperately to will them to turn left or continue straight. Either way, they were taking their precious time.

"Prometheus, patch me through to the asshats below decks."

The god didn't reply. So, he decided just to start talking and see what happened.

"Check, check, check..." he said, happy to see the four people react. They all went to one knee and turned in a different direction. "You are trespassing on private property," Lincoln called out, earning a snicker out of Maggy. "I suggest you vacate the premises before you are jettisoned into orbit."

"Orbit?" one of the men asked.

Lincoln could hear him loud and clear. "As soon as you stepped aboard my love boat, we launched and are currently headed for an exploratory mission deep into Uranus."

Maggy belched out a laugh, getting Lincoln going too. The duo was enjoying themselves at the expense of Osiris and his people. The Prophets team stood, and the invisi-camera focused on the leader's veiled face.

Lincoln whispered. "Show me Elliot and Ava."

A third screen formed and ignited, showing him exactly as he asked. The lights were low, and so were Elliot and Ava. They crept forward, each hugging one of the walls. They were still too far away from the others to do much of anything. So, Lincoln would buy some time and do what he did best. Talk.

"Where is the Cradle?" Osiris shouted.

"Excuse me?" Lincoln asked back. "I'm sorry, but it's hard to hear you through that stylish burqa...Congressman Towns."

Osiris tore the facial covering off and tossed it aside. He gritted his teeth, squeezing his combat rifle hard.

"Who is this?" he shouted, looking around.

Lincoln put a finger to his lips. Maggy finally got her case of the "giggles" under control.

The agent leaned forward and lowered his voice, adding some Batman-like grit to it as well. "I'm your worst nightmare."

Again, Maggy couldn't hold back her laughter. Best of all, the act enraged Osiris. He manically depressed the trigger of his rifle, spraying the empty corridor with bullets until he spent the entire magazine. He was nearly out of breath after he finished.

"You need a minute, Mike?" Lincoln asked. "I mean, if you're not in a rush, I—"

"Who are you?" Osiris shouted, visibly enraged.

"Roswell," Maggy whispered, as another location came in.

Even Lincoln didn't know about that one. As far as he knew, Area 51 had been deemed clear of anything to do with the Cradle or the gods. Lincoln knew there was an alien spacecraft there, but just about everyone knew that. He grinned since most people referred to it as a hoax. The fact that a core was there too sent chills down his spine. It appeared that his organization was keeping secrets from him and the other field agents. *Well*, he thought, *more than usual.* Roswell was his organization's turf. In fact, he'd been there several times. Even though it was the Company's policy to keep most agents out of the loop unless absolutely necessary, it still angered him.

It hurt him.

"Who m—me?" Lincoln asked, stuttering his words. "Oh, I'm sorry, I'm just your friendly neighborhood Prometheus agent."

"You…"

He had an idea and lowered his voice once more, speaking to Prometheus. "Hey, can you do something to rattle these guys?"

"Like what?" Prometheus replied.

"I don't care, but we need them to be as on edge as possible." Lincoln winked at Maggy. "Have some fun with it."

"I'll do my best." Prometheus sounded like he was in pain. "The strain is intense."

They watched as the lights on the first level winked out completely. No one, not even Lincoln or Maggy, could see anything happening below decks. Even Osiris shut up.

But not Prometheus.

"I have come back from the dead to annihilate those who defy my will," the god bellowed. His voice was low, and it rumbled through the Horizon like thunder. "The Prophets will burn for their transgressions!"

Maggy's eyes opened wide. "Woah, this guy is good."

The bridge was unaffected by the special effects and sudden volume increase. It even looked like Elliot and Ava were being spared further down the main hall. Prometheus was solely focusing his sonic assault on Osiris and the others.

All four members of the squad had their hands to their ears. Two of them had even moved back toward the hull entrance a few steps. While Prometheus continued his shouted threats, Elliot and Ava moved on. They were nearing the Prophets strike team but had slowed to a crawl as they got closer. Lincoln would've taken the same approach if he was in Elliot's shoes. They were severely outnumbered and needed to be extra cautious.

"Uluru," Maggy said, typing the word into her phone. So far, she had translated the names for three high-profile places: Chichen Itza, Roswell, and the Uluru rock formation in Australia.

Osiris cringed with every new verbal assault.

“Who,” Osiris said, speaking to the booming voice, breathing hard, “who are you?”

The first-floor ceiling panels bloomed to life, exploding into fireballs, impossibly bright. Lincoln’s eyes flicked over to the other screen and saw that his duo was still shrouded in darkness, but an aura of light could be seen further down the hall in front of them.

“Stonehenge.”

Lincoln barely heard Maggy that time, but he did lean over to confirm her findings. Elliot and Ava were only twenty feet away from the commotion back at the juncture.

“I,” the god roared, “am Prometheus, and you are on my ship!”

“Kill the lights in,” Elliot said, speaking softly, “three,” he and Ava rushed forward, “two,” they lifted their guns, “one!”

As soon as they popped out into the opening of the intersecting hallways, the overhead lights extinguished. It’d take a few seconds for the strike team to regain proper vision. Lincoln was hopeful that his friends could take out a couple of the Prophets during that short window.

On one screen were Elliot and Ava. The other monitor held the four assassins. All were lit by a type of night vision lighting.

Elliot and Ava, along with three of the four killers, pulled the triggers of their respective weapons at the same moment.

# 32

Elliot and Ava did not stop. They got off as many shots as possible and continued their trajectory down the corridor, heading for the stern of the Horizon. From the intel Elliot had gathered while connected to the Cradle, he knew the engine room and defense systems were housed further ahead of them. Neither area sounded particularly safe at the moment. More than anything, they eventually needed to regroup with Lincoln and Maggy above deck.

A tiny screen popped up at the top of his line of sight. Lincoln and Maggy's faces appeared, distracting Elliot. Ava yanked on his arm and sent them barreling down a hallway to the right. It's as if he had his very own Heads Up Display at his disposal. Ava had a HUD too, apparently, and she looked as confused as he felt.

"Uh…" Ava remarked, eyes bouncing around from the hallway up to the HUD.

"We'll explain later," Maggy said. "Looks like you injured two of them and possibly killed another."

"Which ones?"

"Not entirely sure which one is KIA," Lincoln replied. "You winged the big guy. Kinda hard to miss someone that big."

"That's Hades," Ava explained. "He's a fanatic. Osiris' number two. Speaking of Osiris…"

Lincoln shook his head. "No, the giant stepped in front of him."

Bullets tore into the walls around them. Elliot willed a nearby door to open. With a sigh of relief, one did. He and Ava dove through the door to the left just as it closed and was impacted several times by gunfire. The two of them laid there for a second and caught their breath, content in knowing that their pursuers couldn't enter themselves.

Sitting up, Elliot took in the large, empty room. He was filled with dread when he couldn't find another door. They were stuck—safe—but stuck. All Osiris would have to do is park one of his gun-toting henchmen outside their refuge. Then, he and the others could march up to the bridge and attempt to take it by force. Lincoln and Maggy would be severely outgunned if that were the case.

"What is this place?" Ava asked.

He knew where most of the rooms were, but not what they held inside. At the time, the information came too quickly to comprehend fully.

But someone aboard knew.

"You are in my people's training facility," Prometheus announced.

Both Elliot and Ava were silent. There was nothing in the space around them. But there was nothing in the bridge either, other than the capstone.

The god continued. "You would call it a virtual reality simulation."

"Neat," Lincoln commented. He wasn't listening entirely.

"Uh, Elliot," Maggy said, "they're doing something to the doors…"

Lincoln leaned in close. It took him a second to recognize what was being applied to the entrance.

"Get back!" he shouted.

Elliot and Ava darted to the rear of the room as the doors to the VR chamber detonated. Unlike most explosions, this one produced no flack, no shrapnel at all. The material just disintegrated and retreated away from the smoldering hole.

"Activate simulation!" Elliot shouted, wholly exposed, standing in the center of nothing.

"You need to choose an environment," Prometheus replied.

Elliot's decision came to him, deep from his past. It was a place he'd been to several times in his life.

"Jungle!"

Three people rushed into the room, rifles up, just as the lights dimmed, and the room came to life. Elliot tripped as a tree root snaked beneath his feet. He went down and turned the fall into a roll, finding cover behind a thick, half-developed tree trunk. His hand found its surface for balance, and he was shocked to feel rough bark.

It felt real.

He looked all around him. A jungle canopy blocked the ceiling of dimly lit VR chamber. He scanned the foliage and found a gap, seeing only a dark, moon-lit sky complete with stars.

Ava was standing beside him, gun raised. Elliot stood and leaned into her.

"Meet you around front."

She nodded and slunk away. Elliot slipped his pistol into the back of his pants, opting for a stealthier option. Mostly, he needed the use of both of his hands. The ground was covered in gnarled roots and a light layer of fog.

The croak of a frog startled him. It came from directly behind him. The chamber was adding things as the seconds went by, making the artificial environment more real.

*How is this possible?* he asked himself.

The only answer was that Prometheus saw a place like this when he extracted Elliot's memories. The ancient being knew everything about him, just as Elliot knew everything about Ava. When Elliot asked for a jungle setting, Prometheus used Elliot's memories to provide them one via the technology of the VR chamber.

The crunch of a boot stopped him in his tracks. Elliot used his other senses to pinpoint the aggressor's location. A soft breeze kicked up, aiding in his search. Whoever was hunting him was on the other side of a tangled growth that had just popped up. Elliot got lower, walking on his hands and feet like a panther. Soon, he'd spring atop his prey like one.

He sniffed the air, recognizing the slight stench of gunpowder. There was also the coppery aroma of blood. The shooter was injured.

The chirp of bugs grew to a symphony. It was peaceful, to a point.

Elliot edged closer to the growth and spotted the open doorway through an opening. The illumination coming from the corridor was blinding in their current environment. But it backlit the enemy perfectly. His position would be given away, though, and that was a problem. Whoever the person was, they had his or her left arm tucked against their body, with their rifle slung across their backs. It confirmed Elliot's assessment of the attacker as one of the wounded, so much so, that they couldn't lift their rifle, opting for a pistol instead.

Blindly, Elliot felt for something to throw, finding a broken and rotten tree branch off to his right. The stick was real, just like the surface of the tree trunk. Eyeing his target, he felt tiny pieces flake off. He also felt dirt beneath his fingernails.

The tech on display was nothing he could've ever imagined or understood. But here he was in a perfect replica of a South American jungle.

Raising the tree branch over his head, Elliot brought his arm forward but thankfully didn't let go. There, low to the ground, and coming up behind the lone gunman, was another threat. If their surroundings were as real and accurately built as they'd been so far, then the jaguar was too.

And that terrified him.

Elliot ducked back down and watched and waited. The animal moved gracefully, but also with power and purpose. Each silent step was perfectly executed, and the creature's goal was evident.

The mercenary was about to turn and spot the cat. Elliot quickly lobbed the stick, happy to see it strike the assassin in the chest. The dead branch did nothing to the person other than distract the shooter. The interruption gave the jungle cat the extra time it needed to attack. Its shrill cry gave Elliot goosebumps, as did watching it take the killer down to the ground by the neck.

Elliot heard the woman's surprised and horrified, high-pitched shouts dilute once the cat repositioned its jaws and latched onto her throat. Then, all he heard was gags and gurgles.

This "simulation" was undeniably real…and it was dangerous. Prometheus' people didn't mess around when they trained. Based on what the god said earlier, it didn't surprise Elliot in the least. They were a conquering, warring race. It only made sense that they trained as hard as they could.

A snarl refocused Elliot's attention on the gruesome scene. Luckily, it was too dark to see the face of the blood-soaked jaguar, but he could feel it staring down its next meal.

Him.

**After Ava and** Elliot separated, she immediately sought higher ground. Trees had sprouted throughout the immense VR chamber, completing decades of growth in mere minutes. The thick limb beneath her feet was as real as the ones she'd squatted on in the past.

Once, she'd been tasked a mission in Africa against a genocidal warlord that owed the Prophets money. They'd already supplied him with weapons, but he never paid them back.

So, Ava *paid* him a visit instead, convincing the man to come through with his end of the agreement. She did so with a knife to his throat and another blade to his groin.

*I should've cut the monster's throat that day,* Ava thought, spotting her attackers. One of them hung back near the door. Another went right, and the other went left. She was happy to see that the smaller of the two was headed in her direction.

Ava whispered the killer's identity. "Osiris."

She tracked his movements and waited to attack.

It was the kill she wanted the most, but she wouldn't give herself away to get it done. Her training was engrained deep into her mind—similar to Elliot and Lincoln. They reacted as they'd been taught.

*No matter the circumstance, one must always be patient.*

Hades told her that. The man lived and breathed the mantra. He never did more than he was asked, but when he did, it was a sight to behold. He was devastating to observe. No one, not even Ava, could match the man. The only reason she was known as the most lethal of the Prophets' operatives was because Hades wasn't an active field agent anymore.

Osiris weaved his way through the thickening brush and veins, disappearing and reappearing from within the dense foliage and the shadows they cast. Ava gripped her gun but decided against using it. She didn't have a good enough angle and knew if she missed, she'd be a sitting duck to his more prodigious weapon. So, she holstered her gun and shifted her weight, preparing to jump. She'd use her hands to kill the man that had forced her to call him "father."

She didn't regret her upbringing. She'd been given a valuable gift—the ability to end the Prophets. Osiris had trained her to eliminate her enemies, but he never would've guessed that he'd become one of them. It made Ava smile, knowing that he was scared of her. She knew he was. Hades had said as much when he was training her.

"You frighten him," Hades said.

"Really?" replied her seventeen-year-old self.

Hades nodded. "There's a monster deep inside of you that few possess. I have it too. It's what we tap into so we can do what needs to be done. Anyone can end someone's life from afar, but few can do it while their target looks them in the eyes."

*I want that bastard to look me in the eyes when I end his life.*

Ava readied herself, and stood, just as Osiris appeared directly beneath her perch. He moved to continue forward but stopped when the ear-piercing cry of a large cat caught both his and Ava's attention. Ava looked away from her target in time to see a phantom leap on top of the third member of Osiris' party.

If she let Osiris pass below unmolested, she and Elliot could slip through the doors and head back to the bridge with only two Prophets agents left. She liked those odds—but she also enjoyed the prospects of killing them both, right here and now.

*Patience.*

Ava bit her lip and returned to her catcher's squat.

But then, she moved again. Osiris and the big cat both turned to the center of the room. It was in the direction of where she last saw Elliot. A hulking mass came out of nowhere and charged directly for the same spot.

Hades never moved with such reckless abandonment…unless he had his prey square in his sights.

*Elliot!* Ava thought. *No!*

She knew what she had to do.

Standing, Ava yelled, "End simulation!"

Just like that, she fell from the sky as the thick tree branch disintegrated. All around her, from top to bottom, the room quickly withdrew into itself. Falling feetfirst, she raised her knee and struck Osiris in the back. Making the smarter choice, she didn't stay to finish him off. Instead, she got up and bolted for the front door.

"Elliot, run!"

# 33

Elliot did as he was instructed. He ran like a bat out of hell, straight for the front of the room. The doors had already begun to fix themselves too. The blast, as it seemed, only temporarily damaged the regenerating entryway. The nanobots were doing what they were designed to do.

Create.

Pushing himself hard, he bobbed and weaved through the still fertile jungle floor. The room was returning to normal but it was happening above his head first. The bottom half of the chamber was still thick with tall grass and trees. It was still dark too, which was a gift in itself. He used the distraction of the dissolving jungle to his advantage.

The jaguar was still there, however.

There was no way he could draw his sidearm and shoot the agile cat while he ran, and if he stopped to take the shot, someone else would end up shooting him instead. So, he stayed on course and headed straight for the big cat. It had spotted him already, but was nervous, its tail convulsing frantically. It had no idea what was going on and was acting accordingly.

Plus, now its sustenance was advancing toward it.

Elliot was impressed with the reality of the animal's personality. It acted like a real jaguar, not at all like a piece of computer software. The gods knew more about the planet, and its residents, than Elliot ever thought possible.

The cat snarled and lowered its head. Then, with a twitch of its hind legs, it launched itself into the air, jaws wide. There was no doubting its target.

Elliot's throat.

He raised his left arm and ducked his head behind it. He'd take it in his arm if he had too. Then, he'd go for the cat's eyes. But just as one of the jaguar's fangs connected with Elliot's flesh, he exploded through the beast. A cloud of tiny, dust-sized particles covered his skin like a layer of coarse sand. As he ran, they slid away from his body and fell to the floor and were absorbed from whence they came.

A hand found his arm. Ava appeared next to him and helped him keep his footing. Together, they sprinted for the entrance. Both of them drew their pistols and laid down a wild blanket of cover fire as they exited the alien VR chamber.

Both were almost out of ammo now.

Elliot willed the doors to shut, and they did without trouble. The nanobots had fixed them in a matter of minutes. He realized that the doors themselves weren't made up of the microscopic machines. The nanobots were merely what had repaired them. Like the chamber, the bridge was also just an empty room until the nanobots arrived. The basic framework of the Horizon was always physically here. The miniature robots provided everything else.

It was why he could see the corridors and the rooms of the ship, but not what was inside of them. Their contents didn't exist until the room was activated. It was ingenious. The only people that could access the Horizon were people that had a connection to the Cradle—those in Prometheus' bloodline.

*Like Ava and me.*

The revelation made Elliot immediately regret coming to Egypt at all. Even if Osiris had discovered this place one day, he wouldn't have been able to do anything. Now, the only two people that could access the ship and the energy core that powered it were on-site, and it was all Elliot's fault. His blind faith in the Cradle's direction—Prometheus' direction—had overridden his judgment.

Still, the other cores needed to be found. Elliot knew the only way that was happening was with Prometheus' help, and he needed to be plugged into the capstone to locate them. He visualized a comms link between him and Lincoln and was happy to see the screen reappear above his line of sight.

"Status update," Elliot said, not playing any games.

"Screw that!" Maggy shouted. "What about you guys?"

Ava glanced at Elliot as they ran. "What about us?" she asked back.

"Ox, seriously," Lincoln said, "we could see everything."

Elliot's eyebrows raised. His friends saw what transpired inside the VR chamber. It never once occurred to him that Lincoln and Maggy could watch them "train."

Lincoln grinned. "That jaguar was pretty intense, huh?"

Elliot shrugged. "You could say that."

"Is she dead?" Maggy asked. "The woman, I mean."

Ava shook her head. "We didn't stop to check, but I can't imagine someone surviving something like that."

**Blood drained from** the puncture wounds in Kalma's neck. Even Osiris, a man with a black heart, and someone who'd seen everything the world had to offer, was appalled, and not by the injury itself. He was shocked at how it was inflicted.

She, an armed, capable assassin, was taken down by a technologically conceived jaguar on an extraterrestrial spacecraft.

His mind was still attempting to wrap itself around the prospects that something that was created out of nothing could physically harm a human being to this degree. It fascinated him.

Kalma lifted a dripping, shaking crimson hand up to him, silently pleading for help. He didn't take it, however. Instead, he studied her while also replaying what had taken place right before his eyes. The memory of the big cat's piercing scream clawed its way up his spine. This ship, these beings, were more than he ever dreamed of. He already had a list of possible applications forming in his head.

He and Hades were now severely outnumbered. Mantus was already dead. He'd taken two rounds to the chest back at the intersection of hallways. Kalma wasn't gone yet, but she was already pale from blood loss. It was only a matter of time until her heart stopped.

With nothing to be done, Osiris stood and turned his back on his dying subordinate. He stepped away as a gunshot rang out. Pausing, he looked over his shoulder as Hades holstered his sidearm. He took care of what Osiris didn't and mercifully ended the woman's life. Osiris would have been content with letting her die painfully, a fitting way for someone's life to end after failing him. He looked into the dead woman's open eyes and sighed.

*Pitiful,* Osiris thought, stomping away.

He had important work to do and it was not mourning the loss of someone whom he had no personal relationship with. People died all the time. This one was no different than the rest. It was a vile way to think, but it was the truth. NO ONE was above Osiris' goal. His endgame was above all else.

"I want my Cradle."

"Soon, Michael," Hades said, placing a firm hand on his shoulder. "Soon, we will bask in Zeus' light."

He rarely used Osiris' given name. He reserved it for private settings only.

Osiris glanced down at his confidant's side. The wound was closer to Hades' stomach then he'd initially thought. "Is it bad?"

Hades removed his hand from the injury. It was slathered in blood. Osiris knew it would be life-threatening and eventually kill the man unless he received immediate medical attention. Unfortunately, they were a long way from that. It was unlikely that Hades could make the arduous climb back up to the Subterranean Chamber of the Great Pyramid. If he somehow did, then they'd need to make it back to their car and find somewhere that would treat him in privacy.

They required the Cradle that much more now. Not only did Osiris need it to fulfill his destiny, but now, he also needed it to save his friend. If not, Hades was going to die down here.

The big man grimaced against the pain and forced himself to straighten his posture. He was the toughest person Osiris had ever met. Hades' pain tolerance was incredible, something he used to his advantage when he was on the job.

He could take a beating in a fight.

His opponent? Not so much.

"Come, Ardath," Osiris stepped outside of the VR chamber. "Zeus awaits."

**"Angkor Wat!" Maggy** shouted, reading off the twelfth and presumably final location of the missing energy cores. Her hands trembled terribly. It was all too much. Half the words in her phone's file were misspelled because of the lack of control she had on her fingers. In the end, it didn't matter. She knew what they said.

"*Wat*?" Lincoln replied.

He was back at the elevator, tucking himself behind a nearby computer console. And apparently, he still had a joke or two up his sleeve.

Maggy spun around in her chair, which was mostly just an uncomfortable cylinder. "You heard me!" She adjusted herself and failed in the process.

*Did these people not have asses?"*

"Any news on our guy and gal?"

Maggy nodded. "They stopped to check on the bodies. It looks like Elliot grabbed a knife, a rifle, and some ammo."

"What about Osiris?"

"He and Hades made it out of the VR chamber okay, but Hades looks badly hurt." She shrugged. "It's hard to tell, but he's limping and holding his stomach."

"Somebody's coming!" Lincoln yelled, raising his pistol.

Without getting to her feet, Maggy stopped what she was doing and lifted her gun, pointing it toward the lift platform.

The cylindrical elevator came to a stop, and the wall containing it separated to reveal a filthy Elliot Oxley and Ava Towns. Both looked like they had rolled in the mud. Ava smelled like she had rolled in something else.

Ava turned toward Lincoln and held up a finger. "Not a word."

Lincoln kept his mouth shut but also gave the woman a wide berth. The threesome reunited around Maggy. She was trying to get her communication with Prometheus to reconnect. The more time the god spent linked to the capstone, the more jumbled and broken-up his words had become.

It had taken three times to understand his translation of Angkor Wat. First, it sounded like "Anchor Up." Then, "Angry Thought." Finally, Maggy had heard it—Angkor—and immediately knew what he was trying to say. The twelfth core was buried somewhere beneath the Cambodian temple.

If they all got out of this alive, they'd have some work to do, work that would probably take years to complete. With everything Maggy had experienced so far, she was more than willing to leave behind her work in Egypt to help Elliot and the others out.

It wasn't world history.

It was intergalactic history.

*Intergalactic Historian, Magdalen Bitar,* she thought, smiling. She liked the sound of it.

"Prometheus?" Elliot asked, looking up.

He didn't answer.

The section of the roof holding the capstone aloft released. Then, like how it effortlessly rose into the air, it came back down to the floor of the bridge using nothing except pure energy to guide it.

"Prometheus?" Elliot asked again.

After another moment of silence, the god finally replied.

"I'm here..." he sounded tired. "I'm having trouble processing everything. There's...too much information."

"Can you disconnect?" Lincoln asked.

"No," Prometheus replied, "not without shutting down the Horizon."

"And that's bad?" Maggy asked.

"Very bad," pulsed the capstone. "You'd be trapped inside forever."

"Nothing would work," Elliot added. "No elevators or doors."

"No oxygen pump," Ava said, sighing hard.

"What do we do?" Maggy asked, looking to Elliot for answers.

Elliot glanced over his shoulder and looked deep into her eyes. He looked defeated. He didn't know what could be done. Still, Maggy could see that his mind was still trying to work it out. He'd never stop until a viable answer was found.

"Hmm," he mumbled. His demeanor picked up. No longer was he defeated.

Elliot Oxley had a plan.

Lincoln saw it too. "Whaddya got, Ox?"

"Yes," a voice said from behind. They all turned and found two men pointing assault rifles at them. "What do you have?"

Ava stepped back. "Osiris..."

# 34

It was the first time Ava had seen her murderous "father" since her mind was opened up by Elliot and the Cradle. The contempt she felt for the man was boldened with every minute she spent separated from him. Every memory she had of him was now a dreadful one, one she'd never forgive herself for, at the time, proudly going along with.

Terrible things were done. All in his name.

The assassin snarled and stepped forward, balling her fists.

Osiris, just for a moment, looked scared, but she was unarmed. All of them were. Her sidearm was tucked into the back of her pants, as were Elliot and Lincoln's. Even the confiscated rifle was lying atop a nearby table.

The only one that held a gun at the ready was Maggy. She was clutching hers in her right hand, hidden beneath the desk of the alien workstation. Unfortunately, Ava doubted the Egyptologist could get off a shot quick enough. No, they'd need to bide their time.

Osiris' attention went from her rage-filled face to the strobing capstone. His anger was reduced to an expression of pure joy. Ava had never seen him look so happy. She could only imagine what was going through his mind.

Osiris was *the* true believer.

Ava grinned. *Which means he's distracted.*

"Amazing, isn't it?" she said, glancing at the others. "We're still only scratching the surface on what it can do."

Elliot, Lincoln, and Maggy looked at her, but all three figured out that she had a plan and went along with her.

"It's incredible," Maggy said, standing, casually holding her gun by her side. It was still hidden from Osiris and Hades. "The information we've been given will change the world!"

"And Prometheus," Lincoln added. "What a cool guy. Great with kids…better than you."

Elliot stayed quiet. His eyes danced side to side as if he was reading something. His attention was elsewhere, and Ava knew precisely where it was.

He was receiving information from Prometheus.

As soon as his extrasensory conversation began, it ended. Elliot blinked hard and returned to the situation on hand. He looked more confident than before. His eyes met Ava's, and he smiled. Whatever he and the god had cooked up, Elliot was confident it would work out in their favor.

"Finally," Osiris said, "after all these years, I will meet the father of everything."

"Well," Lincoln said, "technically, if you believe everything you read, Prometheus is the father of humanity, so you've already checked off that box."

Osiris' rifle swung toward the special agent.

"Don't!" Elliot shouted. "If you do, you won't get your wish."

Ava knew where he was going.

"Because," Elliot continued, "you can't access the Cradle without us."

Osiris' eyes darted from Elliot to Ava. It was believed that she held the power to activate the artifact based on her lineage, but without the Cradle to test it on, it was just a hypothesis. They had nothing to go on…until now.

"You can activate the Cradle?" Osiris asked.

Ava nodded. "I can, and it showed me exactly who you are." Her eyes narrowed. "It showed me what you did to my parents."

"Ava, I—"

"I'll fucking kill you!" she shouted, charging Hades and him.

Hades leveled his weapon at her, but it was shoved aside by Osiris. "No, we need her alive! But the others…"

All hell broke loose as Hades opened fire on Elliot, Lincoln, and Maggy.

Ava leapt at Osiris and tackled him to the ground. She focused solely on the man who'd caused her a lifetime of pain and regrets. She caught him with a rising elbow strike mid-roll, finding glee when she heard him audibly grunt.

He delivered a strike to her neck and then they separated. The pressure from the shot was enough to cause her to lose her breath for a second. Still, she was a seasoned operative, and an injury such as that wouldn't be the end of her.

Bullets flew all around them as they stood only six feet apart from one another, sizing the other up. Besides Hades, Osiris had taught her everything she knew when it came to combat. The unassuming Congressman was trained to kill, and he had the mentality to do it with no remorse.

*Like what he did to my parents.*

"Why did you do it?" she asked, hunched like a gremlin. "Why did you kill my parents?" She knew the answer, but she needed to hear it from the man responsible.

Osiris stood calmly, arms down to his side. His right foot was set slightly further back than his left.

"I wanted you for myself, and I knew your mother and father were never going to let me get what I wanted."

"So, instead of coming to some sort of arrangement, you killed them."

His lack of rebuttal said much more than anything he could've said. It was all for selfish gain.

"And what arrangement is that?"

"Anything would've been better than what you did!" She leaned in closer. "Did you really think you could hide it from me forever?"

He shrugged. "Killing you was always another option, if and when, you did figure things out. I'm not an idiot, daughter. I knew it would eventually come to this, and when it did, I planned on killing you myself."

Lunging forward, Osiris snapped a punch up to Ava's face. She slapped it away and was caught in the midsection with a strong kick. She didn't go down, but she was knocked back, taking a second kick to her knee and a third to the side of her head.

Ava was sent tumbling to the ground. Woozy, she climbed back to her feet and lashed out violently, getting inside Osiris' reach. She hooked her fingers into talons and went for his face, but he caught her by the wrists before she could make contact and swiftly connected a knee to her ribs.

Never one to fight fair, Ava head-butted Osiris in the nose, breaking it with the single blow. He let go and staggered back.

Ava wanted to tackle him, but she couldn't get a good enough breath to do much of anything. So, she just held her side and waited for her air to return. With one final, deep inhalation, Ava stood upright, but so did Osiris.

The killers were equally matched with one another.

Blood ran from Osiris' nose, and his eyes watered. He quickly cleared the plasma with a forceful exhale through his nostrils, blowing the goop on the floor. He wiped away the combination of blood and snot with his shirtsleeve and returned to his non-threatening stance, hands down by his side, right foot set slightly further back than his left.

"Ava!" Maggy shouted.

Ava turned just in time to dive away. Hades released a stream of projectiles in Ava's direction. Luckily, she now had friends that were watching her back. Regrettably, one of the rounds tore into the meat of her right thigh in midair. In response to Ava's shouts of pain, Maggy swiftly sent a pair of bullets toward Osiris. One of them imbedded itself in his right shoulder, spinning him to the ground.

The Egyptologist's gun clicked empty. Then, she dove for cover, as Hades directed his gunfire her way. Their war raged on, but Ava and Osiris' had been paused. Grimacing against the searing pain in her leg, Ava scrambled behind the closest cover she could find. It was a terminal over near the elevator.

There, Ava sat, leaning against the back of the console. She quickly removed her belt and wrapped it around her thigh, just above the gunshot wound. Ava inserted the end back through the buckle, and as hard as she could, she pulled the makeshift tourniquet tight, jaw clenched.

The agony was blinding, and she forced herself not to black out. She took a deep breath and coiled the belt around her leg three more times, before tucking the loose end under the tightly wound binding.

From a side pocket on her uninjured thigh, Ava produced a silver tube. Inside was a potent painkiller and antibiotic cocktail. She popped the top and jammed the needle into her bleeding leg, only inches from the wound. Seconds later, she pulled out the needle and tossed it aside.

It would take a few minutes for the drugs to kick in, and she needed to be ready to move when they did. Reaching behind her back, she drew her pistol and checked it. She only had a handful of rounds left.

She'd need to make every one of them count.

**In the years** prior, Osiris had only been shot once before. He'd taken a bullet to his other shoulder before he began his career as a politician. He was once a lethal operative like Ava and Hades, but that life was never for him. Osiris was a born leader, and with his father's assistance, an influential Senator of Ohio. He moved on from enacting warfare himself and started directing said wars from afar.

Luckily for him, he was ambidextrous. He had tossed his rifle aside when Ava attacked him, but he still had his pistol. Typically, he was a right-handed shot, but he currently held the weapon in his left hand. The long hours spent training to use it in times like this was paying off.

Ava's shouted cries told him she'd also been hit, but he had no idea how bad it was, or where she'd taken the bullet. On one knee, he quickly peeked out from behind a solid table of some kind and took in the surroundings. The only thing he could see with any life to it was the capstone. The people in the room were still hidden behind cover.

Off to his right, he saw a smear of blood on the floor, and since he didn't hear anyone else get hit besides his turncoat daughter, he knew who the blood belonged to.

*No…*

Osiris jumped to his feet and bolted straight for the trail. He found its owner moments later. Hades was slumped to the side, rifle held loosely in his hands. He was still alive, smiling softly when he spotted Osiris.

"Michael," Hades said, his voice soft and distant.

"Stay with me, Ardath. We're so close."

Hades smiled. "As long as one of us gets to set our eyes on Zeus, I'm happy with the outcome here."

Osiris shook his head. “Unacceptable. We’re both in this till the end.”

“I fear this *is* the end,” Hades said, blinking his eyes awake.

Peeking over the center console, Osiris saw something that could change the tides of the battle. He patted his confidant’s shoulder.

“Just stay with me for a little while longer, okay?”

Ducking down, Osiris circled around to the other end of the large, half-moon shaped command center, he leaned out and grinned. His prize was there for the taking.

So, he moved off and took her.

# 35

Elliot was out of ammo, and so was Lincoln. He had no idea where Ava and Maggy were, nor did he know the locations of Osiris or Hades. Neither man had been shot, but Elliot did jam his knee at some point while running. He remembered circling around to the rear of the capstone and stumbling and falling, but not the pain the fall had obviously caused.

"So," Lincoln said, "you do have a plan, right?"

Elliot nodded. "Yeah, to not die."

Lincoln rolled his eyes. "That's more of a goal, not a plan." Usually, it was him making the snarky comments, and before he could add one of his own, someone else spoke up.

"You have something I want!" It was Osiris, and he sounded pissed. "And it just so happens that I have something of value to you!"

"Elliot!"

*Maggy,* Elliot thought, turning and running.

Lincoln was right on his heels. Both men slowed as they rounded the back corner of the pyramidal capstone. Slowly, they edged further forward, stopping when they spotted Osiris holding a tactical knife to Maggy's throat. It was the same type of blade Elliot had in his hand now.

"Osiris," Lincoln shouted, "you son of a bitch, let her go!"

With no shooting going on, Elliot and Lincoln stepped out from hiding, but not before Elliot sheathed his knife behind his back.

Osiris' eyes burned with rage. "Not until I get what I want."

Elliot held up his hands. "If you kill her, you'll have nothing."

"Neither will you." The killer's eyes burned.

Elliot swallowed hard. His plan was coming undone. He needed to be alone with Osiris in order for his and Prometheus' plan to work. It was a long shot, but it's all they had.

"Elliot?" Maggy sobbed. "Help…"

"Awww," Osiris mocked, "she loves you." He grinned. "Tell him you love him, my darling."

He pressed the blade against her skin, drawing a small amount of blood. Maggy whimpered, terrified.

"Tell him!"

Maggy sniffed back more tears and took a deep breath.

"I… I love you, Elliot."

Elliot's hard expression almost cracked at hearing the words he had missed for so long.

"You'll be fine," he replied. "I promise, he won't hurt you."

"Oh, arrogant, aren't we?"

Elliot shook his head. "No, I'm just truthful."

Osiris looked like he was about to explode. So, Elliot told him what he and Prometheus had planned.

"You aren't going to hurt her, because—"

"Because what?" Osiris asked.

"Because then, you won't get your meeting with Zeus."

Almost all of Osiris' anger diminished immediately. Still, he didn't release his only bargaining chip. Pulling Maggy along, he kept the knife close to her throat and moved to within ten feet of Elliot and Lincoln. Ava was still nowhere in sight. Neither was Hades.

"How?" he asked.

"Like this," Elliot replied, closing his eyes.

When they opened again, the capstone broke apart like before, the top rising high above their heads. There on the pedestal was the Cradle. The plasma within swirled and flashed, alive and anxious.

Feeling a surge of energy roll through him, Elliot held out his hand and told the core to come to him. It listened and undocked itself, shooting over to him like a rocket. He snagged it from the air and smiled widely, feeling like one of George Lucas' *Jedi*. Osiris' hand shook in shock and awe. He was so close to releasing Maggy, and when he did, Elliot would pounce. He had no real intention of trying to send the man to Phobos.

But Elliot needed Osiris to believe that's what was going to happen. Hopefully, the lunatic's mania was so off the deep end that he'd willingly go along with it.

Suddenly, a bloodied Hades tackled Lincoln to the ground. The larger man tossed Osiris his sidearm as he went down. The Prophets leader caught the pistol and then pushed his hostage aside. Stepping away from Elliot, he raised the gun and grinned.

Lincoln gagged. Hades was choking him to death with one hand, roaring into the air as he did.

"Go, Michael! Go meet Zeus and bathe in his light!"

Elliot was stuck between a rock and a hard place. Hades slugged Lincoln hard in the face and dropped the dazed agent. Even if he had intervened and saved Lincoln, Osiris most likely would've just shot them all and called it a day. He could, in reality, return with another member of Prometheus' bloodline.

Slowly, the bloodied goon got to his feet, pale and ghastly. Osiris tossed the gun back to Hades, and he quickly leveled it on Elliot. The tables had turned in the enemy's favor.

"You ready?" Elliot asked, keeping Osiris' attention on him.

"You have no idea," Osiris said, stepping up to him. His aim was steady, and his stare intense. As crazed as he was, Osiris was still in control. If Elliot tried anything stupid, he'd be shot point-blank.

Elliot held up the vibrating core and nodded.

Osiris' hand was twitching, but he greedily laid it atop the artifact. Instantly, something happened. The energy, directed by both Elliot and Prometheus, flowed into Osiris. The other man's eyes flashed green, same as the material within the Cradle.

Pushing hard, the strain on Elliot was too much, and he caved in on himself, dropping to one knee. He was too weak to do it himself. He needed help, but from who?

Hands raised in surrender, Ava skirted around Hades and limped up next to Elliot and lifted her hand. He stopped her, though.

"No…you can't," Elliot croaked.

"Why not?" she asked softly.

"Because I'm pretty sure there's no coming back from this. Remember the Grand Architect? The Cradle needs an energy source to power it properly or it'll default and use the Earth instead. It's what I saw in my vision. The only way this works is that whoever wields it is burned up."

"You are both correct," Prometheus said. "One cannot occur without the other."

She smiled, wincing in pain. "That's why I'm here, remember?" She placed her hand on the Cradle. "I'm here to lighten the load."

With both of them touching the surface of the Cradle, it instantaneously flashed in response. A beam of light shot straight up into the air, passing harmlessly through the ceiling of the Horizon's bridge. It, Elliot knew, wasn't a destructive force. It was a doorway across space and time.

Osiris tipped his chin at Hades. "Take us home. Take us to Zeus."

"You are sure of this?" Prometheus responded. "You are sure you want to see what is on the other side?"

Osiris looked back to Elliot and Ava. "I am."

"I am," Hades agreed, stumbling over to them.

Both men realized that Elliot had somehow tricked them. But the realization came a second too late. Hades went to pull the trigger of his gun but couldn't. His hand had already disintegrated into nothing. The dust was quickly absorbed into the column of bright light and taken away.

"What…is happening?" Osiris cried, desperately trying to peel his hand away from the Cradle. But he couldn't release his grip on the object.

A snippet of Olympus and Phobos flashed across his mind in nanoseconds. It gave Elliot a front-row seat to what Osiris and Hades could expect.

He told them.

"You're going to meet your god…in hell."

The apocalyptic vision he'd been given was of the surface of

Olympus—Mars—immediately after Prometheus and the other gods, as well as hundreds of other survivors, left to seek refuge at their outpost within the hollowed-out moon, Phobos. The planet was a complete loss, devastated, a charged husk of its once beautiful self.

Anything that involved Zeus, Elliot viewed as being in hell based on evidence that had been presented to him. As a leader of his people, Zeus had failed miserably. Instead of trying to save as many as he could, he let the majority of them burn. The only ones he had saved from annihilation were those he deemed worthy.

*It's why I abandoned him,* Prometheus whispered into Elliot's thoughts. It's another reason the immortal being sacrificed himself. He was trying to right a terrible wrong.

Inch by inch, Osiris and Hades were broken down into dust and sucked into the glowing vortex, until *whoosh*, they disappeared for good.

Elliot dropped the Cradle and collapsed, fading into unconsciousness. He was quickly shaken awake by Lincoln, who was slathered in blood. It looked like most of the blood belonged to someone else. If Elliot could've, he would've commented on it. Instead, he stayed quiet and tried desperately to keep his eyes open. A hand found his neck. Someone was checking his pulse.

Desperately, somebody tried to keep him awake, but his eyes shut. Strangely, Elliot felt his heart stop beating. He died, but he wasn't scared. He wasn't alone.

Once more, Prometheus appeared before Elliot in his blue spaceman jumpsuit. The god's eyes were sad.

"This isn't how it was supposed to go," he said, resting a hand on Elliot's shoulder.

"Then, how was it supposed to go?" Elliot asked, angry. "How was all of this supposed to end?"

Prometheus shrunk away from him.

Elliot pressed on with his verbal attack. "You said it yourself. You and your monstrous brethren are responsible for everything."

The god closed his eyes and rubbed them, leaning up against the stone railing of his Egyptian balcony. It was another chilly night, beautiful in several ways. Elliot calmed and leaned next to Prometheus, looking out over the city.

"Look…" Elliot said, knowing it wasn't Prometheus' fault, "I chose to do this. This isn't all on you."

Prometheus shook his head as tears streamed down his face.

"I loved humanity so much, and all I did was bring you pain. Especially you, Elliot. I haven't had contact with your kind in so long." His shoulders fell. "I've been so lonely."

Elliot felt terrible. "You can feel the time going by in the outside world?"

"I can." He gritted his teeth in anger. "Every. Single. Minute."

The room grew hotter again. The last time that happened, Elliot was only in Prometheus' consciousness, not dead.

"Am I alive?"

The god shrugged. "You're close to death."

"That's not what I asked."

"Yes, technically, you are still alive, but you are very weak. You will die in minutes."

Elliot's eyes opened wide. "Then, release me from this."

"I can't. You're too weak to survive the return trip. It takes some of your lifeforce to pull that off, and the only thing keeping you alive is what little bit of it you have left."

"So," Elliot said, "either I die trying, or I die not trying." He laughed. "That's a hard hand to be dealt."

"And that's not what I wanted. I wanted for someone to come along and undo what my people brought upon this world."

"The cores?"

"Yes, they're dangerous and they must be found."

Now, it was Elliot's turn to shrug. "I don't think I'm the guy for the job. I'm dying, remember?"

Prometheus smiled softly. "Even in the face of death, you joke."

Elliot crossed his arms. "When you do what I did in the SEALs, you get used to the prospect of dying. It's one of the reasons I left, to be honest. Ever since I graduated high school, I've had my life dictated to me."

"Until you retired. I know everything about you, Elliot."

"Then, you know that I have more to do."

Prometheus sighed. "I do know. It's why I chose you."

"You didn't choose me. I literally fell into your lap." He laughed softly. "I have the bruises to prove it."

"You may be right, but I'd call it fate. I believe we were destined to unite against Zeus here on Earth."

"What about Zeus?" Elliot asked.

"That's why we need to find the other cores and destroy them."

"Speaking of that…"

Prometheus walked away. "I am the only one who can do it. I can't teach anyone how. It can only be me—in the flesh. I created them to react with my DNA only."

"Which is why only people like me, and Ava can activate them."

He nodded. "Precisely. But you aren't strong enough to do it. My entire lifeforce needs to be present for it to work. It's why I need to be resurrected. I need a living vessel to help me complete my work."

"Because you are the only one who can properly do the job."

The corner of Prometheus' mouth curled up. "Smart man."

"Well," Elliot said, "you did choose me for a reason, right?"

"Again, with the humor."

Elliot laughed, incredibly exhausted. "Call it the demented part of my humanity coming out in crises. I try to make the darkest moments in history just a little bit brighter."

*Brighter... Hmm.*

"What are you thinking?" Prometheus asked.

"This melding of the minds you mentioned. Is it still possible?"

Prometheus stood. "I'm not sure. You might be too weak."

"So, worst-case scenario, I'm going to die no matter what we do. Sounds like a win-win for me either way."

"You're ever the optimist, Elliot."

He stepped up in front of Prometheus. "Do it. What else do I have to lose?" He looked around. "What do we have to do?"

"Nothing," Prometheus replied. "You've done everything just by agreeing to help me. I vowed never to harm your people, though I'm sad that I have. Your verbal agreement bypasses my self-established protocols as a protector of man and allows me to do what needs to be done."

"If we do this, I want control of my life. You'll be in the background, and I'll still be Elliot Oxley, not Prometheus, the alien android god from Mars, okay?"

Prometheus smiled. "That's fine by me. I think I'll enjoy being human regardless of how I do it."

Elliot blew out a long, shaky breath. "Will it hurt?"

"No," Prometheus replied. "You're already dead."

**Watching Elliot die** was the hardest thing Ava had ever endured. It was like watching her older brother pass on, and there was nothing she could do to stop it. As far as Ava knew, she was an only child. It was an easier way to live, having no other attachments to life. But this...this was something she could've never prepared her heart for.

She threw herself into Lincoln's arms, gripping the man tight. He also had tears streaming down his cheeks, just like Ava and Maggy.

Maggy was a wreck, still leaning over her fallen love. She was holding one of his hands while laying one of her other hands across his filthy forehead. There, Maggy stroked his hair away from his handsome face with her fingers.

Smiling, she leaned in and kissed him. When their lips touched, she felt a shock of electricity slap her lips. It was faint, but it was there. It reminded her of Elliot and Ava's description of the way the Cradle felt to them. To Maggy, the artifact felt like a cube—nothing more. She couldn't feel anything else at all.

Maggy lifted her face away from Elliot's inert form and was surprised to see him staring up at her. She'd just felt his heart stop and watched him take his last breath.

She had watched Elliot Oxley die.

This man wasn't Elliot. His eyes were bright green, and they crackled with the same electricity that the Cradle did. Ava glanced over to the artifact and was stunned to see it dark and dormant. She picked it up and looked it over. The plasma within was rock-hard and grey. She no longer felt a connection to it. The energy within it was dead.

But she did, however, feel a connection to something else.

Someone else.

"Prometheus?"

Elliot sat up and looked at Ava.

"Yes?" he said, his voice low and booming.

She brought a hand to her mouth. "What did you do to Elliot?"

Elliot's face twitched, and he blinked hard several times. With each successive opening and closing of his eyelids, his brown irises returned.

The next time he spoke, Ava was relieved to hear his voice.

He groaned and held a hand up. Lincoln clasped it and helped him up. "I'm still here."

Maggy stepped back. "You died."

Elliot patted his chest and legs multiple times. He looked at his friends. "I guess I did, didn't I?" He scratched his head. "Weird, huh?"

"Uh," Lincoln said, "you okay?"

Elliot didn't look quite sure that he knew how to answer his friend. He had just died and come back to life in a matter of minutes. That's a lot to take in.

"I made a deal," he explained.

Ava thought back and recalled him speaking with Prometheus back around the time when Osiris and Hades showed up inside the bridge. His eyes were dancing back and forth, not paying attention to the matter at hand.

"I remember," Ava said. "When we first met Prometheus, he was dressed as Khufu. He said something about being resurrected. He needed a body to make it happen."

"Is that what this is?" Maggy asked. "Are you really just a…vessel…for some alien?"

Elliot smiled at her. "I'm still me, Maggy. But yes, I'm also Prometheus now. His consciousness has merged with mine, but he's agreed to take a backseat to me. He feeds me information when I need it but will never step out of line."

"How do you know that?"

Elliot shrugged. "Because he said he wouldn't."

"And you trust him?" Maggy asked, crossing her arms, holding herself. "You died because of him."

He slowly placed a hand on her shoulder. "And I'm back because of him too."

Maggy tried to stay strong, but she eventually lost it and fell into Elliot's awaiting arms. They hugged each other for a moment before kissing once more.

Ava was happy to see Elliot back and seemingly better than ever, but what about the Cradle?

"What do we do with this?" she asked, holding up the dead core.

Elliot held out his hand, accepting the device. Like they had before, his eyes flashed green, and the artifact's casing went up in flames, like a miniature ball of Greek fire. It turned to ash in Elliot's hand, and just like that, his eyes flashed and changed back to normal.

"Woah," Lincoln said, slapping him on the back. "Those are some pretty cool jazz hands you've got there."

Elliot grinned, knowing everything he was now capable of. "You have no idea."

# EPILOGUE

Chichen Itza, Yucatan, Mexico

To the average person, Elliot Oxley looked completely normal. He walked and talked like a typical American male, wearing his usual Volbeat t-shirt and a pair of abused blue jeans. But, if you knew him like his closest friends did, like the ones standing behind him, you'd know that Elliot was anything but ordinary.

Before coming to Mexico, they'd gone to New Mexico and given Roswell a once over. Lincoln went inside and confirmed that what they were looking for was there. The collection vessel, as well as the core they sought, were on-premise. Deep beneath it, actually.

"How do we get it out?" Lincoln had asked before entering the base.

Elliot replied with a shit-eating grin. "Leave that to me."

Closing his eyes, Elliot imagined the collection vessel in his mind. It wasn't hard, considering the shape of the craft had been iconic in pop culture for over fifty years. Flip one dinner plate upside down and set it on top of another, and you got what looked like a flying saucer.

That's one of the two reasons they had traveled to New Mexico a week after the incident beneath the Great Pyramid. They'd gotten back to the surface without issue, but were saddened to see that Maggy's ex, Dr. Alexander Dukaras, had been murdered. Lincoln was quick to place a call when topside and explained to his superiors what had happened, though, he did leave out all the goodies they had found underground.

Alexander's body was found later, along with Hassam, the head of security. Both deaths were blamed on local terrorist cells since the Prophets weren't a publicly known organization. Without their faithful leader, the group quickly slithered into hiding almost overnight.

Congressman Michael Towns was reported to be lost at sea, after taking a leave of absence due to underlying health issues. His daughter, Ava, would later confirm the story. The boat, one Lincoln and Prometheus made up, would never be found.

After a couple of weeks of preparation and healing, the foursome reunited in Mexico. Ava was still dealing with a sore leg and walked with a cane. Everyone else had made it out of Egypt relatively unscathed.

"Ready?" Elliot asked in his earpiece, knowing Lincoln would be somewhere outside, watching.

Now, instead of tapping into his lifeforce to show off his newfound abilities, Elliot tapped into someone far stronger.

*Ready?* he asked.

*I am,* Prometheus replied.

Digging deep, both "beings" visualized the saucer, the collection vessel, and pinpointed its hangar's desert doors. They sat out in the middle of nowhere, just outside the main Area 51 complex. Beneath the doors was a vertical shaft that would be used as a launch bay, if the scientists could ever get the thing working, which they couldn't since it wasn't designed for a manned flight.

From miles away, Elliot and Prometheus gripped the hangar doors hard and slowly began to pull them apart. Once they were jammed open, they activated the vessel and increased the flow of power to its thrusters. Unlike in the movies, the saucer didn't spin to fly. It just glided beautifully in the sky above New Mexico like a kite.

Until the high-tech camouflage was initiated.

One by one, panels along the exterior of the collection vessel warbled like a desert heat shimmer and reflected the surrounding light and landscape. Just like that, the spacecraft turned invisible. Prometheus would take over and guide the craft effortlessly to Mexico while Elliot took care of his routine, human responsibilities.

Like, restart his relationship with Maggy.

It was as if they never separated, except for the ten-plus years of age and a few new bumps and bruises. The two had been inseparable since their time in Egypt together.

Maggy placed a hand on Elliot's shoulder and squeezed. "You can do it. Light this place up like a Christmas tree."

Using one of Lincoln's local contacts, they were given a private moment in the park and stopped to admire the world-famous *El Castillo,* the Kukulkan Pyramid. The beautiful quartet of stepped sides led up to a square, low-roofed temple. But it wasn't the top of the Castle, nor the pyramid itself, that they were there for. Buried beneath it, hidden at the bottom of a recently discovered cenote, was their prize. Luckily, no one had yet been commissioned to clear the bones at the bottom of the chilled waters. The remains had inadvertently concealed the first of their twelve energy cores.

"Did you know," Elliot said, eyes closed, "that the ancient Mayans would cast offerings into a cenote? They believed it was a portal into the heavens. Whatever was tossed into the water was seen as a sacrifice to the gods." He peeked over at Maggy. "Kinda makes you wonder if they had once sacrificed a glowing cube, huh? It's almost as if they knew where it had originally come from and were trying to send it home."

Grunting, he shut his eyes again, just as the collection vessel showed itself for the first time since it had been *acquired* from the Roswell base. Since Lincoln was on site in New Mexico when it happened, he'd been able to deny being involved in anything.

The saucer was guided into place directly over the temple at the top of the pyramid. While Prometheus held the spacecraft in place, Elliot focused his attention on the core. They didn't call them Cradles anymore. These only held energy. Their "Cradle" held a living being. They decided to keep the two names independent of each other.

Prometheus liked it too.

"Locked on," Elliot said, speaking as Prometheus. His voice was low, and it carried across the expanse of grass surrounding the pyramid.

Elliot let Prometheus speak so the others could hear what was going on in his head.

"Keep her steady," Elliot replied. "And…now!"

The tractor beam that was so commonly associated with UFOs was, in reality, used for harnessing energy from around the globe. In this case, they were depleting "Core 1" of its ability to crater Central America. Eventually, the artifacts would be found by someone, and when they were, they'd be studied without knowing what they were.

What if the discoverer could activate it too?

There weren't any more technologically advanced android-like beings to help. Elliot contained the consciousness of the last one on planet Earth.

What bothered Elliot about this particular core was that he couldn't sense a docking system in the area. The core had been unplugged for a long time, but had yet to go supernova, though, he could feel its energy levels. It was low on power…very low on power.

The ancient Mayans had unknowingly cast a ticking timebomb into the cenote. They couldn't have been the only ones too. Other people had probably undocked their cores without understanding the potential consequences.

*We got here just in time.*

Finished, Elliot opened his eyes and turned to face his friends. As they had before, his eyes had ignited into a vibrant green color. He smiled, blinked, and they returned to normal, just as the collection vessel disappeared.

"One down, eleven to go."

Somewhere

He awoke with a shudder, startled by a bone-chilling sound. Either the place around him was made of dilapidated, moaning metal, or there was something alive out there waiting for him. It sounded like it was huge too. Regardless of what it was, he knew he wasn't on the Horizon anymore.

Osiris didn't know where he was.

Half buried in what felt like petrified wood, Osiris laid still and listened. He tried to open his eyes, but there was a blinding light shining down on him from above. So, he used his other senses instead, investigating his surroundings without the use of sight.

Besides the disturbing noise that woke him, the place was still. It reeked of death, and it was cold...really cold. It was a stark contrast to the desert climate he'd been in only seconds before.

*Or has it been longer than that?* Either way, the freezing temperature only added to how uncomfortable he was at this moment.

Osiris lifted his left hand out of the pile of wood and blocked out the light. The first thing he noticed about the room was that it was the size of the hangar they found the starship in. This one had seen better days, though. The illumination came through a ragged hole in the ceiling, not by artificial means. It was a natural source.

*The sun?*

He blew out a long breath and watched as it plumed into the air. This "hangar" wasn't as elegantly designed as he'd hoped, if, in fact, it was made by the same race of beings as the Horizon's docking station. He hoped it was. If it were, it meant that he'd been successfully transported to Phobos.

"Zeus," he muttered, his throat dry.

Physically weak and a little nauseous, Osiris clambered to his feet and realized he was in a sea of bones, not petrified wood.

Tens of thousands of long-dead bodies covered the expanse around him. It caused him to shudder. He'd read of people sacrificing their enemies to the gods in heaven. In some cases, though the stories were covered up, he'd also read of an emerald light taking them skyward. Some Prophets scholars debated on what the light was. Most believed it was the Cradle destroying their foe. The most faithful of believers, like Osiris' grandfather and father, thought it was a means of transportation.

*Looks like they were right.*

Tripping as he took a step, Osiris looked down at his feet and found what had caused it. Hades had also made the journey, but he'd succumbed to blood loss while en route. He knelt and confirmed his partner's death, sad not to find a pulse. Hades would never know how close he'd gotten.

"Where are you?" he asked quietly.

His eyes again found the bones. Some were tangled in Spartan armor. Others in classic Egyptian garbs. Some were even adorned in Mayan headdresses. Every era of human history was here with him. Osiris was honored to represent his own time. He'd make the others back on Earth proud.

A bone nearest Hades' right foot caught Osiris' eye. It didn't look right. Something about it was off, but he couldn't figure out why. Carefully, he yanked it free of Hades' corpse. It was a femur…and it was broken in half. Whoever stripped this man of his flesh, they'd done it violently, and with brutish strength.

*Men didn't build this place.*

Osiris' internal warning system went off, and he spun in a complete circle. Thankfully, he found nothing. Maybe at one point, there was some ravaging monster here. Not now, though. That's what Osiris was hoping, anyway.

Wading ankle-deep through death, Osiris continued forward, doing his best not to look at what he was stepping on. It took a lot to rattle a man such as him, but this did it. The stench was nauseating as well. Records back home stated that Zeus was the only god awake on Phobos. As the strongest of them, he was tasked with watching over his brethren. If that were true, then it meant he lived in filth.

The Phobos station was supposedly running low on power, so it seemed plausible that they had cut out typically essential things like waste disposal and sanitation. A rumble and a shifting of bones behind him caused the hairs on the back of Osiris' neck to stand up. He spun and raised his fists but found nothing.

There was no aggressor.

And Hades' body was now missing too.

A chill ran down his spine. Something was alive in here with him—something that consumed the dead. These weren't the gods he'd fantasized about all his life. These were the things of nightmares.

*Maybe it's not them,* he thought, trying to convince himself otherwise. *Perhaps something else did all this.*

A sound like a gunshot startled him, but there was no bullet.

Something was thrown into the air, launched from within the mass of bones. It plummeted back down to the grim floor and landed within two feet of Osiris' toes. His eyes opened wide, and he emptied his bladder on himself.

It was the lower half of Hades' left leg. Something broke it in half at the knee and discarded it like a dog's unloved chew toy. Osiris heard the splintering of bone. It was what he'd mistaken as a gunshot only moments earlier.

"Hello?" he asked, speaking in what his people called the Language of the Gods. Ava knew it too. Most of the Prophets' leadership did.

The ground shook again, and from beneath the mass grave, stood an immense being. Osiris pictured Satan rising out of the bones in the same manner. The humanoid was covered in years of filth and blood. Some of the latter was fresh. It was the demon that had consumed parts of Hades.

"H—hello?" he asked again, his voice shaking terribly. Osiris was petrified.

The being stepped into the light. Its upper body was nude and scarred, as were its legs and bare feet. It was injured too, from a battle, maybe? Osiris could even see the creature's ribs through a ragged wound in the beast's left side. The skin around the injury was charred and horribly scarred.

Its bones were made of metal.

*They were androids?*

The realization that the beings he worshiped were robots should've shaken him, but Osiris couldn't properly process what he was seeing. It was too terrifying to do so. Plus, this *thing* might not be who he sought.

Its clothes were a tattered pair of briefs. They looked like they may have been part of a larger piece of clothing. And across the being's chest, mixed in with other cuts and grungy smears, was a wound in the shape of a lightning bolt. The scar ran deep, its form sloppy.

Osiris didn't know how, but he knew it had been self-inflicted. It had carved the symbol into its own chest. He also knew the creature's identity.

Zeus.

And he was a monster to behold.

"My lord!" Osiris said, falling to one knee. "I've waited years to gaze upon you."

Truthfully, Osiris was trembling, scared for his life. He regretted his decision to come here and wished that he could go back to Earth. There, he could disappear and start over. But here… He didn't want to be here.

Elliot's last words rang through Osiris' head.

*You're going to meet your god…in hell.*

Zeus' face was gnarled, and the left side drooped. One of his eyes was grey with cataracts. He wasn't the god Osiris dreamt about meeting. Still, he needed to do the being's bidding—even if it was just to save his own skin.

The thought of being skinned alive sickened him.

"You," Zeus boomed, pointing at him. "You worship me?"

Osiris climbed to his feet. "Yes, I do. I've heard stories of your triumphs and needed to see them for myself." The state of the room told Osiris that Zeus' triumphs might've been overstated.

"Where are the others?"

He shook his head. "Gone."

"How?" Osiris asked, unsure if he wanted to know.

Zeus smiled. "I killed them."

He picked up an enormous leg bone out of the pile and looked it over.

"My brother, Ares." He tossed the bone aside like it was nothing. "I woke them as the eons passed. Sustenance isn't easy to come by here."

"You ate them?"

Zeus hacked uncontrollably. He looked sick and feeble but was still frightening to look at.

"Are you a son of Prometheus?" Zeus growled, not answering Osiris' question.

"No, my lord." He put a closed fist on his chest and bowed, "I'm a disciple of Zeus."

"Did you bring me a viable core?"

If it were possible, Osiris' face went even whiter with fear.

"N—no, my lord, I do not possess the ability to wield one. All I have is my unwavering loyalty and my knowledge of Earth."

"Earth!"

Zeus leapt the distance between him and Osiris and landed with a thunderclap, smashing bones and knocking the horrified man on his rear. With a shaky right hand, Osiris pushed the pain of the gunshot wound in his shoulder aside and held it up in forgiveness. He pleaded for mercy.

"Please, I'll do anything for you! I'll make my failure up to you somehow."

With the speed of a cobra, Zeus reached out and snagged Osiris' outstretched arm by the wrist. With little effort, he lifted the smaller earthling off the ground and held him up to his face. Now five feet off the ground, Osiris was looking into the genocidal eyes of a maniac. The stories of his brutality in war were legendary within the Prophets. It seemed that he was the same way with his own people as well.

Zeus squeezed, causing Osiris to whimper. Then, the monster applied even more pressure and shattered the joint. The normally emotionally stable Osiris was in shambles, blubbering like a child. Smiling like a shark, Zeus showed off a set of disgusting, rotten teeth. He wrapped his other hand around Osiris' left wrist.

Osiris dangled in the air like a crucifix. The pressure in his shoulders was almost too much to bear. Zeus was close to yanking his arms out of their sockets.

"Since you've brought me nothing of value, I see your being here as just another sacrifice." Zeus leaned in closer and sniffed, licking his lips. "And I do love a good, meaty sacrifice."

## ABOUT THE AUTHOR

MATT JAMES is the international bestselling author of more than twenty action-packed titles (published in multiple languages), including the ongoing DEAD MOON apocalyptic series, CRADLE OF DEATH, DARK ISLAND, SUB-ZERO, THE DRAGON, and the upcoming archaeological thrillers, THE JACK REILLY ADVENTURES.

Matt dabbles in some graphic design work as well. He creates book covers for authors all over the world and has designed the vast majority of his own releases.

He lives in Wellington, Florida with his wife and two daughters, enjoying the work of his favorite authors (Greig Beck, Jeremy Robinson, Ernest Dempsey, James Rollins, Matthew Reilly, A.G. Riddle, and Nicholas Sansbury Smith).

YOU CAN VISIT MATT AT:

Instagram: MattJames_Author
Twitter: MJames_Books

Printed in Great Britain
by Amazon

65625739R00132